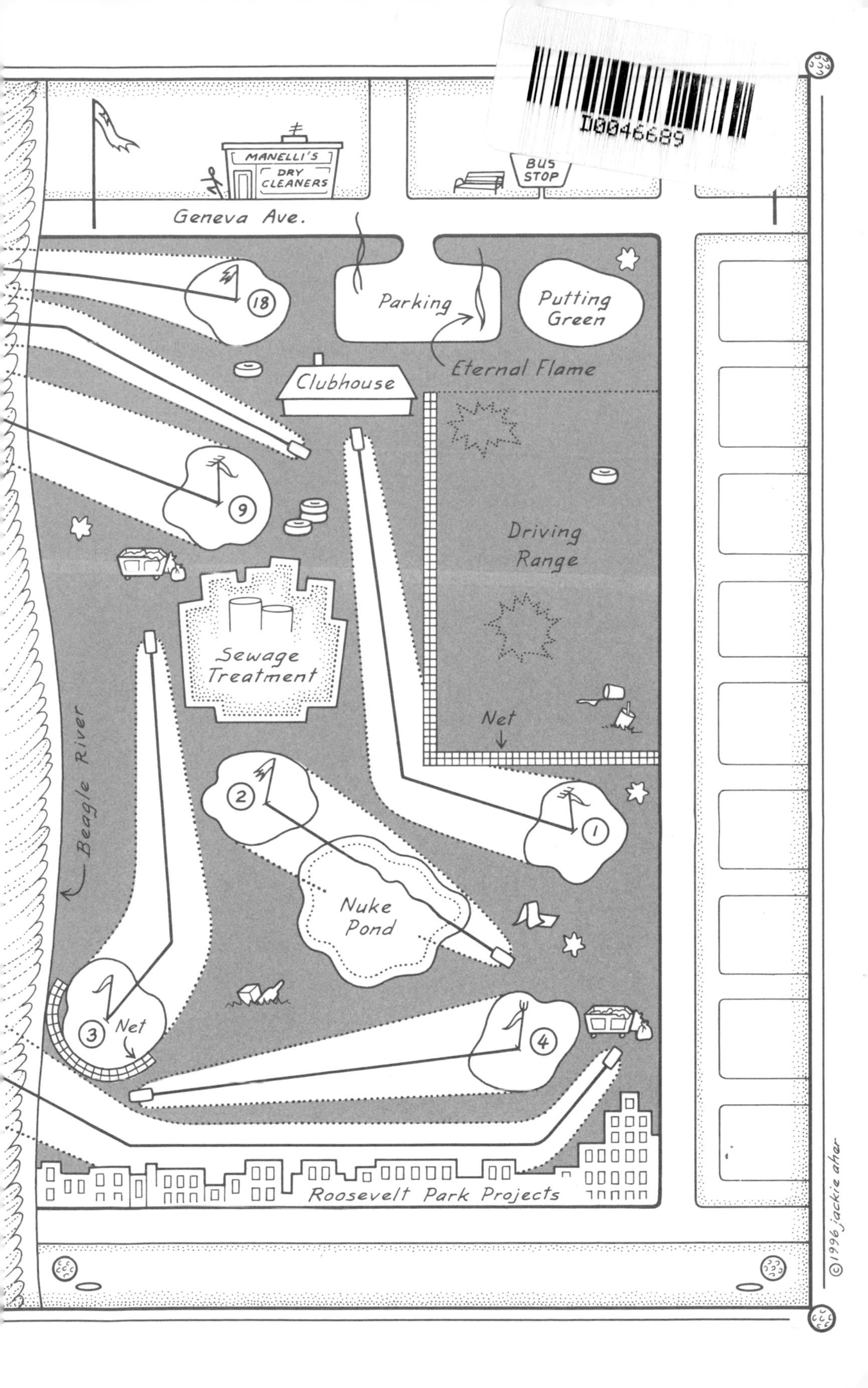
MANELLI'S
DRY CLEANERS
BUS STOP
Geneva Ave.
Parking
Putting Green
Eternal Flame
Clubhouse
18
9
Driving Range
Sewage Treatment
Net
Beagle River
2
1
Nuke Pond
3
Net
4
Roosevelt Park Projects
©1996 jackie aher

MISSING LINKS

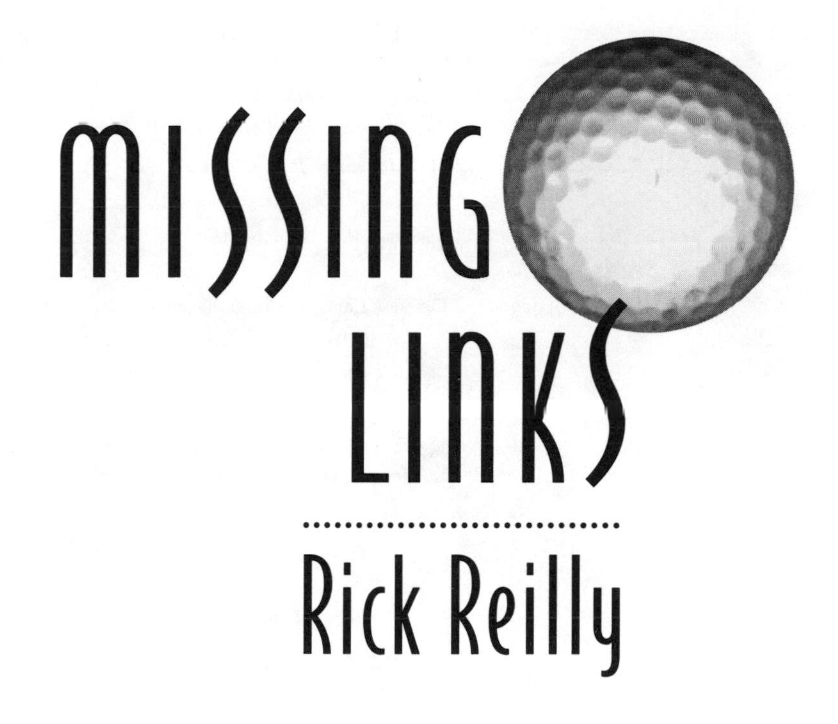

Rick Reilly

DOUBLEDAY
NEW YORK LONDON TORONTO SYDNEY AUCKLAND

PUBLISHED BY DOUBLEDAY
a division of Bantam Doubleday Dell Publishing Group, Inc.
1540 Broadway, New York, New York 10036

DOUBLEDAY and the portrayal of an anchor with a dolphin
are trademarks of Doubleday, a division of
Bantam Doubleday Dell Publishing Group, Inc.

All of the characters in this book are fictitious, and any resemblance to actual persons, living or dead, is purely coincidental.

Book Design by Julie Duquet

Endpaper Map by Jackie Aher

Library of Congress Cataloging-in-Publication Data
Reilly, Rick.
Missing links / Rick Reilly. — 1st ed.
p. cm.
1. Golf—Batting—Fiction. 2. Golfers—Fiction. I. Title.
PS3568.E4847M57 1996
813′.54—dc20 96-10265
CIP

ISBN 0-385-47443-1

Printed in the United States of America
June 1996

5 7 9 10 8 6 4

To Ziggy, Socks, Bluto
and the rest of the addicts
at Ponkapogue Golf Club,
Canton, Mass.,
where golf is way too much fun.

Much thanks and a free complimentary press to Leonard (Two Down) O'Connor, who actually exists against all odds and reason; Kevin Cartin, the best writer nobody ever heard of; Richard Brenne, who baby-sat; David Gernert; Amy Williams (my "buddy"); Bill Thomas in relief; Jacqueline LaPierre; Linda, Kel, Jake and Rae; Dorcester Doris Masten; Ken and Lisa Tyler; Art, Janet and even that temp receptionist; my brother and "The Goons," who are possibly even more ill than the Chops; Mark Mulvoy; Jaime Diaz; and everybody at Zaidy's, whose fried egg sandwiches and coffee kept the beast alive.

1

OTHER THAN WRECKING my best friendships, ruining the happiest time of my life and causing two perfectly good women to give me a free drop (no closer to the hole), The Bet was just one helluva good idea.

Looking back on it, that's the thing that torqued me off the most. The fact that a bet did us all in. I mean, other than sucking down fresh-squeezed Genesees and trying to teach Blu Chao to say, "Fuck them in the neck," betting was all we *did* at Ponky.

Maybe I should mention that Ponky is better known as Ponkaquogue Municipal Golf Links and Deli, named by *Golf Illustrated* as "possibly the worst golf course in America." Ponky is to great golf courses what Spam is to the great chefs of Europe, but it had 18 holes most days, which was all we needed to contest our friendly golfing wagers.

Even when we got bored betting on Ponky the usual way, we started dreaming up ways to bet on Ponky in unusual ways. For instance, we'd hot-wire Froghair's Ford Fairline when he was napping, park it on the side of the clubhouse, open the right passenger window and bet on who could fly an L-wedge in there from 25 yards. Or we'd open the sliding-glass doors of the lunchroom two feet and try to see who could hit 4-irons through the opening out onto the driving range.

When we got incredibly C-SPAN-2 bored, we played Reversals, in which your worthy opponent could tee up your ball, turn around on the tee and hit it as far in the opposite direction as he could, as long as the ball was inbounds. You have not lived until you've played a 674-yard par 4 from the edge of some lake, lying two.

We played Murphys, which allowed, once per 9, your worthy opponent to pick up your ball and hand-place it anywhere he pleased, within two club lengths of its original position. Thud (the Almost Human) liked to stick it directly behind a tree, preferably on a root. Two Down used to enjoy dropping your ball in the water, though this led to the Two Down Corollary, which stated that you had to actually be able to *see* the ball when it was done rolling. Unless the pond was clear—and Ponky ponds were never clear, featuring as they did trash flotillas of half-eaten sturgeons, a Safeway cart, biodegradable Pampers and maybe a murder victim or two—we argued that the ball might have gone outside the two-club limit.

When nothing else would do, I liked to find the ugliest, deepest divot and stick my opponent's ball in the very epicenter of it, which is why I very much liked to play in the group behind Thud, for he and his 394 pounds left divots which would make a backhoe jealous. It is very discouraging, indeed, to be just about to hit the bejesus out of your drive and then have somebody holler "Murphy!" and walk over and deposit your ball in a ball washer.

When we got tired of playing Ponky mostly inbounds, we played it mostly out-of-bounds. We'd play it from the far end of the mats-only driving range, over the net, out to 13, down the T tracks, down 18, through the drive-thru of Manelli's dry cleaners and into the back of the hearse Thud (the Almost Human) drove working for the Peaceful Rest mortuary.

It was one of the great mysteries of life why grown men would actually arrive at 4 A.M. to put their little golf balls in a rusty old pipe outside the pro shop at Ponky and then go back and sleep in their cars, just to play a golf course at eight that would have a hard time making Best of Chernobyl. Actually, we had stuff even Chernobyl never thought of. For a time, the front 9 at Ponky was the Dorchester city dump. Eventually, those 9 holes were built back over the landfill, but we'd still get reminders that Ponky is, literally, a dump. Like you'd find an old shopping cart sticking up out of the ground or your ball would disappear in the fissures that open up in the fairways (a free drop if you could prove it) or you'd get a good whiff of the methane gas that's caused by decomposing trash. Yeah, we did that, too. Somebody would track down a good strong leak of methane and we'd take a Bic lighter and light it and have our little mini eternal flame. Very emotional.

Guys kept coming to Ponky maybe because Ponky was its own world, the kind of place that had its own language. It was never a "cup," it was a "jar," and "jar" was mostly used as a verb, like "I have every notion to jar this on your ass."

Golf clubs were "hickories" or "bats," as in the sentence "Hoover just made a 13. I don't think he's gettin' along with his new bats." Beers were, among other things, "Cloudotto Goldbeers." Money was "zops" or "jing," as in the sentence Two Down often employed when he won big, which was "Boys, if jing wasn't made to be stacked up, how come it's flat?"

You "chased some balata" more than you "played golf." And you did not shoot a "bad round" at Ponky, you put up a "radio station," as in the phrase "Damn, I'm on my way to a serious radio station today."

"Magic 103?"

"Worse. Zoo 105."

It always pissed us off, that "possibly the worst golf course in America." Goddamn media. To us, Ponky was *unquestionably* the worst golf course in America, and if you didn't believe it, you should've come and tried to break 90 on our Astroturf tees and tractor-pull fairways and greens about as soft and puttable as Boylston Street. This is the kind of place Ponky was: We had 150-yard markers that weren't 150 yards from anything in particular.

And why a guy who got into Harvard (but never went) and doesn't have a troop of Cub Scouts in the basement and doesn't quite look like Kevin Costner but isn't bad in a Wayne Gretzky kind of way would hang around a dump like Ponky is a story in itself.

My real name is Raymond Lee Hart and I guess I had no excuse. It's just that Ponky was the only place I had any real friends and golf was the only thing I really *did,* I suppose. Well, except for my lame job, which was writing lame glowing reviews of lame books for a lame outfit called Publisher's Reviews. Other than Ponky, I was about as alone as one sock.

My mother got lucky and out of Boston—which is the same thing, I suppose—and lives in San Diego now. My father, the very respected CEO and part-time kid-murderer of the First Boston Bank, hadn't spoken to me in six years, which was convenient, because I hadn't listened in ten. How the word "trust" got into his title is a backstabber, ain't it? And my only brother, Travis, had been dead, what, six years? Six years. Some coincidence there, huh?

Of course, a Chop was not a hard thing to be. All you had to do was buy us a round once in a while and take on a small golfing wager without being bothered by harmless little gestures like Velcro ripping on your backswing or guys suddenly getting whooping cough as you stood over a four-footer or somebody swinging the flagstick on the backswing of your putt so that the cloth whip sounded like a helicopter.

Not that Ponky itself didn't give you enough distractions. Right in front of No. 8 there was a rusted-out, wheelless, stripped-out, Jell-O-green '57 Chevy, which meant you had to get your tee shot up quick, but not so quick as to clip the half of the *Boston Globe* billboard overhanging the tee box.

We also boasted a very, very bad deli featuring a very, very bad cook—Blu Chao, a Cambodian refugee. Blu Chao's finest culinary delight was her bacon sandwich surprise—Bac-Os, mayonnaise and parsley. Although some would not give you three of those for just one of her eighty-nine-cent fried egg and Spam sandwiches.

The nice thing about Blu Chao is that she went nicely with the interior of Ponky, which looked like it was put together from remnants from a Holiday Inn fire. Most of the red flowered whorehouse-velvet wallpaper was still on the walls but only thanks to yards and yards of blue duct tape that ran all along the ceilings and the seams. Years of grime blocked the view of the course, which we were all thankful for. The tables were from a school rummage sale and thus read "Most Precious Blood" in Magic Marker along the side. The fixtures were done in Early Wal-Mart.

Our showers featured the kind of fungus that fungus wipe off their feet. Plus, we had the single cheapest course manager in the world, Froghair, so named not just for his Wally Cleaver haircut but because in his whole entire life he had never reached one of Ponky's holes in regulation.

It was hell, but it was home. We drank at Ponky, ate at Ponky, argued at Ponky, napped at Ponky, lied about sex at Ponky, rolled Serious Dice at Ponky, schemed at Ponky, got depressed at Ponky, and played golf at Ponky, but usually only 36 a day, unless an emergency 9 was voted upon by at least half the participating Chops.

A "Chop" is Ponky for "hack" or "hacker," which is a bad golfer, which is what many Chops were, but not all. Two Down, Chunkin' Charlie and Cementhead were your basic average golfers—12s, 15s, 17s—though Two Down was patently unbeatable. We called him Two Down because he always said, "Boys, the bets don't start until I'm two down," and sure enough, he'd play like a diseased yak on the first four holes and be down to you on the presses something like three, two and one and then come barreling back, making pars from behind Dumpsters and bottoms of lakes and end up in the Pit of Despair with a pile of jing in front of him.

Thud (the Almost Human) and Hoover were truly horrible Chops, but had redeeming characteristics. Thud could steal you anything you needed stolen if you could find which Wendy's he was currently at and Hoover paid out like an ATM machine in spikes and therefore was liked by one and all.

Crowbar, oddly, didn't play golf at all. He only rode around with us in his cart. Crowbar was this very fat black guy, maybe thirty-five years old, with glasses held together on each side with adhesive tape and patches of white skin all over his face and arms, and a head that just sort of emerged from shoulders. He was the kind of guy you'd like to go up to and say, "Let me know when they find your neck."

We called him Crowbar because he was constantly prying himself into situations, conversations, dinners, parties and other people's lives. He had no redeeming characteristics other than he'd seen every movie ever made and knew almost every line ever said. He had a habit of barging into the conversation with stuff that you did not want to talk about, never even considered talking about, at absolutely the worst possible moment.

Like, you'd be about to try a four-footer that decided whether you ate at Black Angus that night or the science fiction movie in your fridge when he'd out with something like . . .

"All-time worst ice-cream flavors."

And you would have to step away from the ball, unable to block out of your brain whatever the fuck it was Crowbar was talking about.

"What the fuck are you talking about, Crowbar?" you'd ask.

"What would be on the list of all-time worst ice-cream flavors," he said defensively. "That's all I'm sayin'."

"Banana chicken," Two Down would offer.

"Steak tartare," Chunkin' Charlie might add.

Pause.

"Lox," you would say.

"Squirrel," Dannie would offer. "With gravy sprinkles."

We all managed to have no jobs or bad enough jobs that allowed us to waste much of our prime earning years at Ponky. Two Down was a telephone repairman. Cementhead was a plumber who had somehow sniffed too much pipe epoxy over his young years. Every now and then you had to rescue him from a one-hour rake job, in which Cementhead could not seem to understand that the footprints that seemed to be all over the stupid bunker were being made by his own size 13s.

Thud—as his weight kept redoubling, his name devolved, from Thaddeus to Thad to his current handle—worked, like I say, at the mortuary, doing most of the cremating, and having no trouble whatsoever eating a turkey leg while doing it.

Thud lived for food. That's why we always liked to ask Thud for directions.

"Say, Thud, you don't know how to get to the DMV, do you?" Two Down might ask knowingly.

"Sure," he'd say. "Uh, you go down until you see the Häagen-Dazs, go past that to the McDonald's, then go left. Follow that past two Winchell's and then go right at the Arby's. It's about two blocks past Fudge City."

Chunkin' Charlie, of course, was dying of cancer. Any day he could get up and around, he came to Ponky, I suppose because laughs were even cheaper than the fried egg sandwiches and nobody treated him any different than anybody else, which is to say, we gave him as much shit as anybody else. "Hey, Charlie," Two Down might say. "Next time you go in for some chemo, see if they can give you a chili-dip vaccine while they're at it." Chunk was a helluva good man. He was like a father to me. No, wait. That's not true. Chunk actually *liked* me.

Almost none of us had wives or lives or anywhere to go or anything to do except hang around Ponky. We'd stay at Ponky until Froghair kicked us out at eleven, then return with one of Thud's complete set of stolen Ponky keys, hauling a pound of bologna and some Cheetos and a case of fresh-squeezed Budweisers and play Buck and Schtuke and Spit in the Ocean until two.

We were all good people, raised right by our mothers, it's just that over the years I guess we'd all become a little out of round and probably should have been taken out of general play. We were a box of X-outs nobody wanted on the half-price table.

We were not moving up any career ladders, had no socially redeeming values and weren't improving our circle of friends any. But we were kind of a family—probably the most dysfunctional family in modern American life—but family just the same, and if there was one thing I just couldn't give up on completely, it was family. Even if my father had.

Besides, I always had Dannie—the sneaky-pretty pro shop assistant with, as she liked to say herself, "the best real tits in Boston"—but only from the lips down.

Dannie Higgins was a flaming redhead luscious, about twenty-seven, with a cotton-eyed Arkansas accent, a freckled face right out of a Scottish riding stable, this twelve-car-pileup body and a little nose that could've hardly made a dent in a cream pie. Mostly, though, she had these eyes. There have been few sets of eyes in luscious history that made you take a full step back, but these were two of them—a kind of sea green you only see in those postcard pictures of the water off an old boat drifting lazily in the Caribbean somewhere. You could easily dive into these eyes and leave no forwarding address.

Of course, almost nobody knew all that because she wore her hair back in a ponytail all the time and then covered that up with a Titlist hat and Oakleys. She wore almost no makeup and hid those two wonderful girls of hers under the baggiest sweaters in the shop.

We were regular wrestling partners, every Friday, midnight. We'd alternate. One week, we'd go to her apartment and I got to be

Heidi and she had to be the senator. The next week she'd come to my apartment and she got to be Heidi and I had to be the senator. No switching up. If it was my apartment, then the rules had to be the same. I would find my instructions under the mat and had to follow them explicitly. On her weeks, she would find the instructions in her milk box.

Get completely naked except for your baseball hat, a pair of white socks and your black pumps. Face the bedroom mirror. Have the catcher's mitt ready.

All that got started one night after we'd played 36 holes, and I won one up after a great match. Then we played gin until midnight and I won by one Hollywood. Then we had one of our Diehard putting matches on the putting green with everybody's car pulled up around it and the headlights on and I took her for $20 with a 40-foot camel ride on the last hole. It was a rare day. I had beat her at everything. And we were sitting there just the two of us at the corner table, loaded up on fresh-squeezed Gennys, and me beaming and her pissed off and she just looked me right in the eye and said, "Yeah, but I bet I *fuck* better than you."

You can't just let somebody *say* that.

After that, we had a regular organ recital once a week. I guess it wasn't just purely recreation fucking. There was some feelings there. I know there was on my part, though I hid it well because I wasn't sure there were any on her side of the handcuffs. I think she was doing it just to keep the loneliness away. When it comes to hearts, I wasn't going to show her mine until she showed me hers and she wasn't about to.

Anytime we'd get so we were staying too long or letting emotions start to hog the covers, we'd both back off and she'd say something like "Well, you ain't bad. For practice."

You had to be out of the other's apartment by sunrise. No exceptions. And there were some things you absolutely couldn't do.

She couldn't ask about Travis and I couldn't take off her locket or look inside it. No exceptions.

She might be covered in chocolate mousse or be wrapped entirely in Christmas ribbon, but no touching the locket. She could discuss everything up to and including my failed writing career, but Travis was off-limits. Fine with me. Hey, you needed a lot of rules to stay FBs, as we called ourselves—fuck buddies.

It was simpler this way, I suppose. No stupid emotions involved when you're an FB. Nobody pissed off because you used a bath towel getting out of the shower or a shower towel getting out of the bath or didn't hear her say "I love you" because you were watching SportsCenter. Besides, she said I was too irresponsible for her, that I would make the worst dad in dad history and I agreed, so we kept our weekly fluid exchange parties going and left the Harlequin stuff out of it.

Her fantasy was to marry this polite, honorable, outrageously handsome, perfectly dressed blond stud who helped her push her car to the side of the road one day and wasn't wearing a wedding ring but whose name she never had time to get. And naturally, I didn't say what I wanted to say and picked what anybody would pick: a deaf, dumb, blindly loyal twenty-one-year-old Miss Striptease Florida holding tomorrow's racing results in one hand and a pony keg in the other.

Naturally, our arrangement was known only by us for a lot of reasons, the most important of which was that it would've ruined the betting altogether and you never let anything screw with the betting at Ponky. Dannie was one of the guys, the only female Chop in what was otherwise your basic Johnson Fest. She swore and drank and smoked the driver about 240, so she was hard enough to beat without thinking of her as a woman at the same time, so mostly we just didn't.

Those were probably the happiest years of my life. And then

11

Hoover had to go and take his ball retriever and rip a two-foot gash out of the hedge at 17 and from that hole was born The Bet to See Whether the Tag Team of Stupid and Jealousy Could Kick Happiness's Ass, and suddenly everything took a distinct right turn dircctly toward Shit.

2

THE DAY THE BET began to assume its hideous form was the day Hoover lost $208 to his shadow, which is a lot of cash to drop for a man who takes the bus to the golf course.

Hoover wasn't much to look at. Dannie said his mother must've had to borrow a baby to take to church. He sort of looked like that skinny guy in Westerns, the one that's always first out of the saloon whenever it looks there's gonna be gunplay. For somebody who was supposed to be Italian, he was white as plaster of Paris and looked like he tanned nightly under a 40-watt bulb. Two Down saw him in shorts one time and said, "And now, students, your circulatory system at work."

He had this Lettermanesque gap in his teeth, a little red hair that he covered up with one of those Jackie Stewart racing caps, skinny white arms that were mostly elbow and a score counter on his belt, which had been rubbed shiny with use.

Come to think of it, Hoover wasn't even his real name. We called him Hoover because he very much sucked. After most rounds, he was awarded the puke-orange Naugahyde La-Z-Boy in the Pit of Despair, reserved for the day's biggest loser.

Hoover's real name was Alberto de Salvo, which also happened to be the name of the Boston Strangler. That figured. Hoover apparently had all his luck surgically removed as a small boy.

Still, Hoover loved the game. He had every color book Harvey Penick ever wrote, including the Little Red Book, the Little Green Book, the Little Shoebox of Stuff Harvey Penick Forgot the First Two Times, the Little Blue Two-Volume Videocasette featuring the 13 Most Important Things Harvey Penick Asks You to Remember at the Moment of Impact, and the Little Fuchsia Book: New Stuff Harvey's Agent Wanted Him to Include.

Hoover would spend sleepless nights worrying about shaft kick points. He actually knew what his swing weight was. He was obsessed with equipment. He would no sooner have just received his boron-headed, titanium-shafted Big Bertha in the mail than he would banish it to his trunk and bring out a brand-new, French-bubble-shafted, graphite-headed Whaling Wendy, which, unfortunately, the factory forgot to de-shank, and so then he'd have to dump that and go to his mercury-loaded, airstream Colossal Cathy.

He was some kind of MIT scientist and somebody said his IQ was 153, which goes to show you golf is not a game you want to think too much about. Bless his heart, Hoover thought way too much. He believed in a person's inner "chakras" and had his adjusted after very bad rounds. He tried pneumatic balls, which actually *did* add 15 yards to his drive, until it got hot and they started exploding in his bag, which caused most of the guys in his group to dive for cover, thinking the darling youngsters that live in the Roosevelt Park projects off 13 were spraying the course again for amusement. After that, he played nothing but Titlists 8s.

"Wh th fck you nly ply Ttlst 8s?" Thud (the Almost Human) asked him one day with his mouth occupied with his ninth fried egg sandwich of the day.

"Because," Hoover told him. "The number eight is the only perfectly aerodynamic number you can get on a golf ball. Any other number will affect the flight."

"Rt. Nd I'm Jck Fckng Nckls." Thud munched.

As much as you wanted him to succeed once—*just once*—it was hopeless. He would take the club back very, very, very slowly, stop halfway up, raise his elbows straight over his head and twist his body like he was trying to win Hernia of the Month. Then he would come crashing down at the ball in hopes that maybe it would not have time to see him coming. Dannie said he sort of looked like a man trapped in a moving car with a bee. His goal was to shoot his weight, which was 105, but he'd never done it. Of course, he'd only been playing Ponky seven years.

And after each horrible shot or bad break or terrible round of high-tension golf, Hoover would plunk himself down in the puke-orange La-Z-Boy, loose a large sigh, fling his Jackie Stewart cap toward the hatrack, miss and say, "Rats get fat. Good men die."

"What does that mean anyway?" Cementhead asked him once after he'd put up a double radio station.

And Hoover said, "It is the universal and ultimate order of things. It means that hard work, diligence, patience and good deeds aren't worth anything at all. It means the centers of things do not hold. All is chaos. It means karma is dead."

And Cementhead asked, "What does that mean anyway?"

Still, Hoover had a will. You could beat him like egg whites and the next day he'd be back, doubling the bets, convinced the breakthrough was just around the corner. He'd say that "a person's golf swing can only truly be foolproof when tested under pressure," and we'd all very much agree and pretty soon he'd be taking all the action we'd give him.

The day Hoover dropped the $208 was one of those early September afternoons that can't decide whether to be summer or winter and the usual suspects were hanging around. The Stringley brothers, slower than refund checks, had teed off just in front of us. The Stringley brothers were these identical eighty-five-year-old twins who only played against each other and always for the same action: $1 a hole, instant whip-out, although nothing the Stringley brothers did was instant. You'd be behind them and you'd see one of them totter up to his putt and gag it in and cackle what he always cackled: "T-t-t-t-take a s-s-s-s-suck a that!" And then the other one would begrudgingly hand it over.

"Me and Stick in forty years," said Two Down.

We had our own usual games going—giant skins, carryovers, incest, $10 two-downs, double the backs, Alohas (double everything on 18), a game or two of Las Vegas, complimentary presses whenever and wherever the hell you felt like it and unlimited junk, which was anything else that you could dream up.

The usual and absolutely nonnegotiable assortment of penalties and assessments were in place, set forth by Two Down many years ago, encased in plastic and blue-duct-taped to the top of the corner table in the salmonella paradise of a lunchroom known to us as the Pit of Despair.

Schedule of Fines

Hackalooski (player with higher handicap giving player with lower handicap advice) . . . $5
Ernest and Julio (excessive whining) . . . $2
Hit and Whip (player hitting a bad shot and blaming another player in the group) . . . $5
Venturi (analyzing your swing too much) . . . $2
Posing . . . $1
Collared shirt . . . $2
Each logo over the one-logo limit per player . . . $1
Double plumb bob . . . $1
Purposeful, willful and distracting talk of pooni . . . $3

Once in a while, with his 40 handicap and his chakras fixed up nice and his Jackie Stewart on snug, Hoover could get into your Hanes pretty quick. And that's what happened that day.

He had me down $25, Chunkin' Charlie down $40, and Two Down down a good $100, and had accepted absolutely free and complimentary presses from all of us. Not only that, if he double-bogeyed out, he'd break 100, which would be on a par with a lobster climbing out of the tank at Jimmy's Seafood Grill, taking the stage and whistling the entire score of Cats.

"Gentlemen, we shall be stacking up some of that flat tender in the Pit of Despair very soon," Hoover said, beaming.

Chunkin' Charlie was up first on 15. He hit a very good drive and gave it the big Walter Hagen pose.

Charlie: "Boys, if you like golf, you *gotta* like that shot."

Me: "Right. Until you find it in an old Hunt's can."

Two Down: "You'll probably have to play it out backward."

Charlie: "Five says I make par."

Me and Two Down: "Bank."

Now it was Two Down's turn. He hit his patented screaming low hook that would've sailed under a '63 Valiant and not touched earth or oil pan.

Now it was Hoover's turn. He was just about ready to take the club back when Two Down said a very hideous thing.

"Hey, Hoov."

"What?" Hoover said.

"You probably know more about the golf swing than anybody here, right?"

"So?"

He still wouldn't look up.

"Well," said Two Down, "don't you think it's funny that you never see your shadow during your swing?"

"Kindly go fuck yourself," replied Hoover, not moving an inch, head still, knees bent, eyes peeled on his Titlist 8.

"Well," continued Two Down. "I mean, in golf, everybody is supposed to stay perfectly still and nobody's supposed to breathe so you have absolutely no distractions. But then right in front of you, your own shadow is going through all kinds of contortions, going this way and that, all the time, and yet nobody ever notices it during the swing."

"Do you mind?" said Hoover.

"Actually," said Two Down, "I guess if you *did* notice your shadow, it would help your swing. I mean, you could see whether your club face was a little open at the top or whether your elbow was flying or all kinds of stuff."

"Double fornicate yourself," answered Hoover.

But this last was said with a clink of doubt in his voice, as though maybe Two Down's words had seeped into his cranium and were bouncing around with the Pythagorean theorem and double quark pie and everything else he had in there. Here, a scientist who had devoted most of his life to the understanding of golf and all its tangents had never thought about the proper use and purpose of the shadow during the swing.

You could see his mind working. *Why is it that nobody notices their shadow? Had he ever even* seen *his shadow during the swing?* He let his eyes steal away from the Titlist 8 to look. *There it was. Plain as day. Why hadn't his shadow ever bothered him before?*

In a fair and just world, Hoover would've stepped away from the ball and somebody would've told a joke or mentioned the weather or reported the news that Thud recently broke his record for the longest urination in Ponky history last week when he peed so long his foursome had to let two groups through. But nobody did.

Hoover stayed frozen over the ball, had to be forty-five seconds—and everybody stayed quiet.

At last, he started to take a swing, his shadow square in front of him. It looked like an innocent little swing at first and then about two feet back he lurched a little. Then, at the top, he gave it an industrial-strength downward lurch, so that now he resembled more a Navy signalman landing a MIG on an aircraft carrier than a golfer.

The ball, confused, went about 8 feet up and 6 feet sideways, bounced off a sick-looking pine tree nobody had hit in the history of Ponky and drowned itself in shame in the pond in front of the tee box.

I still believe that if Charlie and me hadn't been there, Two Down would have been the first man in Massachusetts golf history strangled by a resonant-resistant, Loomis-blend Meaty Martha.

Hoover stayed silent. We stayed silent. Hoover reloaded and set up again, but there was a fabric of dread draped over the moment. This was not like somebody jangling keys or pumping cart brakes. This was a shadow and it would be back again tomorrow and the day after that. Worse, it was *his* shadow, a sinister prank pulled on him by his own scrawny body. Naturally, Hoover saw it again and pile-drived another Titlist 8 into the pond.

One thing for sure, the synapses and nerve signals that sent messages from Hoover's brain to Hoover's body were completely severed. Hoover was now a man without logic. He could not escape the sight of his shadow. He drop-kicked another one in a glob of mud, smother-toed one into the Murkwood Forest, then sliced one over the Elcar fence, off Manelli's dry cleaners and under a sky-blue '85 LTD. He was lying 10 and still on the tee. Breaking 100 was now history.

Naturally, in a moment like this, any true friend, any caring person, would stay quiet.

Two: "Now you've got it corrected, Hoovs."

Chunkin' Charlie: "Hey, Hoovs. When you go find that one ball, can you check and see if my shirts are done?"

Then Crowbar hit him with some movie dialogue: "You're not too smart, are you? I like that it in a man."

Cementhead: *"It Happened One Night?"*

Crowbar: *"Body Heat."*

Cementhead: "Damn!"

Hoover wasn't listening. He was digging out more golf balls. He Gretzkyed two more slap shots into the pond before he finally bent the Meaty Martha over his knee and snapped it, Bo Jackson style. He took out his 8-iron and bellied one barely over the pond and into the fairway. He enjoyed an 18.

For the next two holes, the brooding Hoover was tormented by his shadow. He could not help but see it. And even when the sun was to his back and he could not see it, he was *afraid* he might see it. He was a very good candidate for the centerfold in *Psychology Today*.

He was on his way to losing all those presses and the complimentary presses and whatever other jing nightmares that hadn't occurred to him yet. The horror of the thing that he'd done was starting to mount up inside his eyes, like somebody was starting a bonfire just behind his forehead.

He sat down on the 18th tee and put his face entirely in the palms of his bony hands and his eyebrows seemed to slide off his forehead and come to rest just level with his nose, and he was basically just a lot of black clouds and red hair. He looked like a man who had just backed over his own dog.

"Rats get fat?" Dannie asked.

"Good men die," I said sadly.

"Don't worry about it, Hoovs," said Two Down helpfully. "You won't have the same problem tomorrow."

"Why?" asked Hoover darkly.

"Because," said Two Down, "it's supposed to be cloudy."

And that's when Hoover went triple O.J.

Chops officially recognize two kinds of mad. Joan Crawford Mad gets you helicoptering clubs and looking for wet places to throw your worthy opponent. O.J. Mad is when you are so mad you begin turning in a circle, trying to decide whether to drive your cart into a lake, rip off your clothes and throw yourself on a barbed-wire fence or calmly walk over to the stone wall and begin smashing body parts against it, some of them your own. What you usually end up doing is something painful like losing a crown biting as hard as possible on your putter or purposely taking one shoe and spiking the other and missing, thereby painfully piercing your ankle.

Hoover stalked over to his bag, took out his ball retriever, telescoped it out all the way and began walking toward Two Down, who backed away slowly toward the eight-foot hedge that ran behind the tee box and protected the Mayflower from us.

"It's just a game, Hoovs," said Two Down.

Hoover had him backed up against the hedge. He set up like Yaz, screamed wildly and took a wild swing at Two Down's head.

Naturally, dodging an eighteen-foot ball retriever is a very easy thing to do and the retriever missed Two and whipped violently into the hedge. But this did not deter Hoover. He continued to whack against the same spot, despite the fact that Two Down was well out of the way. Hoover was not going to take any shit whatsoever from a hedge.

Finally, the retriever felt enough was enough and refused to come out. Hoover and Chunkin' Charlie grabbed the retriever right at the edge of the hedge and yanked. Nothing. Hoover, Charlie and me reached in and yanked. Nothing. Hoover, Dannie, me, Cementhead and Two Down put our feet into the bigger branches of the hedge, called "1 . . . 2 . . . 3 . . ." and yanked.

The hedge said *Scccckrrrackkk!* and we all came flying out—us, branches, leaves, centuries-old trash, eleven golf balls and half a retriever. When we had finished dusting ourselves off, we looked back at the damage. And that is when we saw it.

The yank had left a massive two-by-three-foot hole in the hedge. And through the hole was a perfectly clear view of something we never thought we'd see in our lives—the Mayflower Club.

We were all stunned silent.

Finally, Crowbar said, "Open the pod bay doors, Hal."

"*A Man for All Seasons?*" asked Cementhead.

"*2001,*" said Crowbar.

"Damn!"

3

UNTIL THAT MOMENT, we had never actually laid eyes on the Mayflower Club, which was only the finest, snootiest, private, white, sperm-dollar country club on the eastern seaboard.

Not that we didn't know it was over there. We knew. Right across the twelve-foot brick wall that divided Them from Us. We just tried not to think about it.

Actually, that was easy. Until Hoover gouged out a hole in the hedge, it was more myth than reality. You couldn't see into any part of it without a cherry picker or a helicopter or a court order. Word was, the night guards carried guns.

Even the front gate was imposing wrought iron backed by black canvas. And if you managed a glimpse inside when Ivan, the Gestapo guard, opened it briefly to let a Jaguar or a Bentley pull in, then you were still out of luck, because once inside the gate, the Jaguars and the Bentleys took hard rights to get around another brick wall and then a left to begin what we'd always heard was the spine-tinglingest drive in golf to a kind of green-and-blue Protestant Paradise.

It was like living next door to Howard Hughes. You knew he was there. Everyone told you he was there. You sensed he was there. But he never came over to borrow sugar.

In fact, the only time we thought much about it was every June, when the Mayflower held its Mayflower Carousel, a four-day tournament, party and cuff-link fest, in which there would be so many guests it would overwhelm the Mayflower's small parking lot. No problem. For those four days, they would park on *our* golf course and get shuttled over in long, gray stretch limousines. That's what Ponky was to the Mayflower. Emergency parking.

How a place like the Mayflower Club could exist in the worst part of Dorchester, hard by the projects and the vacant lots and the welfare mothers, was a testament to good old-fashioned Boston machine politics.

When the Mayflower was built in 1896, Dorchester was one of the finest sections in Boston. But as the decades passed and Dorchester stopped shaving and wearing clean shirts, the walls around the Mayflower Club just got higher and higher. They weren't about to *move* and give up one of Donald Ross's finest designs. And besides, the next place might not be so nice about them having no Jews, blacks, Catholics or women as voting members and yet, somehow, owning a nonprofit tax status. This never seemed to bother the Dorchester City Council, who reportedly were warmed by under-the-table grease and tee times during campaign seasons.

And so the Mayflower stayed right where it was. It just constructed a twelve-foot brick wall all around it, accompanied by a thick eight-foot hedge and told the Friday-night orchestras to bring it up a notch to drown out those sometimes annoying noises like sirens and gunplay.

It was a tiny microcosm of life, right there on Geneva Avenue. The Jaguars and the Bentleys turned right into the magnificent grounds of the Mayflower, while the 1979 camouflage blue-gray Pintos and the AMC Pacers kept trundling along another eighth of a mile and pulled into the gravel parking lot of Ponky. It was both ends of the American continuum, laid out on one single street in a Boston suburb.

Actually, I take it back. One Chop had seen the Mayflower before—Cementhead. He was doing a diaphragm flush on a kitchen sink one day when he realized he was in one of the half dozen homes in Dorchester that backed directly on to the Mayflower. Now, some rednecks have guns hung in the rear windows of their pickups. Cementhead has a 2-iron. And a ball and a glove in the glove box. "In case of emergency," he'd say.

When he was finished with the job, he realized nobody was watching him, so he climbed the moss-covered backyard wall, threw a ball down on the 11th tee, a par 3, and hit a great shot to about 15 feet. "Man, that tee was nicer than any green we have!" he always said when Chops would ask him to retell the story. He putted up close with his 2-iron and gave himself the putt.

"I'm even par for the Mayflower," Cementhead always took pains to tell us. "Suck on that, you muni hacks."

As for the rest of us, we only knew the rumors we'd heard. Supposedly, the Mayflower had no more than 150 members, half of which were keeping constant company with an I.V. and maybe a ventilator, too. The USGA was constantly begging them to have a U.S. Open, but the members would just sniff twice and go back to their red beluga.

And yet, for as few people as played it, *Golf* magazine had ranked it fourth in American courses, behind Pine Valley, Pebble Beach and Augusta National. But since no reporter had ever been inside its gates, how could you really know?

We heard that the Mayflower was made up solely of descendants of the *Mayflower* ship itself, no exceptions, which was really a polite way of saying, "The only way you black, Hispanic, Jap, Jew and Catholic motherfuckers are gonna get in here is with a court order."

And since none of us could come up with the $35,000 cover charge to join the Mayflower, to say nothing of faking the *Mayflower* bloodlines, and since we were all hopelessly addicted to the ridiculous game of golf anyway, we were left with nothing else to do but try to forget the world on the other side of the hedge and plunk down our $6 weekday ($8 weekend) to play a course no self-respecting rodent would relieve itself upon.

We just figured we were different from them, not worse. Their names were Wigglesworth, Peabody and Coolidge. Ours were Valentini, Papoulias and Harrigan. They read *Barron's.* We read the *Racing Form.* They came over on the *Mayflower.* We came over on the 51 Crosstown.

Of course, we had an idea how huge the difference was. We'd seen enough Masters to know we were playing a pitiful, dog-meat, kennel run of a golf course, but it was our pitiful, dog-meat, kennel run of a golf course and we defended it anyway. We were sure that Ponky had taught us shots those pampered pussies over at the Mayflower could never dream of.

"Let's see 'em try to hit a cut 3-iron around the light pole onto a rock green while keeping one foot on the sprinkler head that never goes off on 16," Dannie would say.

"Man, I just wish the Numerals would come over here *one* time," Two Down would say, "Numerals" being what we called the Mayflower members, guessing that they were all named either Haverford Livingston III or Stockton Charlesworth IV. "I could refinish my basement."

"They'd get one look at our rough and be back with their fuckin' attorneys," Dannie threw in.

"How do you think they'd enjoy putting on one of Froghair's volcano-hole cuts?" Hoover said, invoking the name of our hideous owner/greenskeeper. "One of those in which he pulls the hole out wrong so there's that annoying little ridge all the way around it? Those gentlemen would have him drawn and quartered."

"Yeah," Cementhead would say. "And then they'd *kill* him."

But Hoover's Hole allowed us to see exactly where we stood on life's food chain. Somewhere just below Ramada maids and just above plankton.

Where Hoover had made his hole was pure whimsy. A four-foot-high electrical control box behind the green made for an interruption in the twelve-foot brick wall and so we could see just enough to make us sick—a tee box, half of a green, most of a pond and half of a fairway as it came gently down a lush hill. It was enough to send us into fits of acute and paralyzing envy.

"I think I'm moist," said Two Down.

The Mayflower was more luxurious and magnificent than even our imaginations had led us to believe. The gloriously green, double-cut fairway was finer than any green we had ever imagined. The lines of that fairway were crisp and clean, the sand in the bunkers baby soft and white, the water in the pond clear and blue. The greens—oh, God, the greens!—looked like $40-a-foot carpeting, the kind God might have in His office.

The flagstick stood tall and shining, with a crisp white flag flying from it. Not only was there not a single piece of cloth hanging from a Ponky flagstick, we barely had flagsticks. Three of them were former rakes.

It was like setting a piece of Beverly Hills down in the middle of downtown Akron. It couldn't possibly be, and yet there it was.

Almost nobody at the Mayflower actually lived in Dorchester. They all moved out to their mansions on Beacon Hill and in the Back Bay a generation ago. But the course was just too good to leave.

What's funny is that Ponky was a Ross design, too—Ronald Ross. The idiots that built Ponkaquogue thought that was the name of the famous architect and supposedly wrote away to the American Golf Architects Association, who sent them Ronald Ross—record-setting nobody from Trenton, New Jersey. Ponky became to golf architecture what the *Exxon Valdez* was to scallops.

The landing areas made no sense (for instance, the land on No. 1 banked right and Ronald made it a dogleg left). The rhythm of the course was stupid. The front 9 was a good length, just over 3,500 yards and a par 36, but about the 10th hole, Ross must've looked up from his twenty-third mulled wine, realized how little land he had left and said, "Uh-oh." The 11th hole actually *bisects* the 9th fairway and became such a hazard to players in the 1950s that the city built a tunnel—a tunnel!—that you had to use to get through the 9th without a Dunlop boring an unwanted orifice in your skullcap. Of course, if you didn't quite kill a driver and your ball happened to end up on the 11th fairway, say a novena.

Modern civilization has only made the colossal gap between Ponky and the Mayflower even more staggering. A cement river was built through Ponky, rubber-stamped through by the City Council late one night. It really didn't come into play much, except that it cut across the 5th fairway, bordered the 6th green, cut in front of the 9th and 10th green and nudged up against the 18th green on your approach shot. Beagle River we called it, on account of a "beagle" being a double par, which is what you might make if you hit into it.

True, there wasn't any water in Beagle River. The City Council decided it was too expensive and killed the project about a mile and a half past Ponky. Still, if your ball went into the Beagle, you couldn't go down and hit it because it was protected on all sides by an eleven-foot-high fence.

As if all that weren't enough, the T ran through Ponky at exactly thirteen minutes after the hour and seventeen minutes before, near the west side—the Mayflower side—cutting right across the 14th fairway, the 15th fairway, the 16th green and, conveniently, just behind the 9th tee box on its way to its stop at Field's Corner.

This made for some very exciting presses, because the T is not a very loud train until it is suddenly upon you. And since the 9th tee abutted Waldeck Avenue, and the noise from the trucks and cars hides its approaching sound, you didn't know it was coming until it suddenly appeared on the elevated tracks above the road and came right up your spine just as you were trying to pull the trigger. And even when it didn't, you were always worried it was going to.

Thank you, Dorchester City Council.

And so it was that the first 9 holes of Ronald Ross's Ponky, meant for a private club, were turned into the city dump and the other 9 were sold off for a time and then bought back by the city, which let the plankton-brains of the Metro District run it. The Metro District decided to "re-create" the same "historic" (awful) design over the landfill and screwed that up so bad that a lummox like Froghair could buy it. Froghair never could afford walls to keep the riffraff out, which was good, I suppose, since we ended up being both the raff and the riff.

Now, suddenly, there were these aliens on the other side of the hedge, men dressed in white linen pants and smart golf shirts, real leather golf shoes and belts. There were caddies with each group, dressed in crisp white overalls with smart blue-and-green caps, and blue-and-green lettering on the backs of their overalls that read "TMC" in some kind of fancy Leona Helmsley script. Caddies wouldn't even come to Ponky to *play.*

But it was more than just the people. It was the peace of the place, the feel of it, the quiet. Somehow, just five feet across this hedge, all the noise and the yelling and the needling and the pumping of the cart brakes and the power Velcro and the silent screaming in your brain that goes on at Ponky just ended. To us, Mayflower players used an entirely foreign language: "Oh, nice shot, Cheddar." And "Good swing there, Brewster ol' boy!" and "Get in for him! . . . Ah, nuts!" If a Chop told my ball to get in, I'd know I just hit the wrong ball.

It was two worlds colliding. Theirs was the world of brass and roses and the pianist playing something by Rodgers and Hart as the waiter brought the *ratatouille à la maison.* Ours was the world where guys in yellow suits and backpack respirators and red rubber boots stopped play now and again to make "a routine methane check." Uh-huh. The grass was not just greener over there; it was greener than any green we'd ever seen in our 64 box of Crayolas. It was so green it turned the faces of the Chops green and that envy ended up in a bet that wound up costing us all a lot more than money.

Slowly, like the flu, Mayflowermania began sweeping over the Chops. The Ponkiness in them started to drain out and envy and depression began to crawl in. What one could see through the hole became a big topic of Chop talk. Crowbar, for instance, would spend hours at the hole, just watching. There was a constant logjam at 18 tee now from guys who wanted to assure themselves that the world on the other side of the hedge really did exist, that it was no dream.

It must've been like what East Berliners used to see when they got on a roof and looked over the wall to the other side, aching for all that color.

But to me, it was just a new cable channel to look at before zapping on, a pretty amusement. It was cute, but nothing I was obsessing over—until the day Crowbar and I were kneeling there, looking through it, and . . .

"People you just can't picture taking a grumpy," Crowbar said.

"A what?"

"A grumpy, a crap."

"Please, Lord, strike this man mute," I mentioned.

"No, seriously. Who are your top five people you can't picture taking a grumpy? Like Princess Diana. I just can't see her taking a grumpy. Or the Pope. I mean, isn't there anybody that you have a hard time picturing taking a grumpy?"

And just then I saw a tall man coming to the top of that lovingly mown hill, walking ten feet in front of his caddie and wearing your basic Numerals uniform: Sansabelt khakis, two-tone Foot-

Joys, logo golf shirt with the big Sister Batrille wing-tip collars. He came to his ball and took one practice swing and it was like watching a home movie you hadn't seen in twenty years.

"God! My father!"

"See?" said Crowbar. "There's two."

4

I WAS QUITE SURPRISED to find out that I was a direct descendant of a *Mayflower* passenger. How else could my father have gotten into the Mayflower? I took a guess that some lawyers had scared them off of the blue-blood stipulation and just made the rules: "Take any rich white male with a velour Rush Limbaugh in his office and no history of voting for a school bond."

Not that it mattered. I would've rather waded through a shark tank in tuna underwear than see my father again. It was nothing personal. I just didn't particularly care to lay eyes on the man who took my brother from me. And my mother. And, you might say, the best parts of myself. I didn't want to see him, hear him, think about him or remember him and so, from then on, I stayed away from Hoover's Hole like it was streptococcus A.

I was the only one.

Somehow, what was on their side of the hedge was changing what was on ours. The talk in the Pit of Despair was no longer so much about who did what to whom and how did you like that high draw out of jail I put on your lard ass at 14, but was instead Dannie saying stuff like "God, I just wanna go lay down on that tee box butt nekkid!"

For some reason, it was Dannie who spent the most time at the hole in the hedge, not so much because she loved golf as because that world over there was even more alien and wonderful to her than to any of us.

The best thing about being Dannie's regular bopping partner was all the long talks we used to have after the Parkay was put away. She'd put her head on my shoulder and I'd hear how her family shared a two-bedroom house in Little Rock with her aunt and uncle and their three boys. I suppose that's where she got so tough, knocking up against those boys every day for bathroom space. Her sister slept on a cot in her parents' room. She slept on the couch. The three boys slept on the floor. And on nights when the broken spring was right in the middle of her back, she'd lie awake and dream about a big fancy house somewhere with a big bedroom of her very own, maybe with a fireplace in it and a couch you only sat in.

And yet, through all of that, she said her father never lost his dignity. He was nothing more than a handyman, but she admired him.

"Doesn't matter how down we were, whenever my mama would come to sit down for supper, he would rise."

He was also the only one who held down a job. Dannie's uncle was laid up with some mysterious sciatica problem and her aunt was arthritic and couldn't even help her mom stitch the pot holders that they sold to the little Ben Franklin store in town.

"But I never heard my daddy complain once," she said. "My sister says to him once, 'Why you gotta pay for them all the time? Why can't they go find a damn Amana box somewhere and give us some chewin' room?' And Daddy got all purple-faced and said, 'We will *NOT* turn our backs on family!' And they was my mama's people!"

Dannie was a natural jock, but she got into golf because she loved how classy it all seemed—she always pointed out that it was the only game in which you called the penalty on yourself. She was one helluva good player, maybe good enough to try the LPGA tour, but that isn't what she wanted. She dreamed of a job at a swank country club where the people were polite and all the neat country-club kids called her Daniella.

That might've been where she ended up, except she hit a speed bump about five years ago when she got a little baby by a no-good lowlife who skipped town when he heard the good news. She was so embarrassed that she moved home, had it, gave it up for adoption and practically had to start over again.

None of this soft side ever leaked out of Dannie around Ponky, though. She acted like somebody that would eat dignity's butt with a nice baked potato and a Chianti. She was the cousin of three brothers at Ponky, as bawdy and rowdy as any of us. She could out-raunch any of us.

She used to come back from dates and we'd say, "Well?"

"Well, what?"

"How was he?"

And she'd say, with a wry grin, "Let's just say his new nickname is Hebrew National." Or "About a thirteen on the Stimpmeter, if you boys know what I'm saying." And you never knew if anything really happened at all.

What Dannie saw looking through the hole at the Mayflower was not what I saw, which was a lot of old men in miracle fibers and possibly Depends. She saw men of class and breeding. And she was dreaming about that life the day she saw, coming over the emerald-green hill, a man straight out of a J. Crew catalogue—crushingly handsome, all tan and teeth, curly golden hair, a 20th Century Fox chin, white linen pants, a gorgeous off-white Polo, just the right belt and a Duke of Windsor sort of walk.

"That's him!" she whispered.

"Who?" I said.

"The guy who helped me push my car!" she said. "That's him! Oh, God! He's sooooo nice!"

I took a gander.

"He's pretty," I said. "Got his number?"

Dannie grabbed me hard around the collar until my face was sort of flush up against the hedge.

"He's *class,*" she growled. "Don't you start on him with all your smart talk."

I said OK already and I looked at Two Down and he looked at me and we both knew something was serious here.

"He's just purdier than a first-place belt buckle," she said.

And then Mr. Goodgolf chipped in and some blue blood on the other side of the hedge said, "Browning Sumner, you are the luckiest son of a gun in the club!"

From then on, Dannie was enrolled at the University of Browning.

....

I still think everybody would have gone back to our cozy little vinyl and nitrate world if it hadn't been for Two Down missing that putt.

Two Down was the best friend I had in the world who didn't occasionally tie me to the bedpost and lick me like a Creamsicle.

Two Down was kind of a living Picasso painting. He had this XL schnozz that just jumped off his face like one of those kids' pop-up books. He had one eyebrow that was mostly black and another that was mostly gray and the black one stopped halfway through and then started again, having been cleaved in half by a hockey puck when he was a twelve-year-old goalkeeper. For this reason, some guys called him Red Light.

He was the only golfer I ever knew who had a "We Accept Visa and MasterCard" tag on his bag. If gambling were suddenly to vanish from this earth, Two Down would melt into a little pile of chits and blow away in the wind.

He would bet you ten zops you couldn't eat six Saltines a minute (you can't). He'd bet you how many minutes it was going to take Blu Chao to make a two-minute egg (he had one the day before: nine). He'd bet whether the guy at the next table was going to go around his ear of corn in a circle or side to side (he's a plant: circle).

He was quite sure he was going to strike it big somehow, some way, and whenever we'd drive somewhere, he'd take little detours to show us this mansion he was going to own or that mansion and always add something like "Of course, those shutters will have to go," or "I'll put the chopper pad on that side of the house." He was serious. No bet, no game, no challenge ever really came off until Two Down walked in about two-thirty every day, ripped off his New England Bell uniform shirt and gave the day's game his blessing, which was not so much a word from him as much as it was that crazy gleam in his eyes.

What's funny is he wasn't even much good. He was a goofy-looking 17 handicap with legs as white and skinny as OB stakes and wiry 110-volt hair that stood straight up and made him look mostly like a barbecue cleaning brush. He was about 145 pounds of bravado and schemes and vodka sodas.

The day he missed the putt, the sun had pretty much clocked out and we were playing by the porch lights on the Ponky clubhouse. Of course, nobody went in, on account of a pretty nice stack of zops still lying around in the balance on the 9th green.

What it came down to was me hoping to gag in a 7-foot birdie snake and then crossing my fingers. Because even if I did, Two Down could still make a 5-footer for a birdie to win about $160 total from me and Charlie. If he missed, he'd lose about that much, which made it about a $300 putt, which is about as big as anybody had ever putted for or ever wanted to at a dump like Ponky.

I was about to put my sweetest little brush stroke on mine when . . .

"You know what's funny?" blurted out Crowbar, jammed into his cart, the steering wheel protruding five inches into his gut.

"Guys getting murdered and dumped in the Charles River for talking while a guy is putting?" I said, backing off the putt.

"No," he said, unfazed. "It's that everything you really needed to know about golf you learned when you were two years old!"

"Crowbar," Charlie tried to interject.

"No, lissen," Crowbar went on. "What people yell on the golf course is the same thing you've been hearing since you were a baby. You know, like 'Sit! Run! Stop! Stop right now!' "

"Grow teeth!" Two Down added. "Hurry! Bite!"

"Get up!" Charlie said. "Get down!"

"Not in the sand!" Crowbar said.

"In the hole!" Dannie yelled.

"That's a snowman!" Thud said.

Everybody was having just a wonderful time, except me.

"You finished, Professor Fulghum?"

Despite the sudden Crowbargram, my happy little putt went in like it was afraid of porch light. Now it was Two Down's turn. This time, oddly, Crowbar stayed silent.

Two Down started giving the putt the full Tiger pace, checking the line from every possible angle, talking to his ancient Wilson putter, Arnie, the whole time. Two Down always talked to Arnie over a big putt, for they had been together eighteen years and made more money together than the Hunt brothers.

Arnie was not just a golf club. Arnie was a person. When Two Down was done with his round, he would not just leave Arnie in the bag. No, he'd take it with him, wherever he went, always saying stuff like "Get your sleep now, Arnie. We got a big match with these fish tomorrow." It was just an old flange putter, but he put it in a long black cashmere cover with the name embroidered on it. He'd go down to Kmart and pull his other clubs out of the barrel half the time, but he treated Arnie like solid platinum.

"Why does he talk to his putter?" asked Hoover.

"I don't know," said Charlie. "Two Down, why do you talk to your putter?"

"Two Down, it's an inanimate object," Hoover said. "It is a collection of inert molecules. It is NOT real!"

"Seriously, Two Down," Charlie offered. "You should consider tripling your therapy."

But Two Down just continued conversing with Arnie. "Don't listen to 'em, Arnie. They're sick, sick people. Now, do the six-inch dunk, just like we learned in obedience school, and I'll buy you a whole new bottle of Armor All."

At last, Two Down settled in over the putt. He drew it back.

"Snake juice!" yelled Cementhead.

"Double snake juice!" yelled yours truly.

The well-behaved spheroid did not listen. It merely rolled true and perfect toward the cup, a sure jar if there ever was one.

Except the ball didn't drop into the little tin hole. For this jar was a Froghair special, which is a hole he jerks out the wrong way, leaving an inch-high lip all the way around the hole, which means you have to charge your putt to get it over the first lip, but not so much that it flies over. Two Down hit a very good putt, except that it ran up the front lip and *didn't quite* have enough juice to climb that small hill. Exhausted, it rolled *backward* toward Two Down.

"Un-fucking-believable," said Chunkin' Charlie.

"Oh, man. That's one of them South American putts," said Dannie. "One more revolution."

"Man, that could only happen at Ponky," I offered.

"That's true, Two Down," said Dannie, kicking the ball back to him. "Anywhere else that putt goes right in."

"Seriously, Two," said Chunk, "if you're putting on the other side of the hedge, that putt is in the damn jar for a straight-up birdie."

Two Down was still standing frozen as a parking meter on the green, so two of us picked him up, stiff as a board, stuck him in the cart, and Crowbar drove him back to the clubhouse.

37

It was Sunday night, which meant it was Cotillion Night at Ponky, which meant bringing out a bit of the old Robitussin, as Dannie liked to call it, over ice if we could get it, smoking some very bad Swisher Sweet cigars, trying to teach Blu Chao "Fuck them in the neck" and taking guesses as to exactly what position they were in on the scrambled porno channel. As to that last activity, I thought I had a pretty good guess: "It's kind of like really good golf. It's not fun until both people are trying to get on top."

I stole a glance at Dannie, but she was staring a hole in her swizzle stick.

Two Down had not yet left his hard-won seat on the puke-orange Naugahyde La-Z-Boy and was, in fact, still brooding. He was not able to get over that putt, the way he'd been Donkeyed out of 300 zops, the unfairness of losing that many simoleons because he misread a volcano.

He sat there silent for at least two hours until I noticed his expression slowly start to change. I could see it in his eyebrows. The bigger the idea Two Down got, the higher his eyebrows would go. This time, they went from deeply furrowed to three-quarters of the way up his forehead in the span of about five minutes.

At about eleven-thirty, the eyebrows had reached their apex. He leaped out of the La-Z-Boy, flipped off the set, jumped up on the beat-up piano bench Froghair tried to tell us was a coffee table and called for our attention.

"This better be good," said Charlie, who was not fond of interruptions in Cotillion Night.

"This is better than good," said Two Down. "This is the best wager in the long and colorful history of Chopdom."

"I'm *not* playing Chip or Strip," insisted Dannie.

"No, this is ten times better. Here it is: Everybody puts up a thousand dollars. Cash. First Chop to play the Mayflower keeps it *all.*"

Everybody just stared at him.

"Son," said Dannie. "Anybody ever told you you're one sandwich short of a picnic?"

"You can't get *on* the Mayflower," I mentioned. "The Mayflower lets *nobody* on. I heard last year they wouldn't let Dan Quayle on. They're gonna let us just walk on? *Hi! We're here to play the course?*"

"Signed scorecards with two witnesses," continued Two Down.

"Fgt it," said Thud (the Almost Human), gnawing on a microwave burrito. "We gt no fkng chance."

"One month time limit," Two Down continued. "The bet ends October 1. After that time, the window closes. No bank will be paid."

"Two Down, let's all hold hands and contact the living," said Dannie.

Two Down quieted the crowd, holding his bony arms out full.

"Don't you see?" said Two Down passionately. "This is the bet we've been waiting for our *whole lives*! Most of us have spent our entire golfing lives playing this patch of scorched earth we call a golf course. We *deserve* to play the Mayflower Club once in our lives. Just because we didn't get to dive into the gene pool and come out with Mumsy and Dadsy and wallpaper made of zero-coupon bonds doesn't mean we don't deserve to play a great golf course, does it? This is really a no-lose bet. If only *one* of us makes it, it will be like all of us making it, won't it? If *one* of us gets through the gates of that blue-nosed, blue-haired Bastille, then it will be like *all* of us did!"

Chunkin' Charlie was the first to no bank. "Count me out," he said, looking more gaunt and tired than I'd ever seen him. He picked up the remote and flipped the set back on.

"I'm ot, too," said Thud, working on a Hostess Snowball.

"But, Thud," said Two Down. "Think of the *meal* you will have in the Mayflower clubhouse afterward. My God! I understand most days there is a buffet line of succulent carved prime rib, hillocks of mashed potatoes, veritable bathtubs of brown gravy."

"Wrte me a fkng pstcrd," said Thud.

Cementhead said no, too.

"Great bet, Two," said Crowbar. "Next week, let's see who can be the first inside Biosphere 2."

But Two Down was not to be denied.

"Hoov?" said Two Down.

Hoover looked seriously at Two Down, thought a while and then said, "Golf is not a physical game. Golf is a state of mind. If your intentions are pure and your thoughts are positive and you swing from your innermost point, then it doesn't matter *where* you are. You are not bound to any golf course, nor even to the land itself."

"Jesus," said Cementhead.

"In or out?" said Two Down.

"Out," said Hoover.

"A man's gotta know his limitations," said Crowbar, with his best Clint Eastwood squint.

"Lawrence of Arabia?" asked Cementhead.

"Magnum Force."

"Damn."

Which left Dannie and me.

"Danielle Patricia Higgins?" said Two Down. "Carpe diem?"

For the first time in three weeks, since she'd first seen the glorious visage of Browning Sumner, there was light in Dannie's sea-green eyes. A thousand zops was some serious scratch to a girl earning $375 a week selling handfuls of tees. On the other hand, the lure was irresistible. This was Fantasy Boy we were talking about, Barbie and Ken get married and a big wedding on the club veranda with real-crystal toasts.

Of course, there was always the chance that Two Down had something mysterious up his sleeve and would remove three weeks' salary from her, not to mention her dreams.

She bit her fingernails. She rubbed her freckled face. She smoothed back her strawberry hair a few dozen times.

"Bank," she said, falling backward on the couch.

The Chops oohed and whooped and bellowed and then stilled as all eyes turned to me.

"Stick?" said Two Down.

My first reaction was sinister. Nobody else knew my father was over there, and if I thought I could somehow swallow a few gallons of pride and ask him for a game, I could pick up a fast two Large. My second reaction was wanting to choke the air out of myself for having my first reaction. My third reaction was that $1,000 was exactly $318 more than I had in the bank. My fourth reaction was that if I had to punch out of one more divot after puring a 290-yard drive down nothing but the goddamn defunct watering-system line of a Ponky fairway I was going to scream. My fifth reaction was how much it chapped my butt that my father never had to. And my last reaction was to think about the day he screwed me out of my golf career, about how nice it would be to play there without his help, how it would just grind his gizzard to see me playing in front of him, bump into him in the locker room and say something like "This dump's overrated."

"Stick?" said Two Down.

I looked him and Dannie in the eyes, twice each. They did not blink.

"Bank," I said.

I never dreamed how all this would affect us.

The Pit of Despair went triple ballistic.

And Blu Chao yelped, "Fuck your neck them."

5

THAT NEXT MORNING, as we were going over the rules of the bet, I could already feel things starting to change.

All of a sudden three best friends were looking at each other like one of us might be wearing Khrushchev's shoe. We were counterespionage agents now. We would be working separately, without help from the other. Come to think of it, we would probably be doing everything we could to sabotage each other's best efforts. For three nobodies like us, $1,000 was serious jing.

It was agreed that Thud would hold the money since he was the most trustworthy Chop and also because Chunkin' Charlie refused to.

OK, so that sounds a little strange to say about a guy like Thud, who had just done a three-month fellowship at Bridgewater State Penitentiary, but with golf, and with friends, that's just the way he was. Thud might jack a Toot n' Moo now and again or ransack a few nice houses out in Newton, but he'd sooner have doughnuts with cops than tamp down a spike mark. He once called a 2-stroke penalty on himself for accidentally breaking a branch as he was setting up over a chip out on No. 11, which is something most of us wouldn't have done if Ken Venturi himself had shown it coast to coast on CBS.

How he got sent to Bridgewater was stupid anyway. It was just a simple little dry cleaners job, except that Mr. Manelli had only $29.73 in the cash register and it just disappointed Thud so much that he tied Manelli up in the back room and started working the drive-thru. He'd give people their garments very politely and sold a whole lot of Mr. Manelli's stock right off the rack. "Hey, you look like about a 41 Long. Tell you what. Here's an Armani, gorgeous, $75." All that worked very nicely until he refused to give some lady change from her $100. She didn't think Thud's service was so wonderful that it deserved that big a tip and mentioned it to the police two blocks down. End of clearance sale.

He tucked our $3,000 inside the black leather waist pouch he never took off. Nobody asked what else was in there, possibly because nobody wanted to appear curious around a guy who looked like Thud.

"And no parking-lot jobs," Two Down said. "Neither of the other two can be in your group when you play. No tag-team jobs either. Nobody can knowingly benefit from one of the other guys. Agreed?"

"Agreed," I said.

"Agreed," said Dannie.

We all looked at each other a second and then scattered. Dannie back to Ponky, Two Down to his telephone truck and me to the bus stop, seeing as how I'd sold my two-tone (three, if you count rust) Plymouth Duster for $450 to pay the bet.

Personally, I saw no way for me to get on the Mayflower course other than to ask my father, which I wouldn't do for a month locked in a Motel 6 with Heather Locklear. I boarded the No. 53 bus back to my little no-bedroom apartment and wondered what the hell I had just gotten into.

As I sat there, watching the potholes and the potbellies go by, I examined the situation.

My advantage was time. I could devote all the time I wanted to the bet, since I could write my puffball blurbs for Publisher's Reviews anytime I wanted with one cranial lobe tied behind my back. Publisher's Reviews was nothing more than an arm of the publishing houses and had never, ever given any book a bad review, up to and including a Martina Navratilova mystery. *Talk about serving up an ace!* It ain't exactly Pauline Kael.

This isn't the way I wanted my brilliant writing career to turn out, but when you have burned your first book of short stories, your second book of short stories and your first novel and a half, you don't have a lot of choices. *Raymond Hart is the hottest writer in America today!*

Two Down's advantage was trickery and a sheer love of the chase. To Two Down, the Mayflower was Jumbo Jing. To him, the Mayflower was the Land of the Cocktail Handicaps, which is what he called a guy who said he was a 9 at a cocktail party and played like a 19. He saw $400,000 lawyers with delicious loops in their backswings. He saw doctors with succulent reverse pivots and well-dressed bank presidents with mouthwatering hiccups in their putting strokes.

As much action as he got at Ponky, we were still Tidewater of the Class D league and through the hole was the parent club. At best, we were $10 and $20 Nassau guys, and at worst, we were guys who played for no more than a cold Moxie.

We were the Peoria Dinner Playhouse. Through the hole was Broadway. Two Down wanted it.

As for Dannie, she had an incentive that was even stronger than mine and Two Down's put together. Whereas I was after my rightful place on a great golf course, to say nothing of a chance to spite my father, and whereas Two Down was after the Big Time, which meant all those vats of money owned by guys with hyphenated last names, Dannie was after love, or a reasonable facsimile. She would be very difficult to beat.

....

My first move was straight and simple. I called the Mayflower and asked for the membership office.

"Hello, this is Mr. Smithson," I said snobbishly. "Mr. Tanner Smithson?"

"Yes, sir," said a woman's voice, "what can we do for you?"

"My wife and I have decided to begin considering clubs and we've heard fairly wonderful things about the Mayflower. It's clear to us that we should make a tour of the facilities, perhaps play a round of golf, have a nibble. When might we arrange for same?"

I figured I could get Patty O'Connell and her plus-5 tits from over at Don's Mixed Drinks to come with me and pose as my wife. And with the member they'd stick with us, that would be my two witnesses. Simple.

"I'm terribly sorry, Mr. Smithson," said the voice. "But the Mayflower is an invitation-only club."

"I'm sorry?" I asked.

"You must be *invited* by the Captain to join. There is no application process."

"Surely just this once."

"I'm terribly sorry."

"Oh. Well, what is the Captain's name?"

"Mr. Considine Roberts," she said.

"Might you tell Captain Roberts I wish to be invited?" I said, groping.

"I'm sorry," she said.

"My dear woman, I'm only asking . . . ," I said.

"Click," said the line.

Plan B.

Dannie's plan was to try to bluff her way in, same as everybody's, and when that failed, she immediately turned to favor fucking.

All previous standards were suspended in order that she might date and quick-strap Chance Weatherot, the unctuous son of the richest guy in Dorchester. He was exactly not her type—fraternity boy, Top-Siders, and a fondness for constantly using the word "ultra."

Chance, you want to get set up with a deb?

"Ulll-tra!"

This was strictly a business boink, Dannie later stoically explained to some very disillusioned Chops, in hopes of getting an invite to play the Mayflower from his dad, a member in good standing. But it was only after the deed was turned that Chance mentioned something very crucial to the case.

"Pops lives in Grand Cayman now, babe," he said. "He never comes back to Boston anymore. You wanna come down there with me sometime? His Lear is so ulll-tra!"

She was dressed and gone before the sheets cooled.

Eventually, though, Dannie came up with a concept to get in the Mayflower that I'd never dreamed of.

Death.

There are a lot of morticians in Boston and Thud knew plenty, or at least plenty in the Cremators Guild. And Dannie knew Thud.

"Hey, Thud," she said one day. "How many trips to the Sizzler would it take to get you to do me a monster favor?"

"Fv," Thud said, polishing off a plate of BBQ wontons.

"Five?" said Dannie in horror.

"Nd a cs of Bstr Brs."

"A case of Buster Bars? You're loopy."

They settled on four Sizzlers, six Buster Bars and the phone number of the fattest girlfriend she had.

Thud faxed each of his friends in the body-burning business a letter with the list of every member at the Mayflower, a list that Dannie had tirelessly compiled off the handicap computer over at Fox Hollow. Attached to Thud's letter and list was this note: "Boys, call me RIGHT AWAY if any of these rich old coots shows up in your ashtrays. Trying to win a bet."

Now, if you picked any list of 150 people, your chances of one of them catching a case of rigor mortis in the next month were pretty small. But if those 150 people were all members at the Mayflower, where the average age of the membership was roughly older than Bob Hope and where the main dining room was known to the help as Forest Lawn, maybe it wasn't.

Dannie got lucky. In about a week, on a Wednesday, September 12, the call came. It was a friend of Thud's in Newton. Louie (Ooze) dell'Appa.

"Dan, I got somebody," Ooze said. "It's a Dr. Dingsby. Dr. Alfred A. Dingsby. He just boxed."

It was about nine at night, so the first thing Dannie did was beat it over to recruit for her plan. Charlie wanted no part of it—Charlie seemed to want no part of any of this stuff—so she settled on Thud and Cementhead, who did it for 50 zops apiece—double if it worked—plus a new shirt from Pro Golf Discount.

At 8 A.M. sharp the next morning, the three of them met outside Ponky in combed hair, clean shaves, best khakis, new shirts and actual socks for the first time since their First Communions. They loaded into a black limo that Thud "borrowed" from his boss to get them past Ivan at the gate.

The limo worked. All of a sudden, they were inside the Forbidden City, the Grand Palace of the Himalayas, Carnegie Hall. The beauty of the place flabbergasted them. They were standing there, eyes the size of spaghetti plates, soaking in the magnificence of the place, the majestic green-and-white clubhouse, the immaculate grounds, the shimmering blue swimming pool, when the head pro walked up.

He was a Johnny Weissmuller look-alike—huge diving-board shoulders, wrinkle-free pants, and Aryan face. He looked like a guy that might have been in the finals of the Styling Mousse Olympics.

"How can I help you gentlemen?"

"We're here for our annual game with Dr. Dingsby," said Dannie. "Eight-thirty, I believe he said. Although I'm not sure. I spoke with him yesterday morning and he said he'd get a time and expected it to be eight-thirty."

"Welllll," said the pro, "there's nothing on the sheet about it. Do you mind if I call him?"

"Why, certainly," said Dannie. "Do you mind if we try a few putts? We've never played here, you know."

"Who should I say is waiting for him?" asked the pro.

Good question, thought Dannie.

"I'm . . . I'm Dr. Higgins," she said, a little shaky. "And this is Dr., uh, Thudstein, and Dr. Cement . . . ius. Excuse me. I'm a little unfamiliar with their last names, because we only see each other once a year, on the day we play with Dr. Dingsby, as I said, once a year."

Now Dannie was a little in over her head.

The pro must've started to wonder who these jokers were. Still, he turned, a little suspiciously, and started to walk toward the pro shop.

"You see," interjected Cementhead. "We play every year here with ol' Doc Dingsby on September 13, for that is the day we saved each other's lives."

Both Dannie and the pro turned to Cementhead. Dannie's eyes were horror-stricken.

"Lives?" the pro asked.

"Lives," said Cementhead. "It was at a convention in Mauna Kea. We were part of a medical group of about a dozen or so that went on a fishing cruise. Unfortunately, a terrible storm came up and the boat flipped. The four of us—total strangers—wound up clutching the sides of one small lifesaver that barely kept us afloat. We decided the only way we could survive the holy terror . . ."

"And the hypothermia," interjected Dannie.

". . . was by taking our minds off the situation," Cementhead continued, much to Thud and Dannie's utter amazement. "We talked about anything we could think of, the future, our plans, anything but the present. We all imagined what we would be doing a week from then, and all four of us said, 'You know what? Enjoying a nice round a golf.' We then spent the next two hours talking about courses we played and games we'd had and still hoped to have. We decided then and there, bobbing up and down in those waters . . ."

"Shark-infested waters," interjected Dannie.

". . . that if we made it out of this predicament alive, we would all four play golf on that date, each and every year, no matter what. It was golf that saved us, so we decided we should play golf to celebrate our survivals."

"Unbelievable!" said the head pro, enraptured by the story.

"Fkn A!" said Thud, polishing off a bowl of free mints he'd found.

"We were picked up by a Coast Guard cutter the next morning," said Cementhead. "Half dead. Yet we survived. We have held true to our promise. Once a year, on September 13, we play some of the finest courses in the country. And now Dr. Dingsby has invited us to his club, which he says will be the finest we have ever enjoyed."

"I can't *ever* remember lookin' more forward to a game a golf than this one," said Dannie, gesticulating wildly.

The pro was overwhelmed. "Well, I'll call him right now and see what's holding him up!" And off he went, striding after his Dudley Do Right jaw.

In about three minutes, the pro came back, ashen-faced. He looked like a man who just swallowed a plateful of leeches.

He slowly approached the threesome on the putting green. He could not bring himself to speak.

Dannie played it for all it was worth.

"My God! What happened? What on earth is wrong?"

The pro swallowed hard. "I don't know how to tell you this," he said. "But Dr. Dingsby is . . . the doctor is . . . dead. I'm so, so, so sorry."

"Dead?" said Dannie.

"I'm so, so, so sorry," said the pro, holding Dannie's shoulder. "He was struck down by an eating accident yesterday afternoon."

The three held their breath for a moment and then began their own peculiar brand of wailing.

"My Godamighty!" wailed Cementhead. "I made him putt that nine-incher last year at Merion! That putt cost him three dollars! Why, oh, why, did I worry about a putt when *life* is what's important?!?"

"Please don't let it bother you," said the pro. "I'm sure Dr. Dingsby knew it was just a part of the game."

"Maybe the stress of setting up this game was too much," blubbered Dannie. "And here I was wondering why he had been so slow to get the tee time!"

"Really, don't blame yourself," said the pro.

"I just can't believe our tradition is going to end this way. It's so . . . incomplete. And Dr. Dingsby was so proud of his course. I know he wanted to show it to us."

There was silence. Dannie looked at the pro from under her furrowed brow.

"Well, I guess that's it then," said Dannie. "I'll have to call the limo service. We'll need to make a sizable donation to Dr. Dingsby's charity. We'll stay a couple of extra days for the services, of course."

"Fkn A," interjected Thud.

The head pro stood there, thunderstruck, watching them slouch back to the clubhouse, when he suddenly raised his head.

"Wait a moment!" he said. "You could still play here! I could rearrange a few lessons and play with you!"

"Oh, no," said Dannie. "That would be so much to ask . . ."

"No, no," said the pro. "I insist. The group should play one more time in Dr. Dingsby's memory!"

"Well," reasoned Dannie. "It would mean so much to Dr. Dingsby!"

"Sure!" said the pro. "I'll just go get my shoes on."

And within five minutes, the threesome was standing on the first tee of the Mayflower Club with their white-overalled caddies about to enter the finest course in all of Massachusetts, maybe the finest in the country, the sweetest, most fertile stretch of succulent golfing ground anywhere.

Dannie was thinking about all the ways she could spend two Large and hoping a certain Mr. Sumner happened to want to play through.

She placed a peg in the ground with delight and prepared to tee off on.

"Rl ns v u," said Thud.

"Yes, yes," said Dannie, letting her eyes take in the majesty of the trees, the flowers, the clear blue ponds. "I am sure Dr. Dingsby is looking down at us now and smiling."

"It won't be easy, though," said Cementhead. "I'll sure miss him. And I'll bet all the fine people here who have been his patients will, too."

"Yes," said Dannie.

"He spoke of them often. 'Wonderful people,' he'd say."

That is when the expression on the head pro's face did a 180. His bottom lip sort of fell off his mouth and his eyebrows started sinking toward his nose.

He walked in front of Dannie, picked her ball off the tee, put it in his pocket and faced the three of them.

"Dr. Dingsby," said the pro, "was a vet."

6

EVERY DAY AT the hole, the same show was on, Lifestyles of the Rich and Over-annuitied.

Dannie was getting more and more dreamy about Browning and missing more and more bluffs in card games and 3-foot sidehill putts for large zops. Plus, she wasn't showing nearly as much interest in me and Coach Johnson, which is what we called my best feature. *Coach Johnson care to do a few laps?* she'd say.

But now she'd canceled a Friday-night Hammermania session, for absolutely no good reason. And when I asked, she said, "We don't need a reason, remember?"

One night, I caught her alone in her favorite booth over at Don's. I was wearing her favorite jeans, the ones with the little hole in the butt, so I'm thinking the Coach is going to get a few push-ups in. I took a dollar bill out of my wallet and held it horizontally across my beltline, then I tapped her on the shoulder. She turned around.

"Know what this is?" I said.

"No, what?" said Dannie glumly.

"All you can eat under a dollar."

She turned back around to her scotch and water. "Hard to believe more people don't mistake you for David Niven," she sniffed.

I was starting to miss her already.

....

To me, of course, playing the Mayflower meant not so much the money, not playing one of the world's great courses, but doing it without my father.

52

William Davenport Hart was graceful and stylish and only slightly less fun than ethnic cleansing.

He was one of two sons of the only doctor in Cross, Massachusetts. I don't know what made him a league-leading drunk, but he was a natural. He retired the undefeated and untied Canadian Club champion.

He learned to drink for attention. The only way he and his brother got attention from their father was by getting blotto and pulling guys out of cars at the town's one stoplight and beating them into piles of lumps and then being bailed out in the morning by him.

The doc would scream at them and ground them and scold them, and they would sneak out and get drunk again two nights later, just to piss him off, maybe just to see what would make him finally stop caring altogether. This is when they were fourteen and fifteen. By the time they were eighteen, they both left home and not together. They couldn't stand each other either.

He vowed that when he had kids, he would be just the opposite. He would be with his kids at every step, the human tour guide, life's live-in coach, the every-moment companion.

And he was. Travis and I couldn't so much as blow a bubble without him offering some advice on it. We could not dive off a boat into a lake without him reminding us to keep our feet pointed or to describe more of an arc. His basic philosophy of life was nothing couldn't be made a little better with a little constructive criticism and helpful tips.

I suppose he was doing it out of love, but he didn't have the calmness or peace inside to let us make our own mistakes or forgive them. "For Chrissakes, Raymond, aren't you listening?" he'd say. "You've got to have the 'want to' in this life. The only people in life who are successful have that 'want to,' you know."

Nothing we did came without hearing his sharp voice cutting through the gyms and the fields and the courts. He would actually come to our gym classes and yell things. "You can't get anybody out in dodgeball throwing like that! You've got to come over the top, not three-quarter!" Or he'd sit on the porch while we played Kick the Can and yell, "Keep circling as you go. You can't leave your back to one side that long." Pretty soon, we just stopped playing.

He would enroll us in three basketball camps, two soccer camps and one strength-and-conditioning camp in a summer and show up every day, coaching us in between the dozen or so other camp coaches trying to drown him out. And not just us. He felt the urge to scold everybody. "C'mon there, Red Shorts! Focus!"

Most kids dream of becoming pro athletes. Travis and I were pro athletes from the time we were six years old. A hit paid 50 cents, 75 if you knocked in a run. A touchdown was $1. A's paid $1, too. B's were 50 cents. C's meant you had to pay him 50 cents.

And so a typical dinner conversation would go like this:

"You got Coldfield tomorrow?"

"Uh-huh."

"Excuse me?"

"Yessir."

"That West kid in goal?"

"Yessir."

"You come down there with me early. I'll tend some for you."

"Yessir."

"I don't want to see any of your hot-dog passes either. Don't embarrass me out there, you understand, young man?"

"Yessir."

"Two dollars for a goal against that West kid. One dollar for assists. He's tough. That's a kid that's got some 'want to' in him."

"Yessir."

We grew to hate the sound of his voice, the sight of his face, the smell of his Aqua Velva. We grew to hate ourselves for taking his payouts, for they never came with a "Terrific job." Or a "Great game." To him, a great game or a winning field goal or a team MVP was just a number. "Let's see. All-Star team. Ten bucks."

"Yessir."

He was so easy to disappoint. One time, the babysitter let me drive the car and I ran it into a telephone poll. He grounded me for a month. The next day, he walked into my room and said, "You know, Raymond, I *really* hate to punish you. It makes me so *angry* when I have to punish you. It's so *unfair*. So I'm giving you two extra weeks."

Anything I can do to help.

The worst day happened in a junior high school basketball game. I was our best dribbler, so I was the point guard. I wasn't bad either. Basketball was my best sport.

But this kid guarding me that day was a little termite, all over me, fouling me away from the ref, slapping my wrists, stealing the ball.

"For Chrissakes, Raymond," Father would say, walking up and down the side of the court, sometimes in front of my own coach. "Are you gonna let him embarrass you like that? Protect the ball with your left side!"

It was maddening and we were losing. The ref finally called a foul and I missed the first free throw badly.

"For Chrissakes, Raymond," he bellowed. "Bend your knees."

I snapped my head his way and looked at him. "Goddamnit! Can't you see I'm trying?" I said, almost in tears.

He marched right out to the court, grabbed my arm and pulled me off without a word. I tried to resist, but there was no chance. He dragged me right out of that gym, in front of all my friends, took me out to the parking lot, slapped me once hard across the face and threw me in the back of his silver Cadillac Eldorado.

I faked sick for a week and never played on a basketball team again.

The night he broke my mom's nose was the kind of thing that

could happen when you messed with Father when he was drunk, which was only six and a half nights a week.

He came home lit up and Mom didn't have two cold Falstaffs ready with his dinner and she "smart-mouthed" him and next thing you know, I was in the bathroom with her, holding a towel to her nose with Travis sobbing and blood everywhere, on the rug, on the mirror and all over my clothes. I made Travis lock the bathroom door in case he came after us. I can't ever remember being more scared than that.

The next morning, after he'd gone to work at the bank, my mom gathered Travis and me in the living room of our little $17,000 split-level and said, "I want you kids to know what to do in case your father tries to hurt you." And she spent the next twenty minutes telling us how we could use the table lamps to brain him.

Like a lot of sons, I couldn't stand little things my father did, but unlike most sons, I still remember them to this day.

I couldn't stand the way he had to rotate his beer bottle perfectly so that the label faced him as he sat at the TV table. And I couldn't stand how he would smoke *one* Newport every night after supper, and I couldn't stand how he would turn the sound up on the TV on the rare occasions when we would try to talk. And I hated the way he put coins in a vending machine according to size, the way he alphabetized the magazines on the coffee table, the way he kept his medicine cabinet organized by expiration dates and the way he'd yell at Mom if the vacuuming lines were not all parallel.

I hated the way he hung his shirts in his closet so they all faced the same way, each top button buttoned, or the way he would back into parking spots, rev the engine one time, very loud, and then kill it, as though this was something the manual said to do: *Rev the hell out of the engine before you kill it so the carburetor can completely flood for no apparent reason.*

And I hated the officious, loud way he'd spell his last name, like this: "That's Hart. Capital *H,* small *a,* small *r,* small *t,*" as though the guy on the other phone might think he's goddamn e. e. cummings or something.

All of which was why it killed me to love his golf swing so much.

My father was a wonderful golfer, with a swing as slow and fluid as 10-W-40. He was the New England military champion three times while in the Air Force and almost won the Massachusetts Amateur when he got out. Might've won it for sure the next year, except he broke his hand on the back of some guy's head arguing over whether or not he should sit the fuck down and stop singing "And They Called It Ireland" at the top of his lungs, especially without any music.

Everybody seemed to love to play golf with my father. They must have. He played every weekend day and usually twice during the week, being the president of a little bank in Somerville, where we lived. I would hear him go early Saturday mornings and hear him come back late Saturday nights looped and pissed off. If he came in your room you'd pretend you were asleep no matter how loud he yelled.

Until I was thirteen, my father never took me to the golf course on any of those mornings. Not once. Not once in the hundreds of times he went. Not to ride in the cart. Not to caddie. Not to watch. Nothing. He always said it was not a game for kids.

"Kids just slow up the course."

But on my thirteenth birthday, he came home and threw two books in my lap: the USGA rule book and a pamphlet on etiquette.

"Raymond, it's time for you to learn golf."

I wanted to say, "No, thanks," but chickened out.

"First things first," he said.

"Yessir."

"You've got to know the rules and etiquette of any game before you can learn it properly. Know the rules and the etiquette and then I'll take you out."

And so I was made to memorize them. And, my God, if it weren't for him, I wouldn't today know such crucial bits of information as: You get a free drop away from a bird's nest or a hive of bees, but not an anthill.

"How about a worm on your ball?" he'd say.

"Dead or alive?" I'd say.

"Alive, but half in the ground and half out."

"It may be moved as a loose impediment."

"As a loose impediment, what?"

"As a loose impediment, sir."

Of course, the upshot of all this is that once I was on the course with him, I immediately wondered why I had been looking forward to it. He was prickly and nasty and had all the patience of a dyspeptic bouncer.

He and I would go out and you could've cut the tension with a 2-iron. He'd give me about three million things to remember during the swing and I'd try it and top it and he'd say, "Just forget it, then, Raymond. You obviously don't have the 'want to.' If you don't want to do something the correct way, then just don't do it at all."

And the emotion of being belittled coupled with the frustration of probably the hardest game in the world just came roiling up. And I'd stomp off the course right in the middle of the round, tears flowing down my face but not giving him the satisfaction of hearing a single whimper.

And he'd always yell the same thing: "Raymond, there's no need to get *emotional.*"

We tried one more time, in a father-son alternate-shot tournament, but when he screamed at me, "You never leave a birdie putt short!" right in front of the other father-son, I dropped the bag and my glove right there and ran in a sprint home.

I made a secret vow that night never to touch him again. Not to hug him, shake his hand, nothing. And I didn't, except for the one time he came home and I was still up and he went after my mom with that horrible poison in his voice. I vaguely remember him being enraged that his dinner had not been left for him in the refrigerator the way he had ordered it left—wrapped in aluminum foil with the dressing left off the salad.

I was fifteen, thinking I was big, and I stepped in front of him, ready to fight, and he fell on me, smothering me. I screamed and cried and he got off me and I got up and pushed him once and ran off to my room, crying as hard as I'd ever cried in my life.

Maybe all those things I could've forgiven. Maybe I could've somehow talked to him as a man later and confronted him and tried to understand him. But not after Travis. I could never forgive that.

7

THROUGH THE FIRST week of the bet, most of the outside money was on Two Down. He lurked like Bela Lugosi. He was the chalk favorite, yet nobody had heard a thing about him. It was like running a Miss America contest without knowing where the hell Miss California was.

Two Down was a kid from a big military family whose dad fought in the first years in Vietnam. With all the friendless moving and his parents' strict ten-hut discipline, he just kind of went nuts when his father was killed. He had a terrific imagination, no money and no curfew. Those things, combined, got me into more trouble at Roslindale High School than girls and Ripple combined.

One Christmas, he talked me into going around town stealing all the baby Jesuses out of crèche scenes. Among all baby Jesus kidnappers in history, we were the best. We must've had thirty-five baby Jesuses.

We had Jesuses that lit up from underneath and Jesuses whose crowns lit up and Jesuses whose hands and feet moved. We had porcelain Jesuses and plastic Jesuses and wooden Jesuses and even a rubber Jesus. We had tiny Jesuses and great big Jesuses. We had naked Jesuses and swaddling-clothes Jesuses. We had sleeping Jesuses, awake Jesuses, smiling Jesuses and one crying Jesus.

Our favorite was a little black Jesus we got from a church in South Boston whose little penis was turned up. The rest of them were turned down. Very cool Jesus.

Once we had absconded with them all, we couldn't decide what to do with them, so we started putting them places. A few made it to the front lawn of the synagogue. We put two in the nursery at

Mass. General. The rest we just put back—in the wrong crèche scenes. Like, we'd put a tiny Jesus in a huge crèche scene, sort of a "Honey, I shrunk the Savior" kind of thing. The last thing we did was put the black Jesus in the biggest, whitest, most bigoted church in Boston.

And Two Down left a note that read: "Somebody better speak to Mary about this shit."

And so I was sure he had a few hundred ideas on how to take my Mayflower money, but as things turned out, Two Down had no more plan than the rest of us.

He first tried the Blitzkrieg Approach, which was to simply drive through the gate, park his car, walk to the first tee, peg it up with some threesome, introducing himself as a new member and go from there. Unfortunately, he could not even get by Ivan, the guard with the face like Upper Siberia. Two Down and his beat-up Pinto with the shattered back window were turned away three different times. The last time the Pinto never even came to a complete stop.

Then Two Down took to hanging around the corner from the club, at the intersection of Waldeck and Grant, near a telephone pole, where he simply parked his New England Bell truck and used New England Bell equipment to tap into the club's telephone lines.

Sometimes he'd tap into the pro shop, sometimes the phone in the clubhouse, whatever he felt like. He would do this for hours on end, hoping to hear some little nugget or chunk of something that might prove valuable.

Mostly what he heard was a lot of "So that's me, Forbes, Jinxy Boy and the Bobster at seven fifty-two? Got it?" or "Yessir, Mr. Paddington. . . . No, it won't happen again. I'll ask the greens-keeper what can be done about getting those geese to stay quiet while you're putting. Yessir."

But then one morning, while Two Down was tapping the locker-room phone and practicing rolling 11s on the floor of his truck and eating a couple long johns, he heard this:

Mayflower voice: ". . . and we've talked so much on the phone over the last few months, it will be nice to finally meet."

Second voice: "Kind of put a face with a voice."

Mayflower: "Yes!"

Second voice: "Plus, I've never played in one of these. I'm looking forward to it."

Mayflower: "Wonderful! So we'll see you here Friday about 7:30?"

Second voice: "Will do. See you then."

They hung up. Two Down flipped open another phone and called a friend of his at work and asked him to check the computer and find out what number the Mayflower voice had called. When the friend called back with the number, Two Down called another phone company office, asked for the reverse index, and got a name to go with the number. It belonged to a Mr. Scott Sullivan, of Chelsea.

Fine. Then Two called the Mayflower to see what in the world the second voice meant when he said "one of these" that was set to happen Friday. This took a little trickery.

"Hello," he told the pro-shop voice. "This is Mr. Sullivan. The darnedest thing just happened. I've just been invited to play in an event there Friday and I never quite heard the name of the event and I'm too embarrassed to call my host and ask again. Can you tell me?"

"The member-guest?" said the voice from the pro shop.

"Exactly," said Two Down. "I feel so stupid. Thank you."

Now he knew that a Mr. Scott Sullivan of Chelsea was going to play with a member he'd never met before in the member-guest on Friday, September 14, at the Mayflower. Only he didn't know the name of the member. Any of the 150 Mayflower members could've used that phone. No problem for Lenny the Brain.

He waited until early Friday morning, about five-thirty, two and a half hours before the tournament was to start, and called up Mr. Scott Sullivan, of Chelsea, waking him out of his upper-tax-bracket dreams.

"Mr. Sullivan?" Two Down said. "This is Avrum Isleworth from the Mayflower Club."

"Uh, oh. Mmmm. Yes?" said Sullivan in a groggy voice.

"I'm sorry to call at this horrid hour, but I'm afraid we have some bad news," Two Down lied. "A water line burst on the course last night and most of the holes are terribly flooded. I'm afraid the member-guest tournament has been canceled."

"Oh," said Sullivan, disappointed. "Well, maybe next time."

"Yes, yes, yes," said Two Down. "We're all just sick about it."

"Well, thanks."

"Thank *you.* Toodle-oo."

Now all Two Down had to do was get to the club early enough Friday morning to look for the name Scott Sullivan on the registration sheet, find out who he was playing with, and he was a dead mortal lock for the money.

By 7 A.M., Two Down had his Pinto with the shattered back window at the imposing Mayflower gate. Ivan the guard looked at him with disdain.

"Scott Sullivan," said Two Down. "Member-guest."

Ivan looked at him and actually laughed at the thought of anybody in a Pinto being invited to the Mayflower Club to play golf. He snapped up his sheet and began looking at it with utter cynicism. But when he came to Sullivan, Scott, his face fell like a gun-club soufflé. He put the sheet down slowly and, keeping eye contact with Two Down, opened golf's Brandenburg Gate.

"A little quicker next time, Ivan," said Two Down. "You want me to miss the buffet?"

And with that, Two Down was inside Eden.

He nearly smashed into a classic Jaguar gawking at the place, but he calmed his nerves for a moment in the parking lot with some deep-breathing exercises and then got out.

A young man, maybe twenty, came up in a golf cart and said, "May I give you a ride in?"

Two Down pointed to his throat and mouthed the word "laryngitis."

"Oh," said the young man. He took Two Down's clubs and laid them across the back of the cart. Two Down had taken all his bag tags off to avoid trouble. He had even used one of those sticker guns to print out the word "Sullivan" and stick it to his bag handle. The man is very thorough. Two Down got in and off they whirred.

"Who are you playing with today?"

Two Down, of course, had no idea who he was playing with today, but it didn't matter, since the young man said, "Ooops. Sorry. I forgot about the . . ." and he pointed to his own throat.

Two Down smiled. Here was the perfect scam. Whatever member had him as a guest didn't know his face and now wouldn't be able to recognize his voice. And he couldn't very well talk business or common acquaintances with a mute, so it would be just pure, simple, silent golf. He would even write Scott (Two Down) Sullivan on the scorecard, so Dan and I wouldn't be able to say it was some guy named Sullivan's card he'd simply stolen to make it legal. All that was left, Two figured, was the very high stacking up of flat tender.

Two Down bailed out of the electric cart at the registration table, where two women were handing out free balls and green-and-blue souvenir coffee mugs with the TMC scroll on them and signing up the day's players. It was a glorious morning and out in it there was the most beautiful golf course Two Down had ever seen without crouching.

"Good morning," said one of the cheerful women.

Two Down pointed to his throat. He gave a little wave. He

walked around the table, pretending not to hear, in order to look at the large pairings placard that was taped to the wall behind the table. Who would be the lucky stiff that would make him 2,000 zops and introduce him, once and for all, to big-time, old-money, sperm-dollar mega-zops? He searched for the name Scott Sullivan and finally found it, second from the bottom.

Mr. Scott Sullivan. He would be starting on the 17th tee. And the member who would be his host for the day?

Dr. Alfred A. Dingsby.

Personally, I thought my next try would've made a good Van Damme movie, if I do say so myself. To pull it off, I needed two Chops, so I walked the two miles from my apartment to Ponky to set it in motion.

It was odd walking into Ponky. There weren't as many games anymore. No more Reversals. No more Mandatory Mulligans. No more Gotcha golf, in which your worthy opponent could nail you from behind in the nads three times a nine, anytime they wanted. Meaningful games like that.

These days, guys were going home after 18 measly holes. Diehard contests were dwindling. Attendance at Cotillion Night was woefully sparse.

When I walked in this time, there were two complete *strangers* sitting at the corner table where Two Down always sat, reading the taped sheet of absolutely nonnegotiable penalties, assessments and fines. I'd never seen anybody sitting there who wasn't a Chop in my life. Two Down might've sprained an eyebrow over it. Froghair was actually walking around smiling.

There were, sadly, only four Chops in attendance—Crowbar, Hoover, Cementhead and Chunkin' Charlie, who looked spent, the cancer starting to get to him.

Hoover was having his usual—Mylanta and vodka—and trying to figure out why he'd just shot 127. His therapist had finally rid him of the dreaded Shadows, but now he'd read an article in the Golf Congress newsletter how scientists have proven a golfer loses one-sixteenth of an inch off his height over the full round of a game. Hoover, therefore, reasoned he should choke up on the club as the day went on. It didn't help.

"Bad day, Hoovs?" I asked.

"Rats get fat," he sighed without taking his skinny hands off his barren scalp. "Good men die."

Charlie was nursing a Claudette and trying to remember why the hell he'd just ordered the Spam melt.

"I hope Blu Chao can get a refund from that cooking school," I said.

Chunkin' Charlie looked up with a big smile. "Yeah," he said. "But at least I'm getting my minimum daily requirement of carcinogens."

"Like you need 'em," I said, rubbing his toupee.

Charlie laughed.

"So, Stick," asked Chunk in a dwindling voice. "How did Two Down want his cash? Fifties or hundreds?"

"Hilarious," I said. "The game still lives."

"Yes, but Two Down will win it," said Hoover. "You'll never defeat a mind like Two Down's. Remember what he did to Dolores Ginty?"

God, Dolores Ginty. It was one of Two Down's finest achievements.

The whole thing started in Dolores Ginty's pants, which is not a place to be starting things under any circumstance. She was this size 22 waitress we had at Ponky who was surly, rude and colder than the ticket taker's smile at the Dorchester Odoplex.

Dolores went about 210 and was constantly dieting and getting nowhere. So one rainy day with nothing much to do, Two Down bet us all $20 that he could make her *gain* 20 pounds in three weeks and *like* it.

He began by buttering her up whenever he could. He'd ask, "You look different to me, Dolores. You look like you lost weight." And Dolores would respond, "Get bent, Polack."

The second thing he did was find out where she kept her supply of FatBeater shakes. Dolores had begun the FatBeater program three days before and it required her to drink three *delicious* shakes a day, especially if you define "delicious" as tasting like spackle. He also found her FatBeater journal, which contained her weight for that first day of the program—219. He gave us all a glance at it to set the bet up. If she got to 239—and liked it—he'd win about 220 zops.

She was trying the Pretty in Peach shake that day, so Two Down slipped Blu Chao a $20 to do his dirty work. Every time Dolores went to make a Pretty in Peach shake, Blu was to slip two scoops of vanilla ice cream into it.

"I make my own shakes, Commie," Dolores growled.

"No, no, no!" Blu Chao insisted. "In America, cook do all cooking. Arrest you government cook not do all cooking."

Dolores eventually just shrugged and let her do it.

"Shake any good?" Two Down asked her after about three days of this.

"None of yah business, Cyrano," she said.

But we all knew the answer anyway, because every time she had one of those shakes she'd finish the blender completely, some days spooning out every single drop and, one day, actually licking the top inch of the inside of the beaker.

Now Two Down got double diabolical. He stole Dolores's keys out of her purse and made copies of them. He had her address from her journal and went to her apartment one day. He took from her closet an ungodly ugly pair of black beltless polyesters that had most likely gone out of style two years before they were made. He zipped them over to a seamstress he knew, had her take the waistline out two inches, then raced back to the apartment, hanging the pants exactly where he'd found them.

In this way, he did every one of her pants and most of her skirts. He got caught only once—by a little neighbor man coming out of the apartment across the hall. There was Two Down, holding a burgundy polyester mid-length skirt with poodles on it.

"Well," Two Down said in his best drag queen voice. "Last time I lend *her* anything."

Little by little, we all could see it. Dolores was expanding. And yet, she *thought* she was getting thinner.

"You look great," Two Down kept saying. "You MUST be losing weight."

"Screw you, Frizzhead," said Dolores. And yet she said it with less venom in her voice than we'd ever heard. She was, for her, happy.

Of course, the day of her first monthly weigh-in came, and when she came back, she looked like she wanted to pinch somebody's neck off. She took her journal out of her purse, ripped it in two hundred pieces, broke three plates and stepped on Blu's toes twice before she went home that night. We fished the journal out of the trash and, after about a two-hour Scotch tape job, agreed that the clerk had weighed her in at 245 pounds, up 26 pounds. The evidence was irrefutable. Two Down had won.

"But what you don't understand," I countered, "is that I have the perfect idea."

This piqued the interest of everybody but Chunkin' Charlie, who got up from his chair and wandered over to flick on the TV set.

"I can't imagine being less interested," Hoover sniffed.

"Look, Two Down said one of us three had to play the Mayflower. But he didn't say when."

"Yes, he did," said Cementhead. "By October 1."

"I know *that,*" I said. "But he didn't say *when* when. He never said what time of day."

Both of them stared at me.

I looked at the moon outside the window.

"You want to play the Mayflower Club, maybe the finest and most exclusive golf course in the country, at night?" asked Hoover.

"Not just any night," I said, pulling out a duffel bag full of tricks. "Tonight!"

I unzipped it to reveal a dozen night balls, three black T-shirts from Woolworth, three pairs of black sweats, three very small flashlights, and two night sticks to plant in the holes to see where we were going. I felt like Martin Landau in *Mission Impossible.* They were duly impressed.

"That's a great idea, Stick," said Cementhead proudly. "Except for one little thing you forgot. The course is *closed* at night."

Hoover and I just stared at him.

"Unlucky break, Stick," said Hoover. "You almost had something there."

I sighed.

"We *know* that, Cement. That's the whole fucking point. We're going to play it at night *because* it's closed. You in?"

"No way," he said, stepping backward. "I got in enough trouble with Dannie."

"I'm in," said Crowbar—a little too fast, I thought. I hadn't even started to beg. What was in it for him?

"Hoover?"

"I'd love to," said Hoover. "But I'm not particularly fond of dodging bullet fire to play golf."

"Ahhh, that's just an old wives' tale," I said. "Mayflower guards do not carry guns."

"Thanks just the same," said Hoover.

I pulled my chair up close to him. I had to have two witnesses, and with Charlie showing no interest, it was down to these two. I never thought I'd be saying this, but I needed Hoover very badly.

"Hoovs, you're not expanding your full energy to the possibilities of golf," I said, locked on to his eyes. "Why limit yourself to playing golf at a certain point on the clock? Playing at night frees your soul from mundane reality. No longer are you bound to the vagaries of shot *results.* It's a Zen question. If you cannot *see* the ball, how do you know it sliced? If you don't know where it lands, how do you measure its success? You can't. Therefore, the *score* becomes useless. The full measure of how you play is the goodness of the swing ITSELF."

He began to look at me.

"No longer can a great shot be spoiled by an unlucky bounce," I went on, "or an overgrown twig that sends your ball off its destiny. Luck is taken out of the equation. Caprice is no longer important. Worth is the only true measure. You could break 100 in your soul!"

"Well . . ." He hesitated. "Throw in a free bunker lesson sometime?"

"Two," I said.

"I shall join the effort," he said.

The Midnight Mulligan Marauders were born.

8

I COVERED MY FACE and Hoover's face in blackstick. We all took off our golf gloves, since they were white and easily seen. I also colored over Hoover's ugly Scottish-style kilties, those repulsive golf shoes with the flap that goes over the laces for no apparent reason. We used one of Thud's cart keys, absconded with a golf cart and set off for our jumping-off point, the hole in the hedge.

We found it using a key-chain flashlight I'd gotten for filling up one day at Conoco. Hoover got through easily. I got through with a scratch or two. Crowbar almost didn't get through at all. Hoover pushed from the Ponky side and I pulled from the Mayflower side, and when he finally popped through, it was as though a very ugly baby had been born into a very beautiful world.

Even by night, the golf course on the other side of the hedge was a different planet; calmer, more peaceful. The crickets' chirps seemed happier, the crescent moon brighter, the smells sweeter. There was room to swing your arms and gorgeous moonlit vistas to take in.

We had stuffed our bags through, too, and began to walk. Suddenly, it hit us. For the first time in his life, Crowbar was not attached to a golf cart. It was like seeing FDR standing next to his wheelchair. We had not thought of this problem. How would he watch us play and be my second witness?

"I'll walk," Crowbar said.

If my 6-iron had jumped out of the bag, tapped me on the shoulder and said, "I quit," I would have been no less flabbergasted. Crowbar would walk?

"All right, Crow, what the hell's going on?" I demanded.

"Nuttin', slob," he said. "I walk sometimes."

"You walk sometimes? You walked one time from the 14th hole when somebody from the projects shot out your front passenger-side tire. And even then you stopped to sit down six times. In five years, that's the only time I can remember."

"OK, if you don't want a witness, forget it," he said.

"No, no, no," I said. "Please. That's fine. Walk. I appreciate it."

I still felt suspicious. I mean, here was a guy so lazy that he had fully admitted to us that when his little schnauzer needed to relieve himself, he never took the trouble of taking him on a walk. No, instead, he'd just open one of his apartment windows, hold out the dog three floors up and squeeze. And now he was going to walk 18 holes?

We started at the one place we knew—the 2nd hole—figuring nobody said what *order* the Mayflower had to be played in either. I was guessing the most dangerous holes would be near the clubhouse, so I thought the later we went through there, the better. We each snuck over to the little stand by the No. 2 tee and helped ourselves to scorecards, pencils and tees. Hoover actually filled his bag with tees. "Well," he whispered defensively. "They're free, aren't they?"

I hit my first shot pretty well, I thought. The night balls worked well, flying away from us like shooting stars. It was a very odd thing to be standing thirty feet from a golfer, and see no golfer at all, only a ball one second at perfect rest and the next shooting off at 100 miles per hour, as though suddenly pulled at top speed by some alien force. I just hoped the glow would hold up for three and a half hours. Woolworth only had the one box.

Then Hoover stepped up. He swung and this huge BEEP went off on his club at impact.

"Hoover!" I whispered. "What the hell was that?"

"Oh, that's the Swingthing," he whispered, pointing to a two-inch contraption on his shaft, near the grip, which I hadn't noticed before. "You set the speed at which you would like to swing, and if you go faster or slower than that, it beeps."

Crowbar and I just looked at each other.

"Can you possibly manage one night without it?" I asked.

"I suppose," he grumbled.

After that, things went smooth as fresh-paved highway. We played silently and quickly. Except, that is, for Crowbar, who seemed to go out of his way to make noise despite all our dirty looks.

One time, on the 5th hole, when we were near the maintenance shack, he came out with "Sentences that have never been uttered in history."

"Whisper!" I whispered.

"Sentences that have never been uttered!" he whispered.

"Shut the fuck up," I whispered.

"That's been uttered," Crowbar whispered. "I mean like 'Sir, would you mind giving me a paper cut in my eye?' That sentence right there has never been uttered before in the history of the world until this very moment."

"Ohhh, I get it," I whispered. "How about 'Crowbar, will you please take off on one of your idiotic, stupid non sequiturs for us, please?' "

"Riiiight," said Crowbar, "Or how about 'Can I have the rest of your okra?' "

Hoover then added, "Or 'The rotund body was found near the 7th green, bound and gagged with a fuzzy head cover.' "

That seemed to shut Crowbar up. After that, he began to fade. He had been anxious the entire night, I thought. He was always looking around, waiting for somebody to come around, nervous. But nobody was near us. No guards, no guns, no night security, nothing so far.

As it turned out, the Mayflower does not return to the clubhouse after 9 holes. Its 9th and 10th are far from the clubhouse, and this was a huge break for us. But we knew we'd eventually be coming to the holes near the grand clubhouse. If there was security, it'd be there. We couldn't afford a peep out of anybody.

We played well and without much incident. This night-golf thing might just catch on. For one, tee times are a breeze. For two, because you don't want to lose your ball, you tend to swing more slowly and evenly and easily, hoping it will go somewhere you can follow. *Golf My Way,* by José Feliciano. Hoover played like a decent hack, which is about three floors up from his usual classification as pitiful, irredeemable hack.

Standing on the 18th tee box—we had now played 16 holes—Hoover was in exquisite shape—only 20 over—which meant he could play the final two holes in triple bogey and break 100. Even Hoover couldn't screw that up.

The 18th is a 410-yard downhill par 4 over a beautiful kidney-shaped pond in front of the green, the majestic green-and-white clubhouse in the back. But because we were so near to it, I told Hoover to ditch the glow balls and use regular golf balls and just hope we hit them straight.

"Raymond, I'm 20 over! I could break 100!"

"Hoov, if you don't switch, you'll be telling your cellmates about the greatest 16-hole round you ever played."

He switched.

We both knocked them down the middle and walked on, noiselessly and slowly, toward the clubhouse. We hit our irons onto the green—by this time our eyes had adjusted so well to the darkness that we didn't need the glow balls. Even Hoover knocked it on nicely. This was all much too easy. Naturally, it was just as I was thinking that very thing, we saw two men.

One was obviously a guard, with his walkie-talkie on his belt, fast asleep in his golf cart, his long legs stretched out over the front. It had to be three in the morning.

The other man, a sturdy-looking guy, wearing black pants, a black windbreaker and a solid-black hat, was doing something we couldn't make heads or tails of. He seemed to be watering the putting green, but in an odd way. One hose was lying on the green with the nozzle end of it in one of the holes. Yet this hose wasn't even turned on. He had another hose turned on full and seemed to be watering the first hose.

We puzzled about him for a time, hiding behind two trees from about fifty yards away. He must have carried on with this weirdness for thirty minutes until he finally stopped, careful to drag both hoses off the putting green.

When he left, the sleeping guard didn't even budge and we decided it was safe. We snuck up and putted out. I made 4 and Hoover 5, which meant if we could just play this last hole, No. 1, I'd win two Large and Hoover could play the hole with a push broom and still break his weight for the first time in his life, not to mention the Unthinkable 100.

Off we slipped to the 1st tee box, crouching low in our black outfits, checking always the status of the tall guard in the cart. Crowbar slunk along, too, as much as a 300-pound man can slink.

Not wanting to wake the guard, I put a very light swing on a driver. It looked rightish, though it was hard to see, but not bad and, best of all, didn't wake Stretch. Then Hoover stepped up to the 1st tee box, a 395-yard par 4, and put the slowest, sweetest move on it this side of Freddy Couples himself. The ball took off like I'd never seen one of his take off—a beauty, with that professional low-to-high trajectory—easily the best shot in Hoover's painful golfing life, over 250 yards.

"Holy, living, breathing Jesus!" yelled Crowbar.

We both looked at him with horrified faces and then to Stretch, who was woken by the voice.

"Hey, you!" the guard hollered, trying to untangle his feet from the steering column.

I looked around the 1st tee, petrified. We were doomed. There was no way we were going to be able to get over a hedge and a twelve-foot brick wall. And we weren't going to outrun a golf cart. We could always beat him to death with our drivers, but he was already on the walkie-talkie, calling for reinforcements.

That's when I noticed a line of carts stored behind the 1st tee and off to the right.

"There!" I yelled, and pointed to the carts. I ran to them, jumped in one and hoped like hell that Thud's key would fit every cart ever made.

I never found out. Apparently, inside the Mayflower gates, they don't get a lot of Midnight Marauder activity, so they just leave the keys in the carts all the time. I stepped once on the gas pedal to figure that out and it fired right up.

Hoover jumped in beside me and we were off like a prom dress. We screeched away toward Crowbar, who was practically dying. His last sprint was twenty-seven years and 230 pounds ago. He tried to sit with us up front but Hoover hollered, "Grab on to the back!" and he barely did. I looked back and Stretch was after us, maybe 100 yards behind us, but gaining. For one thing, he didn't have Captain Criscobutt slowing him down, and for another, he had a faster electric cart. Ours was the older, slower, gas-powered models.

"Stand up!" I yelled at Hoover.

"What do you mean?" he yelled back.

"Stand up and steer this thing!" I said, standing up myself and holding on to the wheel.

Befuddled, Hoover stood up and took the wheel as we barreled down the first fairway. Stretch was closing fast. Hanging on to one of the poles that holds up the cart roof, I reached in my pocket for a tee. Then I pulled the seat open to reveal the tiny engine that was propelling us along. I noticed Stretch was almost on our bumper now. Crowbar was trying to kick at him with one of his stubby little legs. Another five feet and he'd be able to cut us off.

As we bumped along madly, I tried to find the governor, the tiny gizmo on a golf-cart engine that keeps the cart from doing anything much over 15 miles per hour.

It was an old trick Two Down and I liked to commit on the high school golf team. You stick a tee in the governor so that it is permanently wide open and the engine can finally let it out and pretty soon you're doing 45 miles per hour and playing 18 holes of Le Mans. Or we'd play Rat Patrol, in which you get two tee-rigged carts going full speed, right next to each other, and then *switch* carts without crashing. This is a wonderful way to spend your post-practice hours.

The only problem was I'd never put one in while the cart was moving. Stretch was now right next to us and taking swipes at Hoover's sweatpants. Hoover was trying to stand up and steer and kick at the guard at the same time. "Do you very much mind if we do the lube, oil and filter later?!?" he wailed.

Stretch had a good hold on Hoover's shirt when I finally jammed the tee where I needed it. Suddenly, the cart squealed off like it had a 454 Hemi in it. Stretch lost his grip on Hoover's shirt and we were off. Another 50 yards and we'd be at the hole in the hedge, safe and sound.

Not that I wanted to go there.

Just as we came up on the 1st green/2nd tee/hedge hole area, I wheeled our cart around and went back up toward the clubhouse.

"Stick, NOW what the fuck are you doing?" yelled Crowbar, who looked like he might throw up.

Hoover looked at me. He knew. He was mostly petrified and partly thrilled.

Stretch followed me back up, up, up toward the clubhouse, and just as we got near it, I turned back down the 1st fairway. We had a 200-yard lead on him.

"No," said Crowbar. "Goddamnit to hell no!!! Tell me you're NOT going to try to finish the hole now, not with a security guard breathing up our ass!"

"Hey, that's a good one, Crowbar," I hollered. "I'll bet that's never been uttered before!"

We screamed up to my ball in the right rough. While we were driving, I reached back and grabbed an iron. It turned out to be a 5. Too much club, but I could make it work. We screeched to a stop. I took one little knockdown swing at it and the ball knifed toward the green, only left. Didn't matter. The guard was 100 yards back. I floored it over to Hoover's ball. I know I should've just finished my ball out, won the bet and dove for the hole, but I just couldn't bear to not let Hoover finish. He'd played so well.

We found his ball, which was right smack in the middle of the fairway, a 250-yard drive.

"Yesssssss!" Hoover screamed joyously, for he had never hit a ball 200 yards in any direction, much less straight. He had his 7-iron out and he jumped from the cart, and, if you can believe it, took a practice swing.

"Just hit the fucking ball!" Crowbar screamed as Stretch bore down on us.

He did and it went dribbling forward 10 yards.

"We're dead," Crowbar sighed.

Hoover ran ahead and hit it again, this time without stopping. This one was a low, ankle-biting liner that screamed over the green. Stretch was 50 yards behind us, talking into his walkie-talkie. This is when we noticed three more carts behind him, all full of guards and walkie-talkies and all of them in suddenly-awoken-grouchy-guard moods. I waited for tracer fire.

Still, we had some speed up as we raced to our balls. We each had our putters out, too, and I flew the cart right up to the edge of the green—only 50 feet from the hole in the hedge—and we all jumped out. Crowbar ran for the hedge. I slapped my ball up 5 feet from the hole and Hoover hit a nice little approach, considering the circumstances, to within 10 feet.

"Hurry!" I screamed, which has to go down as one of the most obvious sentences in language history. It was unclear who wanted to finish the round worse, me or Hoover, who was about to achieve the finest moment in his life. Unfortunately, the Gestapo was on the green with us and closing in fast.

"Stop right there!" I hollered. I began swinging my putter all around me like Bruce Lee. "Come another step closer and you'll know what it feels like to be overclubbed."

They froze.

"Just let us putt out, like civilized people," I said in a calm tone, "and then we'll talk." I checked over my shoulder for Crowbar. He had smashed his way through the hole, but he was still on the other side, looking back through it. Fine. He was still a witness.

"Partner, I believe you're away," I said, swinging the putter madly at the four guards.

Hoover, shaking, stepped up to the putt and stroked it about halfway there.

"Can't believe that didn't go in," I said. "Go ahead and finish."

He putted twice more and the ball dropped. A 97. He smiled at me.

"Well played," I said. "Now if you'll do the honors for me."

Hoover began waving his putter around madly at the guards with both hands and that's when I noticed my golf ball was no longer sitting on the green. One of the guards was holding it by his thumb and pointer finger.

"Looking for this, asswipe?" the guard sneered.

That hurt.

"I must ask you to put my ball down," I said. "Or I'm afraid I'll be forced to charge you two strokes."

"Come and get it," said the guard.

I was stuck. I had no other ball in my pocket. I had left the Day-Glo balls in my bag. I could ask Hoover to throw me his ball, but then he might stop swinging his putter for a millisecond, which is all they needed to jump us. So much for the bet.

I kept swinging the putter and started backing toward the hole in the hedge. We backed near the cart and got our bags. Hoover took my cue and did the same. The guards merely smiled, thinking they were backing us into a corner. Of course, little did they know we knew the back entrance to an infinitely shittier parallel universe.

When we had backed within 10 feet of it, I screamed, "Oh, my God! Channel 7!!!" and pointed over their heads. They turned just long enough to give us both a head start on diving through the hole, Hoover first, with me right behind him, each of us heaving our bags through the hole ahead of us.

Stretch had a hold of my foot, but, much to my father's dismay, I've never been a good, strong shoelace-tier and the shoe and sock came off in his hand. He started climbing through the hole himself. Crowbar was already sitting in the cart with our bags thrown on the floor.

"The key!" Crowbar screeched.

I threw it to him and, miracle of miracles, he caught it. We all piled in the front this time and took off just as Stretch made a lunge for the bumper, hanging on by his fingertips.

We dragged him along the full Ponky Tour. We whipsawed him through Nuke Pond, off the bumper of the '57 Chevy, off a few fence posts along Beagle River and then, finally, picked him off on the edge of the tunnel on the 9th. There may have been more, but it was difficult to see, since the bulbous flesh of Crowbar's gut was often in my face as I tried to drive.

We raced for our cars and started to pile in them.

"You didn't play a full 18," Crowbar hollered, driving off. "You didn't win the bet."

"Thank you so kindly for mentioning that, Crow," I hollered, climbing in Hoover's car.

As we squealed off, Hoover's eyes were huge and white and stuck out of his blackened face like lightbulbs. That and his huge white smile made him look like Al Jolson.

"Ninety-seven!" he cried.

"Should've gone in on the bet," I said. "You'd be up two Large right now."

His face fell a little.

Poor guy. Even his silver linings came with acid rain.

Sockless, shoeless, scraped, blackfaced, exhausted and penniless, I had one idea left.

Plan C.

9

I TRIED TO KEEP my hands from quivering and rang the buzzer.

"Yes?" said the voice.

"I hear you're taking applications for caddies?"

"Service entrance," said the voice.

My hope was that caddies get to play on Mondays or once a month or perhaps just on the last day of the season. And if they weren't allowed at all, maybe I'd get a feel for the place and be able to smile-beat some member into letting me play once with him. It beat Plan D, which was . . . I had no Plan D.

I was no stranger to the way of the Loop. I had vowed never to step foot on a golf course again with William Davenport Hart, but my mother hated to see me leave a game she could tell I loved. So, when I was sixteen, she said something to my father's brother, Joe, a stocky BarcaLounger kind of guy with a Marcus Welby face. He ran a Chevron station with six pumps and a little car wash in North Boston. Soon, I was caddying every Saturday for him at Fox Hollow, the nicest public course in town.

I loved those days with him. When it got slow on the tee boxes, he'd throw down a few balls and teach me to chip or we'd putt to the ball markers or try to flop shots over trees or punch them under. He'd bet me a bag of M&Ms I couldn't chip it closer to the little maple tree than him and I very much wanted that bag of M&Ms. And then, after almost every round, he'd sit and have a cold Falstaff on the range under a big willow tree and let me hit a couple buckets and watch and give me a few tips.

But the best thing he gave was an absolutely gorgeous wooden driver—a persimmon Tommy Armour MacGregor 693 with a rosewood finish and a red insert.

"Now, don't hit this puppy till you shoot par, Rayboy," he told me when he gave it to me. "Promise me that. Jack William Nicklaus himself actually used this sucker during the playoff with Arnold Palmer to win the Open at Oakmont. Nineteen hundred and sixty-two."

I believe that was my first true sexual experience. I asked him where he got such a treasure.

"Your grandfather bought it for me at some charity auction. Since he didn't play golf, he gave it to me. I'm just a natural-born hack, but I think you could do something special with this baby."

I fell for golf. It was my kind of thing. I could play it by myself, practice it by myself and sink deep into it by myself. I became good at golf, I suppose, thanks to my father. It was the only place I could go and know he wouldn't be anywhere near. You spend that much time at something, you're bound to get the hang of it. And so, by the time I was a junior in high school, I was No. 1 on the Somerville High School team.

When I was eighteen, I finally did shoot par. I went right home and got it out and took it to the range and was nearly shaking. I didn't even use a range ball. I took a brand-new Titlist out for the maiden voyage. Caught it on the center groove, too.

And later, when everybody else on the planet switched to metal drivers—including Nicklaus—I stuck with my Tommy Armour. "The Last Real Golf Club in America," Chunkin' Charlie called it. I was accepted at Harvard—with Father pulling strings—but I also got a half-ride golf scholarship to UMass, which I snapped up, much to Father's dismay. I ended up damn near winning four tournaments, including the New England College Classic. Story of my life. Damn near. In all my life, I never won a big trophy like that. As a kid, I'd get handed trophies just for being on the team. Or I'd play in some little thing and get handed a funny trophy or a plaque, but never a big one. Never.

The Nearly Man. I'd always play great, but always some little thing would go wrong, or I'd get too emotional under the pressure or get to feeling sorry for myself and end up in the chair next to the winner while I perfected my stiff upper lip.

Some days it was easy to see why. There were days when I would play so bad it looked like I was using gutta-perchas, and other days when I could be officially classified as "Scary Good." I had a 66 once at Colgate, and I went one entire week without getting on the wrong side of 72.

Uncle Joe came to all those tournaments when we'd play Boston College or Holy Cross. My father never did. Any success I'd had in golf was despite him and maybe he knew it. He stayed away. But Uncle Joe loved being part of it. Even into my twenties, I'd still caddie for him, and afterward, he'd sit in the shade of that willow tree and give me tips on my swing, even though he hit his ceiling on understanding the swing when I was about nineteen. He was a warm man, a decent man, and the thing I guess I liked best about him was that he always stopped at two.

He made the mistake one day of asking me what I wanted to do with my life after school and I told him the truth, that I wanted to play golf for a living. He wasn't exactly a Du Pont, but he scraped up enough money from his savings and from some of his buddies and maybe even a loan, I don't know, and put me out on tour for a year, with some vague notion that I'd pay him back someday.

I tried for the PGA Tour, but I got killed in Tour Qualifying School, which is 600 guys trying for 50 places, which is the nearest thing on this earth to anesthetic-free dental surgery. Still, I made the Hogan Tour, which was kind of a vo-tech school for the big boys, a sort of Greg Norman Starter Kit set in Akron and Sacramento and Wilkes-Barre, those kinds of places, everybody playing for a $20,000 first-place check and going three to a room at the Red Roof Inn.

It was from those days that I knew caddies. I knew that a lot of caddies leave the northern clubs like Pine Valley, Winged Foot and the Mayflower early in September, take a month to screw around, smoke dope and drive south to Florida and caddie there for the season at classic places like Seminole, Old Marsh and Indian Creek, where the season starts October 1. But that left the northern clubs short of caddies. Clubs like the Mayflower.

I had on my nicest T-shirt and jeans—an upgrade from my usual golf attire of baggy shorts, T-shirts, dirty socks and the old Red Sox hat my uncle had bought for me so many Yazterdays ago. I even shaved. I was going to lose the hat, but I put it back on for luck. Besides, I needed *something* to hide my face in case I saw my father.

The service entrance was another mile walk and on the projects side, too, a ratty little door through the brick wall. It went immediately very high on my list of Places Not to Be Some Dark Night Without Something Off the Banned Assault Weapons List. I walked past the Dumpsters and the kitchen refuse, through a screen door and a dank little room with time cards and boxes and finally through another door to a wheezy little man who directed me to the caddie master around the corner.

The caddie master was this shrunken little black guy with a cigar and an old Disneyland flop hat on. His whiskers were speckled black and white and he had little notes in pen all over the pink palm of his hand. The sewn insignia on his shirt said his name was Fletcher.

"Thought you might be looking for caddies this time of year," I said.

"Don't take no white caddies," Fletcher said, not looking up from a clipboard.

"Terrific," I said. "My lawyer has been dying to file a lawsuit somewhere."

"White caddies don't know nothin' about caddyin'," Fletcher said, still keeping his head buried in the papers. "White caddies always thin' they fonna make some pal in tha club and fonna be able to play tha course or en up a memmer and eat tha turtuhl soup the rest a they life and po tha sheeery innit. No white caddies."

So much for being able to play the course.

"I don't want to be a member," I said. "I don't want to eat turtle soup. I don't even *play* golf. All I've ever done is caddie."

"Bullshih."

"Nosir."

"Where you carry?"

I started rattling off every famous course I hoped he'd never been to. "Out West, mostly. Six seasons at Cherry Hills in Denver and the three at the Broadmoor in Colorado Springs and for a while I caddied at Fort Ord in the service."

"Dju ever see tha plaque at tha Broadmoor war Arnie drove tha foist green?"

"It's not at the Broadmoor," I said. "It's at Cherry Hills."

"What your bes at Pebble?"

"I told you. I don't play."

He finally looked up. "Whatchu do if Tha Man and you be lookin' for his ball and nobody else around and he say ta you, 'Uh, gee, tha group behind are catchin' us up. We better not tarry on too long hair'?"

I snapped my reply: " 'I don't think anyone would deny you a free drop here, sir. After all, we'd have found it if we weren't in such a rush. I've taken the liberty of throwing one down on top of that clump of grass.' "

He looked a while at me. "Whatchu say if Tha Man cain't 'member if he had a 6 or a 7 on tha hole?"

" 'I actually think it was a 5, sir, but if you feel you must give yourself a 6, I suppose there is nothing that can be done.' "

"Whachu say if Tha Man scream at you all ta way round, thow clubs all dee day and then stiff you on tha tip?"

" 'Thank you, sir. Please ask for me again.' "

"Lessee how clain you keeps yo hands," he said.

I offered them. He noticed the many calluses.

"I thought you say you din't play golf."

"Construction work," I said.

"Then how come yo left hand isn't tan like tha right?"

I paused. He looked at me. I smiled.

"Played a *lot* of softball this summer."

He glared at me.

"I got a guy quittin' Tuesday. Lottery is at six ever mornin'. Be hair or you don't go out. No booze. No fightin'. No guns. No knives. You keeps anythin' over $15. Everythin's cash. Fuck wit me and I'll make you wish you'da die as a small boy."

"I'm honored," I said.

I started to make my way out the byzantine maze I'd come through.

"Hey, whas yo name?" Fletcher called.

He definitely had me there.

"Carl," I stammered. "Carl Spackler."

....

The next morning was going to be Sunday and because I didn't have a car and my body was aching for a round of golf in actual daylight, I took the last bus Saturday night toward Ponky, snuck back into the Pit of Despair with my key and slept in the puke-orange Naugahyde La-Z-Boy until about four, when I woke up and realized I hadn't put my Titlist with the purple dots in the pipe. When I got out there and did it, I saw Charlie and Cementhead sitting in Cementhead's plumbing truck in the parking lot and I decided to climb in the front seat with them.

Besides, with Dannie and Two Down as worthy opponents now in the Killer Bet, I figured I could use some allies. Maybe Cementhead might accidentally spill something he wasn't supposed to out of one of the large holes in his head. And Chunkin' Charlie Thompson was one guy I could trust.

Before the cancer hit Charlie, he must've had a friendly, athletic kind of face with a fighter's jaw. Now, though, the cancer was starting to make his cheeks purple and drawn and his big hands were getting skinnier and bonier and his golf shirts looked more and more every day like they were hanging on a parking meter.

I really didn't want to think about it on account of my uncle dying of pretty much the same thing and maybe on account of he reminded me a little of him, too. He was always loose and kind and took nothing too seriously. He took as much crap as he gave out and always with a wink. He was a little different than the rest of us, but I couldn't quite make out how. Maybe his car was a little nicer and his clothes a little newer and he never seemed to have to ever write anybody a chit.

It hurt to think of what was happening to him and yet it didn't seem to be as painful for him. He never tried in the least to hide it. He even had a name for it—the Uglies—as in the sentence "Man, I'd like to play nine more but I gotta go to St. Luke's and let them shoot at the Uglies."

He knew he was dying, which is why he played so much golf. "Where else would you want to die but a golf course?" he'd say.

"Yeah?" I'd say. "So what are you doin' here at Ponky?"

I was fond of him and admired his courage and his love of the game, so I tried to do what I could for him. Usually, when I had a car, I'd put a ball in the pipe and save a space in my foursome for him, knowing it was tough for him to get up. I once tried to make an 8 A.M. tee time for him and he said he couldn't.

"Why not?" I asked.

"Because I don't stop throwin' up till eight-thirty."

But there he was, sitting in there with Cementhead, trying to read a bulldog edition of the *Globe* with his shaky hands by the beam of the flashlight he held in his mouth, since Cementhead's dome light was busted out. Cementhead was asleep, which is when he was his most intelligent.

"Can I see your license and registration?" I said, climbing into the cab.

Chunkin' Charlie spit out the flashlight. "What's the charge?" he said.

"Bein' stupid enough to wait out here at 4 A.M. to play a dog track like Ponky," I said.

"Guilty," he said.

"What are you doin' up anyway, slob?"

"The Uglies didn't feel like sleeping," he said.

"Whaddya suppose Cementhead is dreamin' about?" I asked.

"Probably a nice piece of copper tubing that fits *perfectly* into an elbow joint."

"Nah," I said. "I'm thinkin' 'Barney.' "

Charlie laughed. Sick as he was, he still laughed more than anybody at Ponky, only now his laugh always came along with about six or eight coughs at the end.

"Shouldn't you be dreamin' about breakin' the course record at the Mayflower?" he said.

"Right," I said. "Soon as they let caddies start playing with the members."

"You're a caddie?"

"Startin' Tuesday."

Charlie mulled that over for a while.

"Hear anything about the other two?" I asked.

"Nah, they haven't been around at all," he said, rather quickly, as though he wanted the subject dropped.

"Didn't want any of that big bank, huh, Chunk?"

He seemed uneasy with the question.

"Nah," he said. There was an awkward pause.

"Why not?" I said.

"Jesus," he said, a little ruffled. "I mean, why do you guys care about that place anyway? What's wrong with Ponky?"

"Nothing that about six SCUD missiles couldn't fix," I said.

He seemed to be actually getting pissed.

"This place isn't so bad," he said, finding a little energy. "Christ, think of all the laughs we have! Think of all the good golf we play here! Nobody cheats. Everybody whips out right away. Everybody's a pretty decent player. What more do you want out of the game than that? What more do you want outta *life* than that? You know, there's more to life than what something *looks* like through some stupid hole. There's people. There's, there's friends. There's, you know, common decency toward the other guy. Respect. You look through that hole, but you can't see everything."

He said this with a little bite and his voice kind of rose a little and started getting a little shaky. I guess the whole notion of the bet just kind of sat in his underwear the wrong way. I figured I better let it drop.

Curious, though.

10

FOR ONE OF the finest clubs in the world, the Mayflower didn't seem to give a hairball about the guys who actually *carried* the clubs. Not fifty feet from what we'd always heard was one of the most lavish clubhouses in golf (caddies are not permitted inside), lurked a ten-by-twelve box known as the Caddie Room.

The Caddie Room was done up in Early Slave, with a bare linoleum floor, almost nothing on the walls and two windows, both of which were covered by old pieces of plywood. It was dark, moldy and had no rest room. You were asked to use the portable toilet back behind the Dumpster and that filled up after two days and was only emptied every four, so half the time the caddies had to walk three blocks to Shalakar's African Cuisine to relieve themselves.

Shalakar was a former caddie himself who used to go by the name of Foot. I asked him one time how he got that name. " 'Cause no client of mine ever had a bad lie."

It was unclear who put the plywood over the windows—the caddies who didn't want to see any members or the members who didn't want to see any caddies.

You could see both their points.

The caddies looked like the Lawn and Bottle Club that meets day and night on Tremont Street in the Combat Zone, sucking down 8-balls and four-packs of Ripple. Most of the caddies had variously advancing stages of glaucoma and cataracts, thanks to day after day in the sun without wearing sunglasses, and the lady with the employee health-care plan hadn't quite gotten by the Caddie Room in the last hundred years.

As for the members, it was like my uncle used to say: It's all right to be a member of the Mayflower, but he'd never want to *belong.* Once I was inside, I knew what he meant.

To me, most of these guys looked like they picked their teeth with welfare mothers and wiped their feet on woven children. They walked with that certain erectness that made you believe they could close down your company, jail your great-aunt and take your last bit of hamburger money.

They said a lot of faux chumly things like "You bet, buddy!" and "How's the fam?" and "Where in the *world* have you been, pards?" and yet not listening to or caring about your answer. They never asked a follow-up question. It was never "Really? Do you recommend it?" No, it was always something rote, like "So, how you hittin' it, big guy?"

The members seemed to be all painted in a kind of Lincoln Continental beige, mostly in their fifties and sixties. They were all way over the national logo limit—which is two—seeing as how they had one on their visor, one on their chest, one on their sleeve, two dozen on their belt and, God help us, now some had them on their back pockets.

The Mayflower turned out to be a very cheesy place. There was the lovely Brie Concorde. There was the backslapping good-time boy Cheddar Bradford. There was the elegantly dressed Colby Smithson. Maybe someday Brie would get divorced and marry Colby and they could introduce you to their precious twins, Gruyère and Gouda.

Those were the Christian names. Their nicknames were even more stupid. If, for instance, your name was Dan, you were automatically the Dan Monster and the Danner or Danny Boy, the Danimal, Big D or D Man. Nobody called you Brinks because you won a lot of bets or Provisional because you always ordered a backup entrée at restaurants or Casper for your tan. They didn't know each other that well. They didn't care to. They were too wrapped up in themselves to see anybody else.

The Mayflower had a lot of members from the creamed-corn set, and every night at least one old guy would end up asleep in his mashed potatoes. And so with so few young members, the Mayflower had become almost purely a golf club, which meant the players who could actually still stand erect were pretty good—better than average for a country club—and the bank was steep.

I drew fourteenth that first day in the caddie lottery, which meant I had about two and half hours to kill with a lot of guys named Dogmeat, Professor, Haircut, Shakespeare and First-and-Third, who got his name for the direction his eyes pointed, which is to say, in two opposite directions. Shakespeare got his name because he once brought a book to the Caddie Room.

From the minute I sat down, Professor, sitting next to me on the springy couch, seemed particularly interested in the only white caddie in Mayflower history. I could tell this because he kept staring at me while I was trying my best to resemble an end table. He looked about thirty-five or forty, had a cigarette behind each ear, wore a hopelessly faded Washington Senators shirt that looked like it had been worn while applauding Frank Howard.

"What happened to you?" he finally asked. "Your venture deal collapse or did you get upside down on a naked option?"

It was a very odd question coming from a man who looked like he'd spent the night in detox. I guess my eyes showed it.

"That's right!" he said. "We ain't all Stepin Fetchit round here! I pull *Barron's* out of the Dumpster ever day and read it front to back. Now, what bring a white boy with no dirt under his fingernails to a room like this? You get screwed by yo arbitrage guy?"

"Invested it all in pet mousse," I said. "The market just never seemed to gel."

Professor's stone face allowed himself a slight grin.

"Who you with?" he said. "*A Current Affair* or *48 Hours?* Whatever you gettin', give us a fourth and we'll start makin' shit up. We'll tell how they cane us out on 14 tee box."

"No. Actually, I'm doing a novel. *Black Like Me.* I just got very lousy pigment operations."

Professor stared some more and then laughed.

"I don't know what you are," he said. "But you definitely ain't no caddie."

Professor not only turned out to be the smartest caddie in there, he also turned out to be the best. "Oh, yes, yes, yes," Haircut said that morning. "That boy can tell by the sound what kinda tree you just hit."

"Whaddya mean?" I asked.

"Well, if a member hit one into the trees, he say, 'Shhhhh!' and lissen for the sound. And then he announce real loud, 'Oak.' Or 'Maple.' Or maybe he say, 'Tha sound like a new birch.' And he go right to that maple and find yo ball. One time I were with him and some ol' boy hit one way, way, away right, and Professor say, 'Shhhh!' and wait for the sound. And when it hit, Professor look kinda puzzled for a second. And the ol' boy say, 'Professor, what kinda wood was that?' And Professor say, 'Cedar siding. You hit Mr. Thompson's house.' "

And right then is when Fletcher called out, "Spackler!"

I jumped up.

"You gots Mr. Concorde."

I heard some chuckles in the Caddie Room. Wonderful.

I left the room and came out into the bright of the day. It took my eyes a while to adjust from the blackness of the Caddie Room to the bright sunlight, but I soon realized I was standing in front of a sort of blond George Hamilton—about forty-five, swimmer's shoulders, blond bangs that hung halfway down his bronzed forehead and swept back easily from his face, and the look of white-paper murder in his eyes. He was way over the logo limit, with his Doral hat and his Desert Highlands shirt and his Skins Game Khakis.

"This is Mr. Concorde."

"Hi, I'm Carl Spackler," I said to him, extending my hand.

He put a Titlist HVC 100 in it and didn't even look me in the eye. "If I wanted friends, I'd go to a bar. Now, I read my own putts. Keep up. I like my ball cleaned after every putt. Keep your mouth closed. This is business."

Oh, my pleasure entirely, Mr. Concorde.

When we came out from around the corner on our way to the 1st tee, I nearly had to catch my breath.

I had seen it at night, but the daylight beauty of the Mayflower was another thing. The fairways looked like they were vacuumed twice a day. The lakes were navy blue, outlined in tall green reeds and freckled with yellow lily pads. The clubhouse itself was breathtaking, painted sparkling white with green trim, balconies off nearly every window and the windows protected by white-and-green awnings. There was a huge covered terrace overlooking the putting green and an Olympic-size swimming pool off to my right, bluer than a blueberry Popsicle. There were twenty-four tennis courts behind that. It was a toss-up as to which surface was smoother—the pool or the tennis courts—because not a soul was using either.

The red-brick wall that was so dilapidated on our side looked like they sent a team of convicts with toothbrushes out every day to scrub the mortar on this side. The bunkers were right out of *South Pacific.* Even the white of my overalls shone like I was in some kind of All Temp-a-Cheer ad.

"I said, 'Driver!' " insisted Concorde. We were standing at the 1st tee and I guess I was so awestruck by the place I hadn't heard him the first time. He hit a little draw down the middle, about 230 to the top of the hill, and we were off.

It was a very odd feeling being part of this kind of golf, everybody's shoes shined up so nice and clubs clean and bags so big and new and everybody saying, "Good shot," and telling their worthy opponent's balls to "get in!" Nobody at Ponky would say,

"Good shot," if somebody holed out from 240 yards. "Press!" maybe.

What's weird is that Stone Concorde couldn't have been more polite and kind to his colleagues. He was the kind of guy who always had a pat on the back and a kind word for everybody, especially the guy who just lost the hole. As much as you wanted to hate him, it was hard to find evidence. He was interested in everybody else's shot, praising it like it had come off Greg Norman's grooves, not Wentworth Coddlestone's. He would hit a decent shot and palm it off to luck or closing his eyes or hitting too much club fat or too little club thin.

But there was a hint of evil about him. Like a guy would be in a greenside bunker about 30 yards from the hole and he'd say something like "You're good at this long bunker shot, Evan. I read in *Golf Digest* that it was voted the hardest shot in golf, but you never seem to have any trouble with it."

And all of a sudden poor Evan is thinking, *How come I never have any trouble with it?* And next thing you know he's under some rose bush lying 4. At least at the Donkey, we're up-front with our psyching. In that situation we'd say, "Ten to one you skull it into the grocery cart." But at least we don't do mind fucks.

The charming Stone Concorde was also a born cheater. It took me about three days to figure it out. Reason I knew is they kicked a guy off the TC Jordan Tour for doing the exact same thing.

Concorde had two ball markers, both of them metallic, both of them with "St. Andrews" on them. He'd use the first one most of the time, but every once in a while, when he was on the green away from the others or when he had a longer putt, he'd slip the lightly *magnetic* one onto the bottom of his putter. Then he'd reach down to mark his ball with the legal marker in his left hand, balancing himself with his putter in the right. Naturally, the putter supporting him was three or four feet closer to the hole. He'd pretend to mark his ball with the legit marker in his left hand but he'd never actually put it down. Then he'd wipe the magnetic marker off his putter blade three feet ahead of him and—*voilà!*—he was suddenly three feet closer to the hole.

Nobody ever noticed. Nobody ever came close to noticing. The only reason I noticed was that I was trying to learn the greens and I kept noticing that he wasn't quite putting the putt I'd just read.

This guy Concorde was one clever, cuddly, cutthroat bastard.

From the conversation and the bag tags and the three other caddies that day, I figured out Concorde was a real estate developer, a very good real estate developer at that, if you didn't mind the top of your mountains lopped off to make that terrific finishing hole.

He looked to me like about a 13 or 14 handicapper, but tougher than a Blu Chao steak. He also seemed to like the way I handled the bag—or, more likely, was a bigot and was glad to have white hands on it—because after that, he asked for me plenty, which was not a good thing, since I had no more chance of getting a free pass to play the Mayflower from Concorde than I had of waking up one morning as the House Majority Leader.

I knew it from the way he tipped. He gave me $20, which was about 4 percent of what I figured the cheatin' sloth won.

Not that I was going anywhere. I had seen something that was going to make me stay no matter what—Madeline the Cart Girl.

....

After that first round, I headed back to the Caddie Room, where Fletcher said to me, "You can go to the employee winnow and get yoself sompin' t'eat, Spackler. 'Tain't bad and it cheap."

So I went to the employee window and stood behind another caddie. The prices were decent: $2 for a cheeseburger, $2.50 for the pot roast plate. Unfortunately, the guy in front of me got handed a torched-looking tuna melt.

As the poor caddie was walking away, I heard a very familiar voice say, "All right, who's next?"

And that's when I looked up and saw a very familiar face.

Two Down's.

11

I WAS TWENTY-TWO. I had been on the Hogan Tour only two months when Uncle Joe was diagnosed with colon cancer. It went through him like a forest fire. In two months he died and my father didn't even come to the funeral. After the services, I went back to Fox Hollow and hit two buckets by that old willow tree and let myself cry through most of them.

It was too bad, too, because my golf that year was the best of my life and he would've loved it. I never won one of those big trophies, but I had a second at Lubbock and a second at Ogallala and four thirds. Yeah, Nearly Man, coming to a consolation bracket near you.

Still, it was looking like I was going to make the top five on the Hogan money list, easy, which would automatically qualify me for the damn-straight PGA Tour the next year, which is only a lifetime of cold beers and courtesy cars and trying to fit big-ass novelty checks in first-class overhead storage.

But right around then is when Travis started washing his hands funny.

He was seventeen and that's what Mom noticed first. That he was washing his hands ten and fifteen times a day. It's the kind of thing that sneaks up on you. You don't even notice it and then, bam, an alarm clock goes off inside you and you realize maybe something is a little wrong.

Travis was not the kind of kid who was going to wash his hands ten times a day. You might have to tell him ten times to get him to wash them once. He was a mud kind of kid, always riding dirt bikes and skateboards. He was five years younger than me, but he could hang with me on almost anything. He thought golf was much too Ward Cleaver, but he loved to shred bumps with me on snowboards or to mountain-bomb. You'd get to the top of a hill—a steep hill with rocks and trees and general death—and start running down it as fast as you could. If you slowed down a step, you would lose all personal honor and dignity and would be labeled a Perry Como-listening, rice-cake-eatin' pussy.

But then that wonderful knee-scab kind of kid seemed to change a little. He started staying in his room too long. He would shower for an hour at a time, sometimes twice, three times a day.

The disease kind of slouched up on them, my mom said. First, she noticed that he wanted to always sit in one particular chair in the living room and would pitch a fit if anybody else did. Then she noticed he would only use the back sliding glass door, never the front one.

"Why don't you use the front door like every other erect *Homo sapiens*, Lardass?" I asked him one day from Pensacola.

"Bad luck," he said.

Then he started fixing his own meals. "It's no trouble," he'd tell my mom and so they'd be sitting there together, eating two different meals. Then she noticed he didn't want her touching anything he was going to eat, ever. She'd give him a napkin and he'd take another. She'd pour him a glass of ice water and he'd go pour himself a different one.

One night, he showered for two hours, then finally came down to dinner. When Mom just casually brought his plate over to him, he lost it.

"Damnit, Mom!" he screamed. "Now I gotta do a whole new plate!" And he made himself an entirely new dinner, leaving the tainted one by itself on the table.

I was home for a week off when it got really bad. I'd been there a couple days and he was worse than ever, sitting in his chair and examining his hands all the time, freaking out every time someone opened the fridge, worried that they would touch something on "his" shelf, standing eight feet away from me instead of giving me a hug or shaking my hand. Then, that third night, I woke up in the middle of the night, to find him sitting in his kitchen chair at the foot of my bed.

"Ray," he said, holding his pillow to his chest, "why am I like this?"

....

The doctor said he had OCD—obsessive-compulsive disorder—a kind of a spin-off of Tourette's. He said some OCD patients become terrified of germs, that they believe they will die if they get somebody else's germs, and since germs are on every single thing we touch—doorknobs, laundry somebody else just folded, forks somebody just put away—it can be seriously debilitating. Travis wasn't afraid of everybody's germs, just his own family's. But his fears would grow.

The doctor prescribed Prozac and asked to start seeing Travis three times a week.

But Travis wasn't buying it. It all sounded so *weird* and he was still a teenager. It was better to be anything than weird.

"He's lying! Can't you see that? God!" And he wouldn't go. And when my mom would make him go, he'd just sit and not say a word. Then she found all the Prozacs he wasn't taking, spit into his chest of drawers.

All I did was worry about him. I'd call every other night to see and every other night the reports were worse. My father never answered. He was always at some directors' meeting or a golf boondoggle at Winged Foot or some Toastmaster's banquet. It was more comfortable for everybody when he was gone.

My mother would be in tears. "Now he won't eat our food," she'd say. "He won't wash his clothes in our washer. Raymond, he's getting so skinny!"

She'd call my father and ask him to skip a meeting and try to talk to him. This was no help. Travis, like the rest of us, was afraid of him, hated him. Besides, we made an agreement long ago by the light of the moon coming in through our venetian blinds, each of our faces slapped hard that night, that we were never going to listen to him as long as we lived.

And yet, it did nothing to stop William Davenport Hart. Nothing couldn't be fixed by The Coach, The Guide, Life's six-foot instruction manual.

"Look, just get yourself a game plan," he'd say to Trav. "Make yourself a wall chart. Give yourself a sticker or a check or something for every time you force yourself to walk through the front door. Or for every time you feel like you have to wash your hands and force yourself not to. Tell you what, I'll give you a dollar for every check mark. And two dollars for every pill you take. How's that?"

Travis would just hold his hands over his ears and then run up to his room and lock the door.

"You don't have enough 'want to'!" my father would yell up the narrow staircase with its thousands of fingerprints. "You've got to have 'want to' in this life!"

It got so bad, I skipped a tournament I'd already registered for to come home and talk to him. I had to. For some reason, he seemed less panicked by me.

I'll never forget what he looked like that first night back. My kid brother, the wild and brave one, the one who always got tannest, slept the deepest, laughed the easiest, the one who feared nothing, looked like a crackhead. His eyes were ringed in black and his hands were dried and chapped, the skin red and flaking. He was forty pounds lighter than he should've been. His room smelled because he refused to let anybody clean it. It is a sad thing, to want to hug your brother and not be able to. He was on his own private mountain bomb now, and there was no way to stop.

Still, we made a little progress. He agreed to start taking his medicine and go to two sessions a week if I'd stay around for a month. I said I would. I said I'd stay as long as he needed.

Things went a little better after that. The doctors told us progress would be very slow, if at all, and he was right. I got him to let me flick off his light switch at night, a huge thing for him. He had a job bagging groceries at the local A&P and he agreed to ride in my car to work once in a while.

But in other ways, he was getting worse. Now when he'd get off work and look for something to buy to bring home and eat, he couldn't decide. He would stand for thirty minutes at the bottled water section, trying to decide which brand to buy. Eventually he would come home with nothing and eat nothing.

"Why isn't he getting better?" my father said to me on the phone one day. "This is embarrassing the family. It's all over town."

"It's a long, slow deal, Father," I said. "It might take a long time."

"We need to get him to a psychiatric hospital."

"Maybe. They think he may have to go someday, but he's not ready yet. He'd never go now."

"He doesn't know what he needs."

"And you do."

"Don't you smart-mouth me, Raymond."

Silence.

"Somebody needs to take that young man and bring him to his senses," he said. "Your mother and you just coddle him."

"Gotta go," I said, and hung up.

Two nights later, I came home from the range to the worst day in my life: my mother hysterically crying on the porch; a patrol car in the driveway, a policeman talking to my father.

My father had come home to take Travis to the hospital, like it or not. He had convinced my mother it was the only thing to do.

The sooner Travis got serious help, the better, he said. She never could stand up to him. Even after they were divorced, she let him run her life, buy her the car he thought was right for her, bring her dresses. She gave in. "I was just so scared," she confessed to me later. "I just thought in the hospital he couldn't hurt himself."

He marched into the house that night, fortified by some cash bar somewhere, ran right up to his room and grabbed him, just like that.

My mother said Travis let out a scream that even today makes her stomach ache when she thinks about it. Travis kicked madly, but he was no match for my father. My mother was sobbing.

Down the staircase they came, a horror, my father carrying Travis as Travis groped like mad to grab a handrail that he had refused to touch for eighteen months.

Prying open the dreaded front door Travis feared so much, my father burst into the yard with his screaming son. He yelled at my mother to open the back door of his car, which she did, in a sprint. He threw him in, headfirst, and then lay on top of him, pinning his arms down. Then he screamed at my mother to take him to Boston Psychiatric Hospital.

They pulled out of the neighborhood and onto Linden Avenue, the four-lane road that cuts through town. My father had both his forearms down on Travis, who was suddenly, oddly calm.

"Are you going to behave?" my father apparently asked, out of breath.

"Yes," Travis said, wild-eyed. "Yessir."

"There, then," said my father.

Slowly he released the pressure until he saw that Travis was going to sit up straight in the backseat, quietly. My mother stopped crying a little.

"That's a boy," said my father. "You see, son, sometimes the right thing to do in this life is not the easy thing. Sometimes we've got to just suck it up and do the one thing that . . ."

And then my kid brother Travis snapped open the back driver's-side door of my father's white Cadillac Brougham and threw his skinny, exhausted body under the wheels of an oncoming six-wheel Ford pickup.

....

With his snowy-white chef's hat and his Olympic-ski-jump nose sticking out from under it and a huge white apron that must have gone around his flagpole body three times, Two Down was a vision.

"I didn't know Blu Chao ran a cooking school," I said.

He looked up from his order pad and did a second take.

"Stickman!" he whispered as loud as a whisper will get you. "Who let you in?"

"I own this dump," I said. "You're fired. Nice hat."

"Nice overalls," he said. "Do you mind painting the basement while you're at it?"

"Funny. Gimme a cheeseburger. Keep it from looking like plane wreckage."

"Can you believe this?" he said. "We're inside the Mayflower Club!"

"And we're not allowed to play the course at any time," I whispered back.

"I know!" said Two Down. "You gonna quit?"

"Definitely," I said.

"Me neither," said Two Down.

"Does the phone company know one of its employees is a short-order cook on company time?"

"Nah. I've still got a shot at Employee of the Month. Have you seen this course?"

"This dog track?" I said.

"Have you seen how much jing these guys throw around?" he said, practically pulling an eyebrow muscle.

"How would you know what they do?" I said. "You're back here burning the caddie menu."

"I get around," he said.

We talked while he emasculated my lunch.

"How'd you get hired anyway?" I said. "Looks like you could burn ice water."

"Nobody wants this job," he said. "Half the salary is tips and caddies don't tip. I'm their third guy since the Fourth of July."

"Ten zops says you don't make it to Friday."

"Bank," he said, handing me my cheeseburger. It looked previously digested.

I liked my chances.

What with my worthy opponent infiltrating *my club* already, I realized I had to get moving. Besides, Dannie was giving me the complete FB freeze-out, so I had my Friday nights free. The next day, I asked Fletch if I could get another loop after my morning round and he said no and I snuck him some stacking tender and in fifteen minutes I was out again.

I had to meet *somebody* that might want to take pity on a poor young man whose dad, a decorated colonel, died in friendly fire in Desert Storm and who lives with a good-lookin' tramp of a mother who will boff just about any man she meets who buys her a drink. Unfortunately, it wasn't going to be this next guy. He looked like he was just slightly older than carbon.

We were looking for his ball off the 3rd fairway, when I tried anyway. "You make me think of my late father, sir," I said.

"It's not farther," said the old coot. "It's right around here."

"No, no, sir. Not *farther.* Father. You look like him."

"*You* look. That's what you're paid for, isn't it? Punk kid."

Ohhhhhh-kaaaaaay.

One morning, Fletcher hollered out "Spackler" and I jumped up and he said, "You be with Mr. Hart, he's the tall man in the . . ."

Oh, shit.

"I can't," I said, heading for the back door of the Caddie Room.

"Whachu mean cain't?" Fletcher said.

Too late. I lit out the back door and Fletcher never gave me "Mr. Hart" again. Caddie privilege.

As the days wore on, there were only two vaguely interesting parts of the day. One was Professor, who would pore over *The Wall Street Journal* and tally up his imaginary investments. "Damn!" he'd say. "Professor's ol' Advantage Fund is up 26 percent this year. I'm 12 percent up in bonds and damned if my cattle futures didn't go and double in the last six months. I'm richer'n Jesus."

"Why don't you turn pro?" I'd ask.

"What? And give up niggerin'?"

The other was Madeline the Cart Girl, with whom I still hadn't spoken.

Most fine country clubs don't have a cart girl, a cart girl being a fetching lass who comes around with sandwiches and sunblock and shorts tight enough to reveal the year of the nickel in her pocket. It just looks too muni. But since the Mayflower course didn't come back to the clubhouse until 18, it was forced to have a cart girl, and thank God for that, because then there would be no need for Madeline, who was cuter than a tap-in birdie.

She went along the lines of a Meg Ryan but with a little Demi Moore chocolate kind of hair and a little Julia Roberts sort of little afterthought of a nose and these big pink Barbara Hershey lips set on top of a Grace Kelly athletic sort of body and these Jan Stephensen calves that kind of did the merengue when she walked. Other than that, she didn't remind me of anybody special.

At a SwankFest like the Mayflower, caddies are supposed to say even less than cart girls—forget them saying anything to each other—so those first few days I just sort of snuck peeks at her. Meanwhile, the members snapped their orders at her and then undertipped her and then forget to buy me anything.

After about the third day of watching her, it occurred to me that I hadn't even thought carnally of Dannie in days. More miraculously, I hadn't thought of my first wife, Deisha, at all, Deisha being the failure I hung on myself just in case I was somehow under the legal failure limit for one life.

12

I NEVER WENT BACK to the Hogan Tour that season Travis was killed and yet I still finished eighth on the money list.

I wanted to throw myself into golf to try to just lose my mind for a while, but eighth on the Hogan money list means you have checked into Hotel Bupkus.

It means you are a pocketful of change and two S&H green stamps away from being broke, which is where I was, not to mention depressed. I figured I needed $30,000 at least to get through another year on the Hogan Tour, and that's riding with caddies half the time and going three to a room at Red Roof. My uncle's friends were tapped out.

There was nothing in the world I wanted to do less than ask my father for money. I blamed him for Travis's death. Of course I did. Maybe Travis was going south fast, but I could've talked him into going to the hospital on his own. I know I could've. But no, General Patton had to do it the blood-and-guts way, right now, this moment, no waiting. He had the "want to," even if Travis didn't.

He'd said nothing to me since Travis died. Not a word. And I'd said nothing to him. I wanted to, I had an urge to fly at him that day on the porch, let all my emotion out, perhaps pull his spleen out through his ear. But I knew if he and I got violent, my mother might lose it for good.

She was never the same after Travis. I'd call her up sometimes and ask her a question and there'd be these long pauses you could drive a one-act play through. She'd left him, but she blamed herself for letting my father do that to Travis. I guess I blamed her some, too. But I blamed him the most.

Still, an entire year had gone by and all my efforts to get back on the Hogan Tour failed. I wasn't ready to play at the Q School, finishing 123rd, and that meant trying to play little Grapefruit Tours and Space Tours again. Even if I had made the Hogan Tour, I wouldn't have been able to afford it. It takes a whole lot of fourth-place checks to keep you out there with nobody behind you.

There was nothing left to do but swallow a huge clod of pride, put on my best shirt and tie—my only shirt and tie—and call up the president of the bigger and better Kendall Square Bank and ask him to front me the money. I was ready. My game was back and I was ready for Q School.

When I walked in, I thought I was in Republican Campaign Headquarters. I was surrounded by eight-by-tens of Reagan and Bush and Goldwater. Everything in the place was simulated mahogany, up to and including the stapler. The carpet was Augusta green with a golf hole cut in the corner, complete with a little flag with the bank's emblem on it.

My father sat behind a desk that must've done in about three cherry orchards. He was in a plain blue suit with a red-and-gray rep tie. His forehead was annexing more of his head than the last time I'd seen him, but he looked tan and healthy.

"Well, Raymond, what can I do for you?" he said, without looking up.

Since he didn't seem to want to know how I was doing or *what* I was doing in that last year, I skipped the chitchat. I asked him if he hadn't noticed but I'd had a pretty good year on the Hogan Tour until Travis and would he feel like sponsoring me for another year, since Uncle Joe was dead and since I'd come so close the year before and felt like I was right on the edge of a big breakthrough.

And he started by straightening up the perfectly straight items on his desk. Then he answered the way he always answered, with that pompous habit of asking and answering his own questions.

"Raymond, do I want you to become a great golfer?" he said.

"Of course I do. Do I think it would be loads of fun and good times for you? Of course I do. Do I have the financial wherewithal to sponsor you? Yes."

Pause.

"But I'm not going to."

I felt the tingle burning in my ears.

"I'm not going to because I think this is a pointless road you're taking. You and I both know you don't have what it takes to make it on the Tour. You never won there. You never won in college. If we can't win in college and we can't win on the Hogan Tour, we're just kidding ourselves, aren't we?"

I couldn't even reply. As he was talking, his cheaters were going up and down on his nose and all I could think was what a right cross would do to his face . . .

"I saw your scores," he said. "Those scores aren't going to get you anywhere. Honestly, I think with a minimum of practice, *I* could still beat you."

. . . how much blood there would be, what the eyeglasses would shatter . . .

"Oh, sure, you might make the Tour for a year or two," he said, faking a chuckle, "but you don't *really* consider yourself a Tour-quality player, do you?"

. . . how cut my hand would be, whether I would need stitches, how I would make my escape from his office, past the wide-eyed secretary, down the stairs, go back to the apartment, pack my stuff . . .

"You need to give up this nonsense right now and start making something of yourself, and if it's me that has to play the bad guy and tell you, then so be it."

I would like to say I stared at him one last time, issued the perfect put-down like "You're right. Why should I play golf for a living when I can spend the rest of my life in the thrilling world of trust fiduciary planning and triplicate faxing?" and then walked out, but I didn't.

I was so numb that I muttered a few more lame reasons. I think I even said please. And he told me no again and then I left. I think really that was the day I lost respect for myself, looking across about two acres of cherry wood, in the Boston branch of the Republican Party.

I went down to Florida that next year to play the SpaceCoast Tour, which is basically guys putting up their own money and playing for it. I'd tend bar at night and drink half my check until 3 A.M., and then try to play in the morning, and, gee, I wonder why I never played very well down there?

I boiled it down to three things: (1) I missed my uncle. (2) My father was Joseph Goebbels. (3) I had nobody left I really cared about.

It's goddamn hard enough trying to make birdies out there on yellow-bastard, double-dogleg, 454-yard par 4s with damn 3-irons in your hand without having to wonder if anybody besides you gives a hairball about it.

The end came at the Dairy King Classic in Cocoa Beach. I had a two-shot lead with 4 holes to play. But then I had three straight power lip-outs for birdie. I mean three straight balls that went into the hole, took a look around, picked out the furniture, started to put up drapes and then decided "nah" and came back out.

Then, at 18, I just hit one longer and straighter than I-80, but it landed in a fucking anti-divot, from which there was no escape but a punch 5-iron short. Then I chipped on and put a stroke on my 12-foot-putt par that was just as pure as double cream. Only the ball went *over* the top of the hole like the hole was just a painting on the grass. I just couldn't believe it. I even went up to the hole, got on my knees and dropped a ball into it to see if it was real.

I lost to a seventeen-year-old phenom named, preciously, Conner Kimball Worthington, who merely played the last 4 holes in 3 under, jarring an 8-iron on the last hole to win, nothing too spectacular or anything.

I had jalapeños in my eyes. I took my lousy little check for $312 and threw my clubs in the trunk of my sorry-ass little Ford Capri and drove back to Boston. I drove eighteen straight hours, pulled in at about midnight, drove straight to the Salvation Army, took my sticks out of the trunk, removed my uncle's driver and tossed the rest on the Army's front door. Let the soldiers of Jesus try their luck with the fucking game.

Admittedly, I let the end of my golf career suck the life out of me. I could've made something more of myself, but I couldn't stop believing the thing I enjoyed the most had been ripped out my backbone. I got cross-eyed drunk one night and toasted my father's dying of gonorrhea someday and my putter's "liprosy" and Conner Phucking Phenom. Most nights after that I'd just stay at home with a friend of mine, Glen Fiddich, reading books without the benefit of actually seeing the words.

I could always write, so I took a job writing news copy for a little neighborhood weekly, but hating every minute of it. I wrote freelance for the *Globe* and the *Herald,* but got very tired of making garage fires sound like something Edward R. Murrow needed to see. I finally got the job writing for Publisher's Reviews.

Not only were me and the Coach not getting laid enough; I wasn't even trying.

But then one afternoon I met a luscious and dropped for her. Her name was Deisha Lake. She was an upgrade from me in almost every way. She was better-looking, more inventive, more erotic, more ambitious, more social.

In six months, we were married. I probably overclubbed with her, but she loved me and I loved her. She had short, dark

Dorothy Hamill hair with these oversized Bambi eyes and a "you won't believe what I'm wearing under here" grin on all the time.

She was the daughter of a guy who owned a Boston advertising agency and he wanted nothing more than to spend all his money on his only child. She'd spent a year in France and a year in Costa Rica and wasn't scared to try or do anything. She was the best of what money can bring to somebody, which is that it made her interesting and fun without making her a platinum-plated bitch at the same time.

She and her gorgeous little gymnast's body and I went through two mattresses and most of the Victoria's Secret catalogue in two years. I voted her Best All-Around numerous times.

Things went great for a while, but she always was disappointed in my career ambitions. It seemed like it hurt her more than it did me when the stuff I'd write would end up in the fireplace. "That was good, Ray!" she'd say. Maybe I was too much of a perfectionist, like my father. Maybe I was chicken, like my mother. She did not have much patience for chickens. I guess she just got tired of waiting.

One night she told me, "Ray, if you don't start doing something with yourself in a year, I'm leaving you."

"I've got an expiration date?" I said.

"I'm serious, Ray," she said.

I guess she gave me time off for bad behavior because only nine months later—and me still having written nothing—I woke up with a phone call at 2 A.M. and a man's voice asking, "Is Deisha there?"

"She's, uh, she's asleep," I stammered in that groggy, overly polite tone you use when you're shocked out of REM. "Who's this?"

And the voice was silent for a second and then said, "The man she's sleeping with."

Pause.

"Dang," I said, "and here I thought that was me."

When I confronted her a week later with an ugly phone bill and too many $60 lunches at Chez Lapin, she said, "Raymond, I *warned* you," and a few fuck-yous were lobbed back and forth and three dishes and an ironing board broke, but in the end she packed.

All she said as she left was "Jesus! Everybody has disappointments! Deal with it!"

Over the next five years, I never really came close to caring for anybody else like I cared for her. I'd be some sperm of the moment for some luscious, but I never gave much more than that. I never gave my heart. Mostly, I applied for monkdom. One thing about my job, I could read *a lot* of books.

I am not sure what it feels like to be depressed, but I know there were times, when I'd just spent five straight days in my apartment without ever leaving, that I began to yearn for an even smaller place. I often wondered if this is how Travis started.

I could not see any real point in living without Deisha and I can remember staring too long at a bottle of sleeping pills once or thinking just an extra moment too long about what it would feel like to just gently slide my car off into the headlights on the Mass. Turnpike.

Slowly, I learned to numb out those feelings. I learned to numb out a lot of feelings. Screw facing things. Get yourself a friend like Glen and the only thing you ever have to face is the old morning overhang.

And that's why it was such a UPI news flash when I started having Wesson oil kinds of thoughts about a woman who was selling peanut butter and cheese crackers to geriatrics out of an electric golf cart.

I noticed that none of my instructions under my milk box were being picked up by anybody who wanted to come in and perform circus tricks on my face. I also noticed Coach Johnson getting a little annoyed at same. This is maybe part of the reason Madeline began climbing up the hit parade.

Every time I'd see Madeline, I'd wait until Concorde started walking ahead and quickly buy something from her and overtip some ridiculous amount and she'd smile and I'd smile. I could never talk to her because she worked until five or so and I couldn't get a second loop and caddies were not allowed on the course without a player, so it looked like a stymie. Story of my life.

Finally, one day, on the 5th hole, I was forecaddying about 200 yards up the fairway and there was a wait back on the tee and she happened to be just sitting there, having served everybody she could, and so she started driving up to me.

I had rehearsed all my opening-line possibilities. I thought I'd go up to her and say, "Can you tell me which one of these clubs is the mashie?"

But instead, she outed with "What would you most like to do to these pompous bags of pus?"

"I don't know." I mumbled. "What would you?"

Clever.

She smiled a felony smile. "I would wait till one more of these comb-overs put my fifty-cent tip in my pants pocket like usual and said their usual 'Darlin', what I couldn't do to you,' and have Mike Wallace jump out of the beer cooler with a crew. Then they either sign over power of attorney to me or I start suing."

"Me," I said, finally working through the twelve-second delay in my brain, "I'd like to have one of 'em lie down on the tee box with a ball on a tee sticking out of his teeth and then take out a driver and hit it very fat."

"That would be pleasant," she said.

"It's wonderful to love your work, isn't it?" I said.

"I'm Madeline Wagner." She held out her lovely, muscular, tan arm and pink-fingernailed hand. I shook it and felt a little Black Cat go off in my duodenum.

"Carl Spackler," I said.

She laughed. "Yeah, right," she said. "And I'm Noonan."

I was dumbfounded.

"Carl Spackler. Bill Murray's name in *Caddyshack,*" she said.

She looked at me. I smiled. Odd Social Situation No. 478: The woman you have a large Idaho Russet in your shorts for has found out your secret in less than thirty seconds.

"Exactly what are you hiding from, *Carl Spackler?*"

"A one-armed man killed my wife," I said. "I must find him."

She laughed some more.

Awkward pause.

I noticed that she carried the rule book in her cart. Saved.

"I see you're part of the Great Books Club."

"Oh? Oh, that. Yeah, they won't let me have anything else in the cart. No books. No magazines. No radio. But they let me have that in case anybody needs it."

"You actually read it?"

"Read it? I go hours with nothing to do but read it."

"OK, let's see how good you are."

"Right now?" she said.

"With the rules."

"Oh."

I very much liked this girl.

"Let's say some practical joker digs his own little hole and jams the flagstick in it a long way from the real hole," I said. "Group behind them plays toward the flagstick, only to find out the hole is fifty feet away. Do they get to replay their shots?"

She scrunched her nose.

"No."

"Why not?"

"Rub of the green."

"Right."

"My turn," she said. "Ummmm, OK. Match play. Guy goes into a bunker holding his sand wedge and the rake. He sticks the rake up and down into the sand and plays his shot. Is there a penalty for testing the surface in a hazard?"

"Depends," I said.

"On what?"

"Which end did he stick into the sand? The fork end or the handle end?"

"Handle."

"Yes. Loss of hole."

"Wow. Right."

"Don't you love golf rules?" she said.

"No," I said. "My father made me memorize the rule book before he'd teach me the game."

"Relaxed kind of guy."

"The best," I said. "One more. Is a snake a loose impediment which you can move or an outside agency which you can't?"

I thought I had her stumped.

"Depends," she said. "A dead snake is a loose impediment. A live snake is an outside agency."

I whistled.

"Of course," she said, "that doesn't count Mayflower members."

"You really hate these people, don't you?"

"Square it."

"How come?"

"Ohhh, my uncle got blackballed trying to get in here. They

knew he didn't have any money. He was just the personnel director. It was a gift from his company. They knew how much he loved golf and instead of giving him a gold watch or a golden parachute, they offered him that. But these assholes rejected him."

"What'd they say, that he wasn't a descendant of the *Mayflower?*"

"No, no," she said. "They got sued out of that phony baloney deal years ago. They didn't say anything. They just didn't want anybody in the club whose aunt hadn't left them half the Federal Reserve."

"Lovely people."

"The best."

"How did he take it?"

"Not bad. He'd joke about it. He'd tell people he got turned down because they found out he once voted for Truman. Or he'd say that they rejected him during the physical because they found a pulse. But I think inside it hurt him."

"So why work here, then?"

"Well, I had so many hundreds of offers to consider after graduating with a master's that I came here just to clear my head."

My players were approaching now.

"What's your master's in?"

"Paleontology."

"Oh, so this is field research, then," I said, being witty.

She laughed. "You know," she said, "it's too bad employees are not allowed to date caddies."

"Who's a caddie?" I said. "I'm a member. I just prefer carrying my associates' clubs as a social grace."

"Don't say that," she said, driving off. "I'd have to hate your guts."

13

THOUGH TWO DOWN had no access to the members as the caddie chef, he was allowed inside the clubhouse, somewhere I couldn't go. He also had his job as a phone repairman, in which he rarely did any work, but nonetheless had a uniform. Unfortunately for Dannie and me, he put the two jobs together.

After work each afternoon, he would go into the rest room, change out of his chef's outfit, slide on the taco-brown New England Bell outfit, sneak down the hallway and up the stairs. Up there, where they didn't know him from Yitzhak Rabin, he was allowed to wander in and out of offices, always giving some lame excuse like "Checking on some bad fiber-optic lines here, ma'am."

Mostly, he'd go to the office of the general manager's secretary, hoping to rifle through papers and see what he could see. The secretary was a matronly woman of about sixty-five. He'd just fidget around until she left and then go to her desk, being sure to take apart the phone just in case she came back. He had no idea what he was looking for, anything that might be useful—a carte blanche guest card maybe, or a memo with blackmail possibilities, anything.

And then one day, he came upon the yearly membership book, a computerized listing of all the members along with their monthly charges and he hit himself a gusher.

Under the name of Colchester, Bingsley M. (member number C-39), there were no charges. No dues. No cart fees. No milk shakes. None at all. Just a small pencil notation at the bottom by the secretary: "Retain per GM."

Odd. He hunted through a few cabinets until he found the

membership ledger from the year before. He found Colchester, Bingsley M., again. "Retain per GM." He looked up the year before that and the year before that and before long he had looked through the last seventeen years. Zilch. The last time there was any record of Colchester, Bingsley M., paying for anything at all at the Mayflower Club was in August 1977. This Bingsley character had signed for a cheeseburger and then pretty much disappeared off the face of the earth.

Two Down began to guess. This Colchester had apparently been a fairly frequent visitor that year, his first year, 1977, playing in a few member-guests, having dinner, giving to the employee fund, and such. His address then was in tony Louisburg Square. Since then, apparently, nobody had heard from this guy. He hadn't paid a dime. Yet he was being kept on the books. Why? Why hadn't the club just dismissed him?

That night, Two drove the telephone truck to a gorgeous brownstone with a gold-and-black wrought-iron fence running in front of it. A black maid came to the fifteen-foot brass-trimmed door.

"Yes, ma'am," Two Down said. "We're just checking an old line that belonged to a Bingsley Colchester."

"Oh, well, this is the Smythe residence now," said the maid.

"No Colchesters?"

"Not in the three years I been here."

Two Down even went so far as to ask a friend of his at the *Globe* to check the clip files on this Colchester guy and the friend came back with almost nothing. He found only two clips. One from 1966, when Bingsley Colchester was mentioned as being part of the "mentionable attendees" at the annual Boston Yacht Club Cotillion. And another one from 1977 that read:

> "It's clear that something needs to be done for this part of Massachusetts Avenue," said Bingsley Colchester of the Ju-

nior League. "I don't believe poverty is the kind of image Boston wants to put out there."

And that was it. No other records.

Two Down's eyebrows were starting to do the Watusi, but he did one last thing. He posted a note on the bulletin board in the men's locker room. On the outside, the note read: "URGENT message for Bingsley Colchester." He had folded the note and inside he wrote: "Mr. Colchester. Please call L. Petrovitz, attorney-at-law, 555-1525, regarding a recently uncovered inheritance."

When nobody called Two Down's answering machine after five days, Two Down decided to do an incedible thing. He decided to become Colchester, Bingsley M., long-lost Mayflower member.

He had just passed the fastest, cheapest and easiest application process in club history.

He figured three things: (1) if Bingsley old boy was in Cotillion in 1966, that made him about eleven then, which made him about thirty-nine now, which Two Down thought he could fake, being a hard thirty; (2) the odds against any guy who is gone seventeen years suddenly coming back by October 1 had to be worse than Thud (the Almost Human) getting anorexia; and (3) there couldn't be many people at the club who even *knew* the whereabouts of Bingsley M. Colchester if not one of them would take an URGENT message off a bulletin board.

He decided he would need a few things. One, a story. He would say he had been in Burma and the Far East the last seventeen years, working in the gem trade. These were paper-money people. Not many of them could know much about gems. Or Burma, for that matter. These were not the kinds of people who went to Burma. These were the kinds of people that, when they were tired of playing golf and tennis at the club and lying on the beach in Hyannisport, went to the Caribbean, where they played golf and tennis and lay around the beach in St. Kitts.

He also figured nobody spoke Burmese, so he could fake that, and since he dealt in gems, and quite possibly the smuggling of gems, he could be a little secretive, too. That would actually be fun, thought Two Down, putting a little James Bond in the act.

Diamond-dripping Mayflower ingenue: So, Mr. Colchester, what exactly do you look for in a sapphire?

Two Down: The exact color of your eyes, mon chérie.

But if you are a gem king just back from Hong Kong, you can't readily drive up to the swankest club in Boston in a 1979 Pinto with a smashed rear window. Ivan knew that car too well. He'd rat. He needed a new ride and new clothes if he was going to pull this off without getting arrested.

And this is when Two Down came up with a second very good idea.

Every year, the Shriners of Boston put on a colossal golf tournament at the Charles River Golf Club. It is a monstrous event in which teams of four play a scramble and there are giveaways on every hole. And every year, on the par 3 16th hole—164 yards over a lake—they give away a car to anybody that makes a hole in one. This year, that car was a brand-new Lexus.

Now, giving away a car for a year for a hole in one is just a marketing idea to get foursomes to enter the tournament and cough up the $250 entry fee. The Shriners pay Lloyd's of London about $800 for hole-in-one insurance and if somebody wins the car, Lloyd's takes the bite. Plus, the tournament gets an advertising fee from the car dealer. Of course, most Shriners are serious chops and nobody had ever won even an ashtray with a hole in one on that hole in all the Shriner tournaments I'd ever heard about.

Until this particular year.

Two Down had a plan, but he needed four other Chops to help him. By offering to pay the entry fee, he enlisted Thud (the Almost Human), Cementhead, Hoover (who was now starting to enjoy the bet a little) and Meltdown. Meltdown was a part-time Chop, maybe nineteen, tops, with pierced eyebrows, nose and tongue and spiked green hair. He'd show up in grunge shirts, a leather jacket and green Converse and he'd still shoot 75. He'd learned the game before he went rebel and he still loved it, though he had to do it on the lam because if his friends saw him playing golf, they'd kick him out of the Mao Youth Club.

Crowbar came along, too, mostly because he did anything Two Down did, and besides, how many chances in his life did he have to ride along in a golf cart?

Two put everybody but Thud in his foursome and told the registration office that Thud would have to play in the group directly in front of him. "He's a diabetic," Two Down told the lady. "And I have to give him a shot every hour. It's vital that he play in the group *directly* in front of us." The lady nervously wrote down everything he said.

When they arrived at the Charles River Golf Club the next Monday morning, the batting order was just as Two Down hoped. He, Meltdown, Hoover and Cementhead were in the group behind Thud, who would play with three guys he'd never met in his life. It was a shotgun, and they were to begin on the 4th hole. Everybody had their instructions.

Two Down had played in enough charity scrambles to know how they work. There is an 8 A.M. shotgun and a 1 P.M. shotgun, with two foursomes planted on every hole, which means 144 players in the morning and another 144 in the afternoon. On the Lexus hole, there would be somebody's wife, whose job it was to verify a hole in one on the million-to-one chance that it would happen.

It sounds fun at first, watching hacks try to make a hole in one, but it gets numbing very fast and so, after about two hours of this, Miss Verification is usually sitting back in her lawn chair, reading Danielle Steel and turning her tan every twenty minutes.

So by the time Thud's group came to the 16th tee at about 4:30 in the afternoon, the woman was lying on her lawn chair off the right side of the green, wearing sunglasses and needlepointing. Thud's group hit their shots, all of them oblivious to what was about to take place except for the bulbous Thud himself, who was as nervous as if he were among cannibals, sweating through his golf shirt on a 65 degree day. None of them came close to a hole in one—in fact only one of them even hit the green.

Since it was a scramble, all four players putted from where that one ball wound up, Thud making sure to putt last. After he putted out, a chubby sort of man in his group put the flag back in and the group began to walk off the green. Only that's when Thud suddenly stopped and announced to the group, actually enunciating for once in his life: "I'm gonna try it again." The other three stopped at the fringe to watch him. Nervously, he took his ball and plopped it down on the green and putted.

As the ball rolled, he secretly reached in his pocket and took out another ball—a different ball, a Titlist 1 that bore the imprint "Leonard Petrovitz." He took this ball and hid it in his right hand, next to the putter grip. The putt stopped rolling two inches from the cup and Thud brushed it into the hole with his putter, his right hand still holding Two Down's ball. Now Thud reached into the hole with his right hand and *switched* balls. He took *out* his ball and put *in* Two Down's, all of this unseen by anybody because his hand was covered by the hole.

Thud walked off the green, muttering, "Tht fkng ptt," or somesuch thing, in a shaky voice, enormously nervous and relieved. The verifier, who looked to be about twenty-five with curly brown hair and a pair of purple jogging shorts and matching T-shirt on, never even stopped stitching.

As Two Down's group prepared to hit their shots, the woman looked up and watched, though it was not easy, as the sun was somewhat behind the players, off their right shoulders. Meltdown went first. His 7-iron came up short in the front bunker. Cementhead, to whom Two Down had entrusted absolutely no responsibilities, hit second and his 8-iron landed nicely about 20 feet left.

The needlepoint lady went back to her stitching.

Hoover went third. His 7-iron landed on the right fringe.

Now Two Down stepped up. He had two clubs in his hand, his driver and his 7-iron.

The needlepointer kept stitching.

Two Down gave the 7-iron to Meltdown, then teed the ball higher than he usually does, ready to hit his driver on a 164-yard par 3. He aimed for the woods far left of the green. Taking a deep breath, he coiled and swung. He smashed one deep into the woods, easily 75 yards over the green and far, far left of it. The woman never looked up.

Quickly, Meltdown took the driver from Two Down and gave him back his 7-iron. Then Two Down whispered, "1 . . . 2 . . . 3 . . ."

"YEEEEEEEEEEESSSSSSSSSS!!!!!!!" he and Meltdown screamed.

"IT'S IN THE HOLE!!!!!!!" Hoover shrieked at the same time.

"IT'S A HOLE IN ONE!!!!!!" Cementhead roared.

The woman made such a lurch out of her chair she nearly stabbed herself with her needles.

"What?!?" she shrieked. "Who?!?"

The group on the tee was leaping and hugging and dancing as though Paris had just been freed.

"AYYYYYYYYYYYEEEAH!!!!!" Two Down was screaming.

"UNBELIEVABLLLLLLLE!!" Crowbar roared.

"Did you see that hole in one?!?" Cementhead bellowed.

The woman was still flabbergasted. "Who golfed a hole in one?" she hollered.

"He did!" yelled Cementhead, pointing to Two Down, who had pretended to be so overwhelmed by the incident that he was now lying flat on the tee, wiggling and kicking his extremities like his brain stem had been hot-wired to a power line.

"He did?" stammered the woman excitedly, not sure what to do next. "Well, wow! Really? Dahn! I didn't see it!"

"Check in the hole!" yelled Hoover.

As the woman made her way to the hole, the fivesome clambered into their carts, continuing to whoop and holler, overdoing it, and started for the green.

All eyes were on the woman as she walked to the hole and looked in.

"Here it is!!!" she screamed. "You made a hole in one! You just won a cahh!!!"

Two Down leaped out of the cart while it was still moving, ran to the woman and hugged and danced with her ravenously. Then he ran over to the car and got in it.

"I just won a new Lexus!" he hollered, and began honking the horn. "Can you believe this?"

"Worked just like you said it would!" bubbled Cementhead.

Hoover and Meltdown and Two suddenly stopped for a fraction of a second and looked at him. The woman looked at him, too.

"Of course it works, you idiot!" yelled Two Down. "It's a Lexus!"

And with that, the woman laughed and everybody laughed, except, of course, Cementhead, who suddenly felt the very sharp pain in the butt that comes when somebody like Crowbar jabs you with a ball-mark repair tool.

"When I want your opinion I'll beat it out of you," whispered Crowbar.

"*Terms of Endearment?*" whispered Cementhead.

"The Shootist," whispered Crowbar.

"Damn," whispered Cementhead, rubbing his gluteus.

I didn't know it, but I suppose I was losing The Bet very quickly. I also didn't care.

This is mostly because Madeline and I managed to find time to sneak away from the Gestapo and speak more and more. Some people have a romantic Italian restaurant at which to meet. We had the 5th hole.

I learned a few things about her. She was twenty-eight, from Grove Hall, was divorced once, never drank, was far too cynical, was smarter than me, actually loved being outside every day but truly hated most of the members.

When you are falling in deep lust, there is this feeling you get in your heart, which beats too fast, and your ratchet, which is very close to learning to unzip your Levi's from the inside. It was something I hadn't felt in years. Something was lighting up inside me, like a match you strike twenty times and, just when you're about to give up, ignites. *You're a real boy, Pinocchio.*

I had forgotten Two Down's lunches and spent most of my money buying $7 sandwiches and $3 Mountain Dews out of Madeline's cart. We seemed to stand a little closer every time we were together, careful not to be seen but too far gone with our little unspoken game to really care.

Oh yes, the more we saw each other, the closer we stood, until one day she put my change in *my* front pocket and said, "Darlin', what I couldn't do to you."

"Speak into the beer cooler," I said.

She laughed, but if she'd done it again ten seconds later, there wouldn't have been any room.

The next morning, God or Destiny or somebody brought in a thick Boston fog. It rolled in, blanketing the course. Fletcher told us play would be delayed at least an hour, maybe two. And right away me and the Coach thought of Madeline. I came outside the Caddie Room and wandered around the corner, unable to see ten feet in front of me. I walked up by the pro shop and down by the kitchen and never saw her.

Then, suddenly, coming out of the mist, like Ingrid Bergman in *Casablanca,* was Madeline, on her golden electric chariot with the mustard and mayonnaise packs up front, wearing a Mayflower cap with her hair pulled back to show off her perfect pink lips and those Walt Disney eyes. At first, she looked as stunned to see me as I was to see her. Then she looked intrigued. Then she looked like she wanted to commit a misdemeanor.

I didn't say a word. We were in as public and dangerous a place as we could be—twenty feet from the main window of the formal dining room—and yet we were all alone.

She knew it and I knew it. She tilted her head up at me just a little with those pink lips thick as strawberry shakes and I held her face in my hands and kissed her like you read about.

Then she pulled away and took a deep breath. "I *told* you. We're not allowed to date caddies," she said.

She started to drive away. Then she stopped and turned back.

"But nobody says we can't fuck 'em."

The ride we took in that cart was maybe like the ride St. Peter gives you once you're past the Pearly Gates.

Blanketed in thick, rich clouds, I had no idea where we were and no idea where we were going, but knowing that when we got there it was going to be wonderful. She knew every inch of that cart path and so, even though there seemed to be no path ahead of us, she always made the right turn.

And then, there we were. She picked the 5th green, not far from our first meeting, a lusciously thick green with big willows all around and a creek running in front of it. Nobody ever *really* gets laid on a golf course. Getting laid on a golf course is one of the great myths in America. It is in the empty Smithsonian display case along with "*Penthouse* Letters That Really Did Happen." But, may I get the incurable yips if I lie here. Basically, we got all over each other like Right Guard.

I will only say that seeing a gorgeous woman strip in front of you on an immaculate green while you put up a very nice flagstick of your own and then consummating your lust for the first time by rolling madly around in a rich, warm blanket of fog until you both end up sweat-pooled in the luxurious white sand of a bunker is a good bit better than a kick in the throat with a frozen shoe.

Big rake job, though.

That night, that whole next week, felt like a Wilt home movie festival. Madeline ran one of the great penile enlargement services around. We had sex on the cart late at night. She committed wondrous lockjaw on my pipe while we hid in the range tractor, golf balls from 200 yards away raining down on us. I committed acts illegal in seven states upon her in the trees just off the 12th.

I heard her whole story. Straight-A student. Fell in love with a med student. Married him. Helped him through med school. Hated all the gowns and the hors d'oeuvres and the hospital parties and the functions that she needed to go to with him on his way to someday being Chief of Thoracic Surgery at Boston General.

Fell out of love. Divorced. Alcoholic mother. Dad finally got smart and divorced her. She was sticking it out in Dorchester, waiting for the job offers to come flooding in, waiting for the straight A's and all the good med school karma and all the politeness to rich, polyester jerks to pay off in the round world of space.

We'd screw, talk, screw, talk, not screw, talk, whatever. We'd hardly leave the bed except to answer the door for Thai delivery.

I don't know why I didn't quite tell her my whole story. I mean, I told her most of it, I just left a few parts out. I told her how much

I hated my father, I just didn't mention that he was a member of the Mayflower Club. I told her all about Travis, just not that I sometimes felt weird things going on inside, too. I mentioned Deisha, I just forgot to mention that it took me until two weeks ago to throw away her old sleep T-shirt. And I didn't mention Dannie at all.

I mentioned all my buddies at Ponky, I just forgot to mention about the bet. I didn't want her to think I was sneaky, I guess. Maybe I was trying not to make any mistakes and have another Deisha not on my hands. I never thought it would matter.

Other than that, things just couldn't have been better. So, naturally, I screwed it up.

MY CADDIE CAREER ended the day I got this pure, unadulterated hack for my loop, a balding little guy who was so bad he made Hoover look like Nick Price.

Fletcher rolled his eyes when he gave me the bag, because it was the approximate size of Delaware and, as all club caddies know, the bigger the bag, the worse the player. This thing would've floated a boatload of Cubans.

Now, at the Mayflower, the 11th tee box was way up a hill, which allowed us to forecaddie, which meant that the caddie could give his man the proper club and then go and stand about 200 yards down the fairway and wait for the Man to hit, thus saving the poor, underpaid caddie the long walk up and back down the hill with the bag on his back. Well, my yo-yo got up and jerked one over the trees, over the maintenance shack, over the wall and over the hedge, clean into Ponky, totally O'Brien, which is golfgeek for out of bounds.

"Carl!" my guy hollers. "I need the bag!"

It was obvious what had happened. The cheesebrain didn't think to put another ball in his pocket in case this happened. And now he wanted *me* to lug his condominium bag 200 yards back up that hill so he could get a ball out and then lug it all the way back down. Wrong.

I took his 3-iron, got a ball out of his pouch, tossed it down, squared up and hit one to him. As Dannie might've said, "I hit a purity," because the thing took off with that pro trajectory, starting low and then climbing straight up, landing soft as left-out butter about twenty feet in front of the guy. It hopped twice, skidded a little and rolled, calmly and sweetly as you please until it stopped dead right between his spikes.

He looked down at the ball, looked out at me, looked at the others and laughed an embarrassed laugh.

The one thing I didn't know was Fletcher happened to be over in the maintenance shack, watching the whole thing. He walked over to me.

"Good goddamn thing you doesn't play the game," he said. "You and your Gene Littler ass perfect swing just fucked up. Only way yo ass is gettin' back inside these walls is wid a parrychute."

Seeing as how I was out of ideas, I very much believed him.

The failure of Dr. Alfred A. Dingsby to get Dannie on the Mayflower course hit her like dysentery and it was almost a week before she was on her feet again.

But it wasn't until her Tuesday mornings were ruined that Dannie got serious. After the misadventure of the Midnight Mulligan Marauders, the Mayflower erected a green fence, three inches thick and solid, in front of the hole in the hedge. Naturally, the rest of the Chops saw this as tragic in that they could no longer sit by the hole and dream.

But to Dannie, it meant they had pulled the plug on BrowningVision. She realized she might never see her prince again and her desperation went off the charts, all the way to inspiration.

Remarkably, that inspiration came from a very odd source—Blu Chao. She was trying to practice her English with one of Dannie's unwanted and unsubscribed-for *Ladies Links* magazines, which offers hard-hitting features like "How to Make the Perfect Centerpiece for Your Next Nine-Hole Event" and "Golf and Cooking: When to Use the Spoon."

Dannie was moping around the Pit one day—when she saw the back of what Blu was trying to read. It said,

Show us that your club has one of the 10 best-dressed men in golf and we'll feature you on the cover of our January issue!

Dannie snatched it from Blue and said, "Sorry, but I gotta borrow this," and sprinted out the door.

Dannie camped outside the gates of the Mayflower for three days, each day looking absolutely nothing like she did at Ponky. She actually let her hair out from under her Titlist hat, wore some makeup, got out of her usual baggy golf shirt and into a swirly miniskirt thing, actually let her wondrous cleavage have a look around, not to mention the pegs that won her ten straight Indian leg-wrestling championships at Ponky. Most Chops could've happily been stuck in a phone booth with her and not recognized her.

On the third day, she finally caught Browning cruising out of the gates in a red BMW convertible, his blond locks blowing back in the breeze, wearing a light $300 cashmere Polo sweater, a Bill Blass blazer with crest, a pair of screw-you Ray-Bans and the perfect pair of pleated pants. Dannie was so absorbed in the vision of him that she nearly forgot to follow him at all.

Browning Sumner lived in a sprawling four-story mansion that overlooked the Mayflower course, one of the rare old homes inside the course grounds itself. It was all stone with wrought-iron everything and about fourteen chimneys.

Dannie got her courage up, rang the doorbell, cleared her throat and waited for her opening.

But when Browning answered the door, Dannie went deaf-mute.

She had been in love with him before, but this was different. This was a spell. Dannie thought his face was evolutionary checkmate. "Evolution just hit the wall with him," she said later. "It ain't going no further than that." She had almost forgotten about his perfect nose, his *GQ* chin and those blue eyes you could easily go snorkeling in. Apparently, it would've buckled the knees of the entire graduating class at Swarthmore.

"Yes?" he said.

Silence.

"Uh, yes?" he said again, louder.

"Yes. Yes, I'm Dannie, Danielle Higgins." Her voice was cracking. She was perhaps the worst liar on the eastern seaboard and she knew it. "I'm a photographer and writer with *Ladies Links* magazine and I was told at the Mayflower Club that you . . ."

"Oh, magazines?" he said. "No, thanks." And he closed the door quietly.

End of bet. End of love. End of life.

Dannie knocked louder.

He peeked his head out of the etched Steuben door window.

"Yes?" he said, only fractionally less polite.

"I don't want you to *buy* our magazine," she said. "I want you to be *in* our magazine." And she held up the page with the contest in it.

Browning's eyes brightened, if that's possible.

"I get that magazine!" he said, delighted. "You know, the golf tips for women are often better than the ones they give for men. The swings aren't so huge, more in control, you know?"

"Oh, oh, well, hell yes, we know!" said Dannie. This was actually working out well.

Dannie proceeded to explain the whole thing, how she'd been told that he was among the best-dressed men in the entire Mayflower Club and, possibly, the nation, and how magazines run these contests, but of course, to make them succeed, they have to scout out real talent themselves or they'd end up with four men who dressed the way most golfers dress, which requires a plaid vaccine to cure.

"Very nice," said Browning Sumner. "Come in."

Inside that old stone home was the most gorgeous, postmodern, spare decor any *Metropolitan Home* magazine could have found. It was done entirely in black and white, with unsittable but beautiful chairs next to unusable tiny cone-shaped tables, which were situated next to spartan steel lamps that shot their light at the ceiling, which did nothing for your ability to read, but made a very dramatic impression.

"Cozy," said Dannie.

"Yes," said Browning.

Over the next four hours, Browning and Dannie got to know each other and discovered how much they had in common. Dannie's wealthy Atlanta heritage, the boarding school in Maine, the debutante party at the Rainbow Room. The deeper she got, the worse she felt, until she was almost bursting with guilt, squirming in her chair. To do this to this lovely man who had helped her, to lie to him for money, was almost more than she could bear.

At last, Browning asked about the magazine contest.

"The contest?" said Dannie.

"The contest," said Browning.

"Oh, oh," she said. She could feel her bottom lip start to quiver the way she does when she cries, which is almost never. "You see, to get out to that ol' course out there and shoot some snaps, why . . ."

She began to wave her hand in front of her face to try to dry the tears.

"Are you crying?" said Browning, leaning forward, stunned.

"No, don't be crazy, just allergies . . ."

And right about then she burst like a dam.

"What? What?" Browning said, taking her against his chest, but not so close that she might dampen and thus shrink the Polo. And Dannie heaved, "Oh, none of this is the truth! I'm so crooked I could stand in the shadder of a corkscrew. I just made all this up to meet you!"

Browning pulled back a little. She pulled a little further away, too, to show him her face.

"Don't you 'member me?" she said. "I was in a gold Plymouth Duster and it stalled out right in front of the Mayflower and you were just nicer'n you could be and you helped me get it to the side and I just felt stupid as a box a rocks because it was only a stuck butterfly valve but you just showed so much kindness that day that I just haven't been able to forget you and then one day Hoover, that's this little guy over at Ponky, which is the club right next to yours, though it's really nothing, made this hole in the hedge with his ball retriever, which I personally have regripped three times now for him, and we could see into the Mayflower through the hole and there you were and when the bet came up to see who could play 18 holes here first I just thought well, maybe if I stood to lose a lot of money it would force me to act on the one thing I wanted to do in life, which was to come and meet you and so that's all it is."

And Dannie Higgins hoped against hope that a nova might melt her this very minute and save her any further embarrassment.

And Browning Sumner said, amazed, "*I* pushed a car?"

Well, after another two or three hours of talking, Browning could not remember pushing her car out of the road, but did admit he liked Dannie too much to be mad and, why not, he'd help her win the bet and they'd celebrate together. He arranged for the first tee time he could get, which was two days forward, on Thursday morning.

"Might be fun," he said.

Dannie was beside herself.

"You're just sweeter'n Sugar Babies," she said, and she offered her lips for him to do with what he liked.

He kissed her on the cheek. "I respect you too much to rush things," he said, gallantly.

Dannie swore she heard a harp.

With me out of the club and only four days left until The Bet was over, I got itchy. I hated not seeing Madeline during the days. I missed rummaging around the course, boinking in interesting places, having her sidle up to me and say, "Pssst, caddie. Want to get it up and down?"

I had no car, no caddie job, no money and I couldn't concentrate on these idiotic reviews.

The inside story of the Royal Family as only the sister-in-law of the cousin of the Royal Hairstylist can tell it!

"I know," Madeline told me, "But we're still together."

But that night, waiting outside the club for Madeline to drive out and pick me up, I saw something that changed my mind—my father.

He didn't see me. He was very enraptured with the way he was pulling out of the Mayflower in his biggest, goldest Cadillac with whitest leather yet. It had personalized license plates: BLUTEES.

For some reason, it fried me, my father inside those gates where I wanted to be, where I deserved to be, where Madeline was, and me outside, waiting like a gardener for his ride.

That whole night I thought about him. I thought about how he had tried to explain Travis. How he had said it was an emergency situation, that Travis would've never gone to the psychiatric hospital on his own. That the doctors were considering forcibly taking him themselves. That if he hadn't tried to do something, he would've surely tried to kill himself. The doctors all said he would try soon enough, he'd said. He actually called it a "blessing, when you really examine the situation."

I held my tongue, but just barely.

Travis changed us all. My mother just sank into a kind of little ball. She stopped going to movies with her friends and stopped working at the hospice. She hardly spoke to my father when he called. She hardly spoke to anybody. Eventually, she fell in love with her therapist and they moved almost as far away as they could from that day, that car, that moment, to nearly the furthest point away from Boston, and started over.

I never spoke to my father after that day, but people told me that he was a little humbled. He no longer tried to coach them on where to park or the proper way to tie a Windsor or assault them with all the little sayings he had on life that were taped to every edge of his bathroom mirror.

And it occurred to me that he and I were the only two that were alone now. Travis was wherever muddy little boys go, someplace with no soap, I hoped. My mother was happy and gone. It was only he and I now, skeletons of that old life. He'd gotten what I guess he deserved. Loneliness. If a man lectures in his home alone, does he make a sound? Me, I'd gotten loneliness, too. Is that what I deserved?

Madeline was asleep when it hit me. How bad could it hurt? How much self-respect could I lose if I just asked him? I didn't have to be cordial. I didn't have to forgive him. I only had to *use* him. Come to think of it, wouldn't that be the ultimate revenge?

The next day, I swallowed two blimpfuls of pride. I took a Mayflower Club directory Madeline had and looked up the First Boston Bank.

I was off. When I walked into his office, the size of a small par 5, I got hit by the Republican Hall of Fame again, only this time everything in the office was two notches past cherry up to mahogany, up to and including the painting frame that opened up into a bar and sink in the back. The entire office had the smell of one Newport and Aqua Velva and suddenly I was thirteen years old again.

I felt vaguely like yakking right then on his lush green carpeting, but I kept it down. Suddenly, this all seemed like a very bad idea. The very thought of coming back to this man after six years. *Me* coming back to him.

I was about to bolt, when the secretary greeted me with the big hello. I had her announce Raymond Hart to my father. She laughed like I was making a joke.

He took a minute to let me in. Maybe he was gathering himself after not seeing me for six years. I know I was shivering with nerves.

And yet when I walked in, it was like I'd been to camp for two weeks, nothing more.

"You're looking healthy, Raymond," he said. That was a puzzler, since he never looked up from his paperwork. The bald spot speaks. "Did you get an outdoor job?"

Lovely. His way of saying, "How much does mowing lawns pay anyway?"

"I've got to get the cabana boy to give me a higher SPF," I said, trying to be clever.

He motioned to sit down in a plush chair in front of his desk. "Now," he said, finally looking up, his eyes older and sadder than I ever remembered. "What can I do for you?"

So that is the way it was going to be. No "How's your life?" No "Heard from your mother?" No "Are you married now? Do I have any grandkids?" Just "Now, what can I do for you?" as though I were applying for a second mortgage.

I took a deep breath.

"Well, Father," I said. This was definitely going to hurt. "I passed you on the street the other day. You were coming out of the Mayflower Club. And I just wondered if I might invite myself to play a round of golf with you there someday. I'd pay my own way, of course."

I cursed the moment I ever agreed to this satanic bet, a thing that would make me do something like this.

He gave a dramatic pause. Five seconds. Ten seconds. Thirty seconds.

"Well," he said. "I'm pretty busy."

Great. Wonderful. That was my out. I got up to leave. "Well, don't worry about it, then," I said. I really meant it, too. This was fine with me. I really wanted to sprint out of that office as fast as I could; spring down the stairs and out onto the street and go home and burn the clothes that had been soiled by his office furniture and bathe in lighter fluid the tongue that had uttered the terrible words.

"But—it has been a long time since we've played golf together," he said. "As I recall, we didn't get along too well."

"I think I was a bit too controlling," I said.

"Always the smart talk," he said. "You just want to pop back into my life after all these years, eh, Raymond? And I'm not supposed to ask any questions?"

"Well, it's just golf, Father. If you'd rather not."

I got up again.

"But I don't suppose it can hurt anything. . . ." He flipped on the intercom. "Lois?"

His hunched secretary came in with the scheduling book. "When could my son and I play golf together at the Mayflower?"

"Your son," she said, confused.

"Yes. My son. When?"

"Your son?" she asked again, blankly.

"Yes, yes, Lois. This is my son, Raymond."

She was trying to put her jaw back near her mouth. She looked at this son she'd never heard of and then she looked at the scheduling book and she tried to get a breath, all at the same time.

"Well," she stammered. "You are completely booked tomorrow. You could play Thursday," she said.

"Good. Block it out, then, will you? Something in the morning?"

"Yes, Mr. Hart," and she left.

"That all right with you, Raymond?" he said, without looking up again. The bastard.

"That would be fine," I said. "Call a couple of your friends?"

"I'll get a tee time for eight-thirty," he said.

"Well," I interjected, "actually, could we make it earlier than that? I, uh, I've got a lot of appointments for that day."

"Really?" he said. "What is your job, by the way?"

"I'm a writer," I said. "I write fiction."

Lois looked uncomfortable enough to faint.

"Oh," he said, as though I'd just stuck my thumb in his soup. "And you have appointments for this kind of *job?*"

"Yeah," I said, quite stuck. "I've got to see a couple guys about a metaphor."

But he had lost interest by then and was back at his paperwork.

"Well, anyway, I'll try and get one for seven-thirty."

"I'll see you then," I said, almost leaping out of my chair to get out of his smell, sight, presence. Thursday was in three days. With any luck, I had just sold my integrity, self-respect and soul for $2,000.

Once he had the Lexus, Two Down bought a couple nice outfits, some new shoes. Then he changed the tags on his bag yet again. He ripped off "Scott Sullivan" and inserted "Bingsley M. Colchester." Then he called the club's kitchen and told them to take their job and shove it. Then he drove immediately to the front gate in his new Lexus, where he waved at Ivan, who let him in like he'd been going there his whole life.

"How you like me now, Fang?" he said under his breath as he drove by.

He jumped out and practically ran to the pro shop.

"Hi," he said in a blind rush, offering his hand to the young man behind the counter. "Bingsley Colchester, member C-39. Been gone a long while, gems, Burma, you know, but I'm back now and I think I'll play tomorrow, first thing, what say about 7 A.M.?"

The young man was trying to hold the paperwork on the counter down, so that Typhoon Bingsley wouldn't blow it off.

"I'm sorry, Mr. Colchester. Tomorrow is Employee Day. The members voted last week to let all the employees of the club play the course once a year. Tomorrow is it."

"All the employees?" said Two Down, not believing his ears.

"Yessir," the kid said. "Isn't that great? This'll be my first time."

"Even the kitchen employees?"

"Yessir," the boy said.

There was a cold pain in his heart. "Even the caddies?"

"No. Nosir. They're not considered employees."

This gave him some relief. "Well, how about Thursday?"

"Yessir, what time would you like?"

"The first time you have, I think," said Two Down.

"Yessir. Thursday at seven twenty-two. You're down, Mr. Colchester."

"Very nice. Line me up with a game, will you? It's been a while."

"Certainly, sir."

"Thank you."

He had a temptation to walk around the clubhouse, put his feet up on the coffee table, maybe have a vodka in the men's grill, read *Barron's* naked in the steam room, pick his toes on the cushiony towels, but he thought he better not push his luck. He would stay away until Thursday. Thursday would be a very good day.

The next night, Wednesday night, all of us ended up at Ponky again, just like old times, only with daggers behind our backs, deceit in our hearts and jing on our minds. All three of us sure we had the cash won.

Hoover was in the corner, trying to rub Ben-Gay on his back.

"What happened?" I asked, sitting down.

"Pulled his lumbar," said Chunkin' Charlie, who was no longer well enough to do much more than hang out in the lunchroom.

"How?"

"Well, he just got the new *Golf Digest* and it said, 'Release the awesome power of your left side.' Only, I guess, just as he was going out to try it, somebody reminded him that only last May they ran that cover that said, 'Harvest the hidden power of your right side!' So he went and got that one and he came back and I guess he got out there on the range and tried them both and now he might have to go to his HMO."

"Oh."

Charlie was in a good mood and I knew why. The bet expired at sunset the next day.

"Looks like that stupid bet is gonna come a cropper," he said. "And it was such a *good* idea."

"Yeah, looks like nobody's gonna win it," I said.

"Yep," said Dannie.

"Yep," said Two Down.

Pause.

"Of course, if somebody could pull it off now, it would go down in the all-time annals, don't you think?" Two Down said.

"Hell yes," said Dannie.

"Hell, hell yes," I said.

"I mean, if a guy could pull it off with one day left, it ought to pay more, don't you think?" said Two Down.

"God yes," said Dannie.

"Jesus God yes," I said.

"Press?" said Two Down.

"Bank," said Dannie.

"Fuckin'-A bank," I said.

All three of us looked at each other suspiciously. Now there was six grand on the table. Chunkin' Charlie coughed twice and left.

15

"SELLOUT," IS BASICALLY what she called me. "Low-character, no-character, spineless, sellout mollusk worm no-life."

Basically she invoked a country song on my ass: *From the Gutter to You Is Not Up.*

Apparently, she had picked up the phone in my apartment that morning while I was in the shower and heard . . .

"Good morning. Is Raymond in?"

"I'm sorry, but he's in the shower," she said. "Can I take a message?"

"Yes, thank you. This is his father. Tell him we're all set for Thursday morning at seven-thirty sharp."

"This is his father?"

"Yes."

"And you're all set?"

"Yes."

"For . . ."

". . . golf at the Mayflower Club. He'll be my guest. I just wanted to tell him that they don't allow cutoffs and only collared shirts. And perhaps he should wear a belt, too."

"He's playing with you at the Mayflower tomorrow morning at seven-thirty?"

"Yes. Will you let him know?"

"Oh, I'll let him know."

"Thank you. Goodbye."

"Goodbye."

It was difficult to tell, when she threw open the shower door, her face set in deep, dark granite, which torqued her off the most. The fact that in all our long sessions of pillow talk I hadn't told her my father was a member at the Mayflower or that I was going to actually *play* golf at the one institution in America she hated the most, or that I hadn't mentioned I had been in contact with my father for the first time in six years.

Apparently, she did not think it was such a wonderful idea to ask my father for a round at the club. She did not like Mayflower Club members in any way, shape or form, and apparently she liked suck-up sons of Mayflower Club members even less.

Now, right here is when guys like me sort of gag. I was trying to think of the perfect thing to say and, in doing so, only said a worse thing. I explained the whole bizarre incident away by finally telling her about The Bet. "So, Mad, it's not that I want to be with my father. I *despise* my father. It's just that I really want to win The Bet." This was sort of like trying to put out a fire with an aerosol can.

"You slime!" she screamed. "That's the whole reason you came to the Mayflower? A bet?"

"So what? We met, didn't we? Things worked out!"

"Oh my God! You totally lied to me! The whole reason we met was this stupid fucking bet and you weren't going to tell me! You were just using me! And now you're using him, too! Your own father!"

"Wait a minute! How did I use you?"

"How? How? You just wanted me to help you meet some guy who would get you on the course!"

"No, that's not . . ."

"Oh, bullshit! Liar!"

She started to throw her stuff in a bag. She was going to leave wearing my bathrobe and my Red Sox hat.

"Besides, how could you?" she said at the door. "After all you said about him. How could you have such little respect for yourself that you'd *do* that?"

Personally, I could think of four thousand reasons. But I could hardly bring that up. Besides, I suddenly had a lot of particle board in my face. The door had slammed.

Me and Glen Fiddich went out that night and put some serious hurt on my liver and most of my cranial cells. About midnight, I knocked on her door, with her favorite, a bag of chocolate-covered potato chips behind my back. When she opened it I could see she'd been crying. I offered up my bribe.

"Sorry?" I said.

"You're drunk."

"That's not true," I said. "I think if you test me, you'll see there's still some blood in my alcohol stream."

She apparently did not like drunks in any form either, even clever drunks, perhaps because her mother was a drunk, proving once again that they have yet to find the family that isn't dysfunctional, up to and including the Martha Stewarts.

"I'm so happy for you, Ray. You are turning out just like your father. You play golf at elitist, racist, bluenose country clubs and now you've got Mickey Mantle's liver. Congratulations."

If anything pushed my button it was people comparing me to my father. I had lived my whole life—at least I thought I had—trying to be the polar opposite of him. I was starting to get pissed.

"What business is it of yours what I did tonight? You left a doorprint on my nose this morning, remember?"

"Look," she said. "If you'd wanted to patch things up with your dad, I would understand that. If you'd done it honestly, I could respect that. But this way, using him, using yourself, to win a stupid bet, that's disgusting. You're worse than him. You're worse than any of them."

Her face was turning a kind of burnt orange and she looked like she might just do a Mount St. Helens any moment, so I smoothed things over.

"A few guys try to feel your butt and you think the whole gender is Hitler."

I was out on my gluteus inside of a minute. Basically, she told me I could go straight to the Mayflower Club and fuck myself on the flagpole. She also mentioned something about never coming near her again or I'd need the number of a good urologist.

There are days in life when I am quite sure testosterone is ruining civilization and this was one of them. Women do not understand how overpowering a hormone Testy could be. Among hormones, Testy is U.S. Steel. Even though it was four Large, it was more than money. It had become a contest and males were evolved to try to win contests.

This particular contest was starting to affect my relationship with my two closest friends and now a woman I was in love with, but, goddamnit, what was I going to do? Go against my entire evolutionary path? If Madeline felt angry about me sucking up to my father, imagine how I felt. Didn't she think I felt like a warm pitcher of spit? Women just don't understand how *weenie* it is to lose.

I lay high that night in my water bed set for two. Even seven or eight more fresh-squeezed Gennys didn't help me sleep. Finally, I threw on a pair of khakis and a white shirt with a hole in it, called a cab, and, once Ivan checked the day's play list, was on the Mayflower putting green the next morning at six-thirty. Professor happened to see me and walked over, surprised more than very.

"Pet mousse sales is up, I guess, huh?" he said.

"Yeah," I said. "I'm doing hot tub elevators now. Get you in on the ground floor."

"I get it now," he said. "You was never a caddie. You was a spy for the members. Trying to see if we was smoking crack between rounds or maybe frying up goats in the back."

"No, I was trying to win a bet."

"Didju?" he said.

"I think soon."

"In that case, don't forget to call me for all your financial investin' needs," he said. "I cuts Schwab's ass off at the ankles."

Professor then headed over to the Caddie Room for the day's lottery. At that moment, with my stomach staging the Acid Olympics and my emotions kicking me in the groin, I think I'd have given half the money I was sure I was about to win just to play with him instead.

But when I got to looking for bright spots, it occurred to me that not only might today be profitable, but I was finally going to play the Mayflower in the daylight, without benefit of blackface or night balls and without being chased by a squadron of toy cops.

Of course, I'd also have to play golf with my father, which I hadn't done since I was prepubescent. The worst part was knowing that no matter how much I wanted to, I wouldn't be able to walk off the course this time. Or punch him out.

I was bent over a long putt when I felt a tap on my back. I figured it was my father, but when I turned around, I noticed a very firm hand grab me on the shoulder.

Stretch.

"Your smart ass is mine, night stalker," he said.

"Hello," I said, looking up at a man who had to go six-eight. "I've missed you so."

"Come with me, asswipe."

"Sure, sure," I said. "It's so interesting to see you up close. You look so much better than you do in pictures."

He kept dragging me. "What pictures?" he growled.

"Oh, a couple of our guys are shutterbugs over at Ponky," I said. "Yeah, this guy has some of the best equipment."

"That's nice for his mother," said Stretch.

"He really took some beauties of you," I said. "There's this classic one of you, stretched out asleep in your golf cart. Oh, it's hysterical!"

He stopped dragging.

"You're lying," he said.

"Maybe," I said. "But my father is a member here and I think I could talk my way out of almost anything. It's a bitch to talk your way out of a photo."

He let me go.

"You suck, asswipe."

"Lovely to see you again."

And then, not five minutes later, I felt another rip on my shoulder and the words "I'm afraid you'll have to leave."

I turned around to find Two Down, dressed in a Sherwin-Williams store—hideous lavender pants, bright daffodil yellow shirt and a paisley yellow-purple-and-pink sweater. "Members only."

My first reaction was shock, and not just at his ensemble. My second reaction was shock.

"In that case, we'll go together," I said, wondering what the hell he was doing on *my* course.

"Wrong."

He pulled out a business card that read:

Bingsley M. Colchester
Gems

I looked at it. "All right. Where have you hidden Bingsley? Dolores Ginty's pants?"

"Better question," he said. "How did you get past Fang at the front gate?"

"Just drove by," I said. "They let guests in."

"Who is that hard up for a guest?"

"You wouldn't know him."

Then a new voice behind us said, "Try us." It was Dannie, standing with Mr. Hole himself, Browning Sumner.

"Oh, uh, fellas, this is Browning. Browning, this is Two . . ."

"Too damn good-lookin'!" interrupted Two Down. "It's Bingsley Colchester, but you can just call me Bingo."

"Uh-huh," he said, yawning.

"I'm General Colin Powell," I said, offering my hand. He just yawned again.

Dannie steered both of us away from him. Like the rest of us, she was in a cute position. The money was going to go to the first one to play all 18 holes of the Mayflower and now here we all stood, stupefied, unsure how it had all happened and who would be the winner. A whisper-thon ensued.

"What the hell are you guys doing here?" Dannie whispered, pissed.

"Two Down is suddenly a third cousin of Mr. Standish and I'm playing with my father."

They both stared holes in me. Dannie tried to whisper and scream at the same time. "You can't stand your father!"

"I can stand him for four hours and four Large," I hissed.

"Not if I'm in the group in front of you," Two Down whispered.

"Or if I'm in front of *you,*" said Dannie, pointing at Two Down.

"Chances of playing through our group will be very slim," I said, holding up my undefeated and untied putter.

"Multiple violation," said Two Down. "We said no family members."

"No, we didn't!" I said.

"Well, I'm saying it now," Two Down said.

"Nice try," I said. "Oh, I need two IDs with your check."

"Ray," said Dannie. "You told me you hope your father dies of earwigs."

"I do. As soon as I putt out on 18."

"If your father really is a member, which I doubt, what took you a month to play a round with him?" asked Two Down.

"I like Alcoa Fantastic Finishes," I said. I looked at Dannie. "Does Mr. J. Crew know you're using him just for his membership?"

"I'm not," she said defensively. "This has a future."

"Yeah, he's just glowing," I said. He was now half asleep, sitting against a tree.

That's when my father showed up in stitched polyester pants and some horrendous Buick 23rd Annual Mixed Senior Calloway Low Ball Classic shirt. He introduced me to the two guys we'd be playing with. One was Considine Roberts, the Captain of the club, a plump man born tragically without a chin, eyes set wide apart, no hair to speak of and a fuck-you-commoner quality to his voice. The other was my old best buddy, Stone Concorde, everybody's favorite real estate mauler.

Stone Concorde was just about to give me the big hello and the huge double-handed handshake—the sure mark of the phony—when his eyes got big. He was just about to blow my caddie cover when I interrupted him.

"Yes, yes, Stone is a *business* associate of mine," I said, giving him the two-handed shake back.

He could hardly believe his eyes, but he didn't say a thing. He was storing it away, just in case.

Father gave me a look like I better introduce some people.

"Uh, Father, this is Bingsley Colchester. He's, uh, he's a member."

"My pleasure, Bingsley," said Father. "You're a new member, then?"

"Well, yes and no," said Two Down. "I've been overseas for seventeen years. Gems, y'know. Burma. Thailand. The Golden Triangle. And I just never wanted to give up my membership. I finally gave up the gem dodge and . . . here I am!"

Stone looked at him curiously. Then he looked at me curiously. Screw him. Right then I couldn't worry about Stone Concorde. I had to worry about getting on the tee box before anybody else. Nobody had started ahead of us, for there were no footprints in the dew on the first tee box. There was only a wrinkled starter standing near it, going over the day's tee times on a weathered clipboard. I was just about to go hand him $20 to make sure we went off first, when he hollered out, "Mr. Colchester?"

Two Down pulled his right fist down like on a slot machine. "Yes!" he said.

"You're up, Mr. Colchester," said the starter. Two Down was practically floating to the first tee.

End of bet.

I looked at Dannie. Her jaw hit her sternum. Two Down was shooting each of us a little six-gun finger when the starter yelled, ". . . and you'll be joined by Mr. Sumner and guest."

Two Down walked another three steps before it hit him.

Rules were rules. They were playing together, which meant they were both disqualified. Two Down himself had said it that very first day standing by the T. We'd all agreed. Neither of the other two can be in your group when you play. They canceled each other out. I'd won.

A horror came to his eyes. He looked like a man who'd just had a rattler slide up his pants leg. God, it was delicious to see. Then I looked at Dannie, who couldn't decide whether to cry at her own problems or grin at his. It was one of the great freezers of all time. I tried not to smile too big, only the size of a cantaloupe slice.

"That is so *nice* that you two get to play with each other," I said.

"Munch me," mentioned Dannie.

They both went over and pleaded their cases to the starter, but he would hear none of it. I could've kissed him. This was a record. I'd made $4,000 in Chop cash and I hadn't starched my first drive yet.

For two guys who had spent a month trying to get to this very position—being the first Chops ever to play the Mayflower—Two

Down and Dannie looked like they were heading for an appointment at the Kevorkian Center.

All I had to do was play 18 holes and the money was mine. Sure, one of them could try to back out, or fake a sudden injury, allowing the other to finish first before me by himself, but that would fall under the heading "parking-lot jobs"—giving aid to another—which we had specifically mentioned as against the rules, and it would still revert to Yours Truly.

The only person who could fuck it up now for me was me and I made sure I wouldn't do that by taking my father in the little best-ball game they played. Twenty-dollar, automatic two downs. I knew I could beat Concorde giving him 13 shots—I'd been on too many rounds with him. And I didn't much want to beat my father and run the risk that he'd get pissed or go ballistic and throw me off the course.

I was a 2. My dad was a 2. Concorde was a 15. And the Captain was the full 36, or, as the caddies used to call him, the Mayflower Max. We all had caddies, each of whom I had to wink at when I shook their hand. I got First-and-Third. He was so surprised to see me, he moved his head twice from eye to eye to make sure each one was telling him the truth.

I must say, except for the company, I never had more fun playing than I did that day. For one thing, it was so wonderful to play along and look up ahead of me and see Dannie and Two Down and know that there was absolutely nothing they could do now to whip me.

One time I think Two Down, using his patented controlled shank, tried to pick me off with a skulled driver off the 7th tee while I was standing on the 6th green, but he missed by a good six yards. He also tried to pick Dannie off, figuring if she was injured, he'd win the thing, but Dannie was too quick. Then Dannie let go of a 2-iron once that almost caught Two Down in the knee, but Two Down high-jumped it.

Me, I made the happy discovery that all my years spent at Ponky had improved my game. For instance, to sink a putt at Ponky you've got to roll it at one tiny spot on the hole and firm everything and half of those hit a hole or a rock or buried pop-top and jumped four inches off line anyway. But these putts, oh, Lord, they stayed sweetly on line all the way and dropped right in the little cups like polite little Von Trapp children going off to bed. I must've one-putt ten greens.

At the Donkey there were many fairways you'd try to *avoid.* Like on 6, you wanted to be 20 yards left of the fairway because the best patch of grass at Ponky was there. And at 15, you wanted to be way right of the fairway and into 13 fairway because 15 fairway looked like a Stephen King movie. But at the Mayflower, I suddenly had entire fairways to aim at. It felt like standing in Kuwait and having to hit one in the desert.

I made a couple bogeys out of the bunkers, mostly because I hadn't actually hit out of real sand in so long and kept fluffing everything. Naturally, this is the only part of my game that my father chose to comment on.

"You still haven't learned that bunker shot, have you, Raymond?"

"This is the first one I've ever been in," I said wittily.

My father had a new annoying habit he'd picked up. He was always squirting breath spray in his mouth every ten minutes or so. He must have had lovely breath, though I never found out, mostly because he said almost nothing to me most of the day. But he did have a few conversations with my driver, the Last Real Golf Club in America.

"Where'd you get this club?"

"Uncle Joe," I said.

"The Tommy Armour MacGregor 693," he said, conducting some heavy petting with it. "Rosewood finish. Red insert. Original shaft."

I nodded.

"I wonder where Joseph ever got it."

"Your dad gave it to him," I said.

You could see this sting him a little. "Oh. Oh, no, no, no, no," he insisted. "My father probably threw it away, the fool, and my brother took it out of the trash."

I took it back out of his hands. Never let bad karma handle your clubs. It will only bring you unspeakable hooks.

"No," I said. "It was *given* to Uncle Joe and Uncle Joe *gave* it to me."

The only person colder than my father all day was Madeline, who came by twice and never even looked me in the eye, even when I was buying.

"I'll have one of those cranapple-grapes and some of that homemade garp you sell," I said.

Everybody looked at me.

"I thought this was your first round here," the Captain said. "How do you know what she has?"

Very good question.

Concorde looked at me slyly. Here is where the whole thing turns to dookie, I thought.

"Oh," I said. "Oh, well, we used to have a cart much like this at the Charles River Country Club, where I belong."

Madeline's face turned a kind of maroon with anger.

When we were done and walking away, Madeline "accidentally" ran over my toe. This is not a woman you want mad at you.

Anyway, I was on my way to a cute little 68 and we had Concorde and the Captain out, out, out, down one and down two standing on 16 tee, when my father sidled up to me and said, "We need to back off now," he said. "It's impolite to beat the Captain this badly."

I don't know why I did, maybe because I thought it'd be nice to play Paradise again, but I started to dump. I turned my grip over about a half inch and started to hit some serious fishhooks. I double-bogeyed 16 and 17 and bogeyed 18 and shot 73. Meanwhile, my father, very conveniently went par, par, birdie, and shot 72, giving himself every putt inside five feet the rest of the way. We ended up winning $80 anyway.

Afterward, he was totaling the scores up and announcing them as always. "Well, I managed to nip you by one, Raymond," he said with a Dentyne grin. The bastard.

He offered his hand in a shake. I walked right by it.

"Nice leather you got on that putter," I said.

Now that the bet was finally over, I walked over to Dannie and Two Down with an open hand, hoping to shake, collect and forget about it. They walked right by.

"White folk need to *work* on that handshake shit," said First-and-Third.

I was so hot at my father for the bullshit stunt he'd pulled over the last 3 holes that I could've eaten bees, as Dannie liked to say.

I walked straight to Ponky and sat there by myself and let about a dozen cold Claudettes get a view of the inside of my neck. I was just about to get up and go sit outside Madeline's and tell her how goddamn right she was and would she please run her car back and forth over me if I ever did it again when Two Down and Dannie and Thud walked in. Thud handed me the $3,000 and said, "U cst me a hndrd."

"Never bet against genius," I offered.

Then Two Down walked up and said, "Luckiest prick I ever met," and handed me the extra $1,000.

"Next to Browning's," said Dannie, handing me $1,000.

Then Two started to walk out.

"Two?" I said. "Let's all of us go over to Don's Mixed Drinks and try to set the standing Robitussin record."

"Sorry, I gotta bolt," Two Down said at the door. "I got your guy Stone at two-twelve. *Varsity* match."

"Hey!" I hollered after him, "be careful of that . . ." But he was already gone.

I turned to Dannie. "Well, bet's over. Wanna get a half gallon of butter brickle and play Good Humor man?"

"Nah," she said. "I need to get over to Browning's."

Suddenly, it was just me again. I looked around the lunchroom and got depressed. I looked at my stack of jing. There was really only one thing to do with it.

IT WAS AS though someone had taken Ponky and switched it with a loaner course until repairs could be made. The fun meter was at zero.

Two Down was so thrilled about the way the Mayflower was going to make him a Rockefeller, he never came around Ponky anymore. And because he didn't come around, neither did a lot of guys who came to Ponky mostly to enter Leonard's World.

Chunkin' Charlie didn't come around much anymore either, because, as he said, "the Uglies are four up with five to play."

Crowbar was home working on his pet project, completing an index of all the dialogue ever spoken by Fred MacMurray. Hoover was at a two-day golf seminar entitled "Golf's Hidden Secret: Mass-to-Surface Ratio." Thud was usually in the corner, conducting a torrid romance with Blu Chao's wonton tamales.

When I'd see Dannie, she and Browning were always on their way to his parents' for dinner or she and Browning were going to a client's formal party or she and Browning were going to a gala.

"Uh-oh," I said. "He's afraid to be alone with you."

"Jealousy is eatin' you up, Ray," she said.

"There is not a whole lot left of the FB club," I mentioned. "We don't F and it seems like we're not even Bs anymore."

"This here is the big one for me, Ray. The fantasy is in living color now. Be happy for me."

"I'm sick to death of being happy for everybody," I wanted to say, pettily. "I'm sick of being happy for Two that he's discovered the land of the arbitrage pukes and I'm sick of being happy for you that you finally found Mr. Blow-Dry Universe."

Instead, I just said, "I'm tingling."

"Jesus, Ray, I think I'm in love with this guy. Don't you think that beats appointment sex with a guy that won't let anybody deeper into him than his tonsils?"

This came as kind of a shock.

"Tell me one thing," I said. "Truth or consequences. Have you shown him what's inside the locket?"

She stared at her new $200 Joan and David shoes.

"Well, no," she said.

"I knew it!" I said. "You don't love him!"

"He never asks!" she said. "For your information, we haven't even seen each other nekkid yet."

"What is he? Sir Walter Raleigh?"

"No, it's just that he's such a gentleman, he doesn't want to rush things. He wants to make sure the moment is right. For you, the moment is right if the day has at least two syllables."

"Yeah, but I take the extra day in leap years off."

When she was gone, it was basically just me and a bunch of people carrying Day-Glo golf bags I'd never seen before. I hit balls, putted, played by myself, played with Chunk when he felt up to it, played solitaire, moped, whined to myself, fidgeted and spent time in the puke-orange Naugahyde La-Z-Boy, reserved for the day's biggest loser, which was looking more and more like me.

The rest of my time I just wasted.

Man, what I wouldn't have given for the way things used to be. I longed for our Midnight Dice workshops, in which Two Down would bring the dice, Thud (the Almost Human) would bring the bologna, I'd bring the beer and Chunk would bring the porno.

I longed for a few sucker bets. Like the time Two Down bet Cementhead that he couldn't make a 4 on the 6th, a pretty easy par 4. Cementhead did him one better, he birdied the hole with a 3.

"Whip out, Two Down," said Cementhead.

"What for?" said Two Down.

"You know what for. I made a 4."

"No, you didn't," said Two. "You made a 3."

We were explaining that one to Cementhead for three days.

Or the time Thud was supposed to deliver the ashes of the dearly beloved. The family wanted the ashes put in a special vase they had at home, which meant Thud had to bring the remains in a plastic bucket and then transfer them to the family's vase. This was not unusual, except this family happened to live right off Ponky's 5th hole, so Thud thought what the hell, he'd just play a few holes on the way. Except that on the 4th hole, Thud suddenly remembered his little errand and looked into the bucket. He was somewhat surprised to find no ashes in it.

"Cementhead?" he asked. "Do you have any idea what became of the stuff that was in this bucket?"

Cement looked at the empty bucket and said, "Whaddya mean?"

"The contents of the bucket. What happened to them?"

"Used 'em in the divots. What else?"

"You used them in the divots?"

"Un-huh."

"Cement," said Thud calmly, "do you know you've been filling your divots with a Mr. George O. Tibbles?"

Ever since that day, the Tibbles family has been coming to the fireplace mantel and saying a soft good-night to a vase full of divot mix and the divot mix in our carts has been known as "George," as in the sentence "Hey, Cement, hand me over the George. I got a doozy here."

I got so desperate that I actually had a conversation with Froghair.

"Slow day, huh, Froghair?" I said.

"I'm glad," he said. "I've had time to concentrate on selling this cesspool."

"Why do you want to sell Ponky so much?" I asked him. "You never spend any money anyway."

"Do, too."

"Do not. Your wife told me one time you take two-ply toilet paper and separate it into two rolls."

"That's a lie! I only tried it once. It took too long."

"OK."

"Besides, I've got a friend that can let me in on an idea he's got. Discount Surgery Centers. You know what those doctors charge nowadays? Our guys'll do you for half the price. A course, you don't get as many of the frills, like all the big staff in the operating room and everything, and they do it in half the time, but still."

"Oh, sure," I said. "Imagine what you could save in anesthesia alone."

"Exactly," he said.

Sigh.

Personally, I was torn between the two places. My two sporty little Mayflower rounds—by night and by day—were starting to give me that old feeling again. I was looking at 68 or 69 at the Mayflower easy until my father moosed me out of it, and a lot of 68s at places like the Mayflower could get my butt back out there on some kind of junior varsity tour, where I might just have a chance to shake some steel and rip some cloth and get lucky and wind up in Courtesy Car Heaven, a.k.a. the PGA Tour.

Not only that, I even started believing it.

Besides, Madeline wouldn't answer my calls and wouldn't come to the phone. If I couldn't have her, I was going after my golf career again. And if I lost that, too . . . well, I didn't want to think about it.

The one time I thought it was her, returning my one hundredth message, I was stunned to find the voice of Lois.

"Please hold for Mr. Hart."

Suddenly, there he was.

"Raymond, how would you like to come out to the Mayflower again?" he said.

"Uh, well," I said, not quite believing my ears. "Sure."

"Tomorrow, nine-twelve?"

"Mmmm, uh, yeah. I'll be there."

"Unless you have a lot of appointments?"

"No, no appointments."

"Or a game at the Charles River Club."

"No, no."

"That's fine, then. Oh, and maybe you could buy a new shirt."

"Oh, thank God," I said. "For a minute there I thought you weren't going to say anything to piss me off."

"Raymond, I'm just saying . . ."

"Forget it. See you tomorrow."

I felt like a bit of a rodent playing again with the one person I would most like to see sucked into a 747 engine, but, like I say, I had that *feeling* again. Playing on a great course could do nothing but make my game better. And besides, what did I have to lose? At least I could maybe explain things to her there when I saw her. And not only that, but could it *possibly* be my father wanted to start making things right with me?

The next day, my father and I, not saying too much, played a pharmacist and some toy-making tycoon in a little alternate shot game ("Makes the game go so much faster," said my father), and me and the Last Real Golf Club in America were getting along wonderfully well—I hit every fairway and my father played pretty well, too, and I made enough jing to keep me in purple-dot Titlists for a long, long time.

The strangest thing was that my father and I never argued over how to play a hole or a shot or which way a putt broke, as though we had been evolving on parallel golf universes this whole time without knowing it. You could bring up a thousand subjects and there probably wasn't a single one we'd be able to agree on, but golf somehow was. And I thought maybe, just maybe, that was a start. Somewhere deep in the iciest part of my heart, maybe I could feel a little thawing going on.

The more I played with him, the more I realized that maybe Madeline was right. In a few ways, I *was* like my father. For instance, I learned to suck down scotch from him—my first wife might tell you that—and I learned to swing a golf club from him—low, slow take-away like Billy Casper, full turn like Couples, never getting it to parallel like Norman, dropping it a little inside like Trevino and a nice, high finish like Weiskopf. It was his brother, Joe, that taught me to *play* golf, but it was always Father whom I pictured in my mind's slo-mo.

He didn't say much to me, but he seemed to be trying the way awkward males will, keeping it within the confines of golf. For instance, he would pick up my MacGregor every now and again and say, "So you say Nicklaus used this to win the Open in 1962?"

"Yeah. They say he never missed a fairway with it in the playoff with Arnie."

"How did your grandfather get it again?"

"Bought it at a charity auction that year. Paid $550 for it."

"It's awfully gorgeous," my father said.

He took a very long time giving it back to me.

It was the most civil conversation I'd had with my father in probably ten years. It felt very odd not being ignored by him, like suddenly speaking in another language. I kept wanting to look over my shoulder and ask, "Are you talkin' to *me?*"

Luckily, Madeline was doing a wonderful job of ignoring me.

"Stupid girl," my father kept saying. "Why doesn't that girl ever stop?"

We played twice more together, my father and I, always alternate shot, which was curious, until I realized he either didn't want to get beat by me or didn't want any more fights.

The third time we played, I arrived in the parking lot to find that our opponents were Bingsley M. Colchester and his guest, a sturdy-looking gent named Barton Dunlop, known more familiarly to me as Cementhead.

Curiously, this Bingsley guy did the same thing in the parking lot that a friend of mine named Two Down used to do, which is carry about fifty trophies in the trunk of his car. He didn't win them, he collected them. And he didn't care as long as they were big and cheap. Whenever he was in a big match, he'd show up in the parking lot about five minutes late, all rushed, and say, "Sorry, sorry, lemme just get my shoes." And he'd open his trunk and start taking out all these trophies and setting them on the ground. "I gotta get a bigger den," he'd say. And the poor guy he was playing would get eyes like Barney Google and go out and lose about eight $20 presses.

I mentioned to him that it was just me and he didn't have to go through the whole trophy act. He seemed disappointed.

As for this Cementhead character, he had apparently been having a hard time making the adjustment from the world's worst muni to one of the world's finest private clubs. For instance, when he arrived, he refused to allow the bag boy to take his clubs from his truck, certain the boy was going to steal them.

"Whaddya think I am, *stupid?*" he roared.

Then he put the clamp on the shoeshine man in the locker room, whom he thought was stealing his shoes. The man had to quickly explain that he would shine his loafers while he played and if he wouldn't mind unclamping his shoulder because he was starting to lose feeling in his fingers.

Then Cement walked into the pro shop, sank one of his massive paws into the basket of tees on the counter, slowly guided it over to the man behind the counter like a building crane and handed him a dollar bill with his other hand.

"Uh, the tees are free, sir," said the man.

"Oh," said Cementhead. "Sorry." Still, he kept them and walked out of there like there was a porcupine in his pocket.

But once Cementhead got a little used to the place—his first putt on No. 1 went past the pin, over the fringe and into a pond—he was fine. It was this Bingsley guy who turned out to be the gold-plated prick.

It was almost as though somebody *really* had switched Two Down for this jerk, because there was no Two Down inside this guy. There were no fun bets, only $20 one-downs—no Las Vegas, no bingle, bangle, bongles, no jokes, no lines, no laughs. I'd never seen Two Down so serious in my life. He looked older, somehow, and worried. His skin was pasty white. He barely said a word to me or Cementhead the first 15 holes, which was good, because if he had, I would've put an overlapping grip on his throat.

All he did all day was try to screw me. He dropped his car keys on my backswing twice, pumped the cart brakes on my backswing about seven times, coughed over my putts three times, sneezed twice and, with about $200 riding on the final hole, asked me if I exhaled or inhaled on my backswing.

"I am not sure if I inhale or exhale," I told him. "But at least I don't suck."

Even for Ponky, it was over the top. You expect it at Ponky—you're ready for it—but not at the Mayflower.

I was so pissed off, I hit a two-cheeker about 295 down the middle and we birdied the damn hole on him.

I was beginning to wonder why I used to like the guy so much. Two days before, Chunkin' Charlie told me that Two Down brought Crowbar to the Mayflower, just to ride along, and the guard called

Two Down inside the guard shack and told him, "With all respect, sir, your guest isn't welcome." Definitely a black thing.

And Two Down just took Crowbar home and went and played anyway. Here's a guy that is with Two Down maybe five days out of seven every week for I don't know how many years and now when it really counts, Two Down stiffs him. Beautiful.

After the round, my father said, "Sorry, Raymond, I just don't have time for that drink."

"Oh."

That made four times in a row I hadn't been invited inside the club. He was either ashamed of me or wanted some way of punishing me. Maybe he just felt I should *earn* it.

"Maybe some other time," he said.

....

I was thinking about all that as I was leaving the parking lot—learning to hate Two Down and, come to think of it, myself a little for being a cog in the machine that was changing him—when there was a knock on the window of the little Escort I'd bought myself for $500. It was Two Down himself, noted Dorchester humanist.

"Look," he said. "I'm in trouble."

"Good," I said, rolling up the window.

"No, Stick, please. I'm serious. I need your help."

I let him inside the car.

"What's wrong? You accidentally swallow a cough drop?"

"No, Stick, please."

I'd never seen him so shaken.

"Stick, I'm down eight Large."

"You can't be," I mentioned. "You don't have eight Large."

"I know! But I am!"

"Impressive. How'd you manage it?"

"Dice and putting for dollars."

"Big dollars."

"Big."

"Two, you don't lose at dice and putting. Thud doesn't lose ham-eating contests and you don't lose at dice and putting."

"I've already cashed Jane's Christmas Club," he said.

"Smooth," I said to him. "So sell the Lexus out. That's gotta be worth $35,000."

"Thirty-six," he said. "I already did. But it was more complicated than I thought. I had to pay $12,000 in taxes right off the bat and the insurance was $4,000, which I didn't have, so I sold it and that left me $20,000. I blew a lot of that on new furniture for Jane and a buncha clothes for me and then I lost the rest of it *plus* the $8,000."

"Jesus Holy Christ!" I said. "Where's Arnie? Fiji?"

"That's the thing," he said. "I *had* Arnie. Arnie never putted better. That's why I kept doubling it. This guy Concorde just always drained one more than me. Most unbelievable long-range putter I've ever seen."

"Stone Concorde?" I asked.

He looked lost, running his hands through his bristle-brush hair, his skin kind of clammy. "Yeah. Great guy. Couldn't be nicer. Why?"

Something about this didn't make sense. Two Down was twice the putter Stone Concorde ever hoped to be.

"On the putting green?" I asked.

"No, over at Macy's, you moron."

"So just disappear," I said. "Who's gonna find Bingsley M. Colchester?"

"But, Stick, I can *beat* this guy," Two Down said. "I don't want to disappear. I've wanted to be in the majors my whole life, I don't want to give this thing up. If I can just get back to even with this guy, I'll stay away from him. Then I'll be set at this club for *life.*"

"So whaddya want from me?"

"I don't know. I just . . . I'm goin' against him in a half hour. Stick around—luck?"

"Jesus! Are you taking stupid pills? What's this guy gonna do when you tell him, 'Gee, uh, I'm a little short on cash, but I can hook you up with free lifetime call waiting'?"

"I ain't losing."

"Oh, well, no problem, then," I said, exasperated. "Forget it, Two. I can't watch this shit. You got in over your head this time. This ain't you and me and Chunk chipping into Manelli's drive-thru window. This is lawyer whip-out stuff. These guys floss out chunks of guys like you."

"Buy you the greatest dinner afterward you've ever had."

"I thought you were tapped out."

"My bill doesn't come for another week. By then, I'll either have the cash or I'll be toast."

"Hello? Leonard Petrovitz? Are you listening to anything I'm saying?"

"Please? For old times? As a Chop?"

Just then I saw Madeline squeal off. What plans could I possibly have?

I pretended to be hanging around, just putting, when Concorde came out to join "Bingsley" on the putting green.

"Bingo!" Concorde said. "Gonna put it to me tonight, aren't you, buddy? I can just feel it."

Two Down had none of that old chip-on-the-shoulder bravado he had at Ponky, that face that said, "I'm about to become your new installment loan officer here in about ten minutes."

"That's it, Stoner," Two Down said weakly. "Gonna get back my little IOU right now." But he said it like he was reading a cue card. It was as though when he became Bingsley Colchester, he automatically absorbed this Colchester guy's personality, which appeared to be that of a throw rug.

They started with $100 a hole, aces only, which means if you don't sink the putt on the first try, you don't win and the bet is carried over to the next hole.

"All right, Arnie," I heard Two Down whisper. "Let's play hide Whitey."

Two Down may not have been his usual self, but Arnie was. Arnie was taking it to the hole like Charles Barkley and before long Two Down was up about $600. Then Concorde doubled the bet to $200 a hole. Two Down promptly sank a bunch of putts, a 12-footer and a 22-footer and even a 16-foot right-to-left no-chancer that hung on the lip about five seconds before dropping.

Two Down turned Arnie upside down and grabbed him by the throat. "Arnie! How many times have I told you not to show off? No teaser putts."

A rare sighting of the old Two Down. Now he was up $2,200. Still, Concorde didn't look all that concerned.

"Let's try some long ones," Concorde said.

Two Down got a panicky look on his face.

Stone set up about 30 feet away. "Ten putts from here. A grand for every one you make."

"Right," said Two Down.

To me, it seemed like a stupid bet. Any putt that goes in from 30 feet is just pure, unfiltered luck, a no-brainer, and not much else. You might as well put a dime in a phone booth and hope it pays twenty to one. Of course, Two Down was born with an extra luck gene.

Two Down went first. Nobody I ever met made more no-brainers than Two Down, but in his five chances, all he did was lip one out and miss the rest. It was starting to get chilly and so while Two Down was putting, Concorde put on a black windbreaker.

"Nice try, Bingo," Concorde said in that faux friendly way of his. "Thought you might get one."

Then Concorde stepped up and simply *dunked* the first one. Dead center of the hole. I was mortified. So was Two. He missed the second, but he *made* the next two, an impossible feat, an incredible feat. Now he was up $800 for the night.

"Whooo!" he said. "I am one lucky sonofagun."

"Rats get fat," whispered Two Down.

He missed the fifth badly. Still, he was up $800. Two Down had his head bowed. Then he snapped it up and said, "Double or nothing says you can't make your next two out of three."

"Forget it, Bingopolous, I got no chance," said Concorde. "That was just lucky."

"Triple or nothing," said Two Down.

"OK," said Concorde.

I smiled. Why Concorde would take a stupid bet like that was beyond me. Yeah, he'd just made three out of five, but it was just a tear in the fabric of reality. No possible way he can make two out of the next three. A true sucker bet.

Still, there he was, setting up to it, and knocking his first bomb right in the jar. He missed the second badly. He straightened up a moment before he tried his third.

It was right then, something about the way he looked at the hole, that it hit me. *It was him.* It was the man in black we'd seen in the middle of the night weeks ago, the guy doing the weird things with the hoses. The sturdy-looking build. The black jacket. The black hat. All he was missing was the black pants.

I wanted to yell, but before I could Concorde's third putt was on the way. And going flat dead in the hole.

"Whoooo-ahhhh!" he yelled. "Unbelievable, huh, Bingo?!"

"Good men die," whispered Two Down. He was now down $2,400 for the night, $10,400 altogether. His face went white, his eyebrows sank and he looked like he'd just eaten a curtain hook.

"I'll be," I said, walking over to the hole that held Concorde's two balls. "A guy makes five out of eight 30-footers, all to the same hole, all on the same exact line, all five of which go dead center in the hole. What are the odds, huh, Bingo?"

Concorde gave me a quick dirty look and reached into the hole for his balls. I stepped hard on his arm with my high-tops so he couldn't move it. He collapsed to his knees.

"Hey, motherfucker!" Concorde yelped.

"C'mere a second, Bingo," I said. "Feel the grain right next to the hole."

Bingo brushed the grass.

"Do you feel a little indentation?" I said.

"Yeah," said Two Down. "I do!"

I stepped harder on Concorde's arm.

"Now, follow that indentation and see where it goes."

Two Down got on his knees and brushed all around the cup. Pretty soon, his hand was following a path that led to the exact point where Concorde had putted from 30 feet away.

"There's a fucking little gully all the way to the hole!" Two Down screeched. "I got moosed!"

Suddenly, Concorde swung his left leg around and kicked out my legs from under me. He jumped up.

"I don't know what you gentlemen are talking about," he said, rubbing his arm. "But I do know Mr. Colchester owes me $10,000."

"Up yours horizontally, Concorde," I said, on my feet again. "You know exactly how that little gully got there. It's an old Titanic Thompson trick. You come out here at night and lay the hose down on the green and then soak it. I've *seen* you do it. It makes a perfect indentation on the putting green, but nothing big enough to see. You can only feel it. And it feeds every darling little putt right into the cup. That's why every putt you hit went in hard, dead center, except, of course, the ones you missed badly just to make it look legit."

By now, Two Down had made two in a row by feeling exactly where the path was, putting his ball down in the gully and simply hitting it hard. When the second one went in, Two Down had manslaughter in his eyes.

"I don't know who you saw," Concorde said to me. "Or what you were doing on the grounds at night. But it sounds like a drunk greenskeeper to me." He began to walk off. "I'll have to speak to the Captain about it."

Two Down rushed him, but Concorde spun around and stung him with a straight right hand that looked like it might just cleave Two Down's other eyebrow. The blood was gushing from his head when Concorde said, "I'm sorry, but you had that coming. Now, I want you to know. I have associates that think welching is in *very* poor taste."

"How do they feel about rat-fucking cheats?" I asked, Two Down's blood dripping into my lap.

He spun on his heels and walked toward me. "I think I know who you are now," he said. "You're not just a caddie, are you, Carl? I'll bet you were the young man who snuck in here late one night and did about $25,000 worth of damage to the course flying around here on your golf cart. They said he was tall and skinny, like you. In fact, they've still got the guy's ball up in the Captain's office. I think it was a Titlist 1 with three purple dots on it."

I swallowed a little.

"Yep," he said. "That's right. That's what you played the other day with me. Titlists with purple dots. What say we check your bag right now to see if that's what you play, want to?"

"Get bent, Concorde," I said, picking up Two Down in both arms and taking him to my car.

"Oh, really?" he said. Then he turned and hollered, "Security!"

I started to run with Two Down.

"I can't tell you how little I want to jog just now," moaned Two Down.

"Security!"

I opened the car door, bumped his head on it, threw him in and squealed off.

"So," I said, over his moaning. "Where we going for dinner?"

17

IN THE EMERGENCY room, Two Down and I drew up a list of his options. It's an old trick my Uncle Joe taught me. Whenever you find yourself in the deep end with cement flippers, write down what possible solutions you have left and the right one will jump off the page and pop you in the nose.

Seeing as how the doctors didn't think Two Down's condition was any rush and seeing as how the blood trickling down from his gashed forehead was inconveniently blurring his vision, I offered to do the writing:

What Two Down Can Do Now to Save His Skinny Butt

1. Tell the truth. Explain to Concorde who he really is. Mention that, although he does not have much liquidity currently, he would be happy to set up an easy payment plan. Hope he isn't jailed for forgery.
2. Leave America forever.
3. Kidnap Concorde. Nail him into pine coffin borrowed from Thud. Pay him back with his own ransom money. Laugh.
4. Ask nurse for hemlock IV.
5. Disappear. Inform club of Bingsley's demise in Burmese elephant accident. Move.
6. Blackmail Concorde's sorry ass.
7. Sell house. Move to Chicago and live with brother.
8. Sign up for instant Mafia membership. Ask for complimentary rub-out.

9. Play Hoover $5,000 Nassau. Press the back.
10. Bleed to death.

Unfortunately, what seemed to bop Two Down in the nose was No. 3, the pine-box route, and I couldn't talk him out of it.

Personally, I was not all that worried about myself. Even though I was pretty sure Concorde was bluffing about any damage the Midnight Mulligan Marauders had done, I had taken the precaution of removing all my purple-dot Titlists from my bag and throwing them in the Ponky Dumpster on our way to the hospital.

Besides, it was a Dorchester standoff. I didn't think Concorde would rat on me, because he knows I could start asking around at the club how many people had lost money to good ol' Stone on three-day-camel-ride putts. And maybe I couldn't prove it, but at a country club, being called a horse thief is pretty much the same as being one.

Two Down, though, refused to go to the members, because he had this feeling Concorde knew he wasn't quite who he said he was, especially now that his ex-caddie had come to his aid by stepping on his arm. We could call up a few members and get them to the club the next morning and hope to show them the gully, but with watering and a mow, it would be gone by tomorrow. No good.

I admit, I was looking out for myself a little here. I didn't want my ass thrown in the mix, not right now. All that could do is screw up my comeback and if I was going to lose the best woman that had ever happened to me over golf, then I wasn't going to screw my golf up over a little guy with one and a half eyebrows.

If that sounds like a sellout, I guess it was. My new middle name. I had decided to bet everything on rebuilding my golf career. And if I was going to talk my father or some other rich

Numeral friend of his into sponsoring me for a season, causing a large scene at the Mayflower wasn't going to help my chances. I *needed* the Mayflower.

Not only that, but as much as I hated the people, I was kind of enjoying going there. I'd been using their killer practice facilities for two hours before every round I'd played with my dad. You do not appreciate the feel of a good range divot until you've been without one for six years.

"If I were you," I told Two Down seventeen stitches later, driving him home, "I'd go with No. 5. Disappear, come back to Ponky a few months later and hope you never see Concorde again as long as you both shall live."

"He'd find me," said Two Down. "He knows I know you. He knows I know Dannie. He'd find me."

"Then tell him the truth and work it off over a few years," I said.

"He'd have me arrested. I'd lose my job."

"They still need a caddie cook."

"Hilarious. Get your own cable show."

Two Down was locked in on kidnapping. I told him I wouldn't help him, so he called Thud himself. He agreed to buy him one of Don's famous cellophane-wrapped burritos if he'd meet him at midnight.

I took it upon myself to try to end this thing once and for all. Our lives were a joke. Dannie and I were hardly even speaking anymore. I never saw Cementhead and I was worried about Chunkin' Charlie. So as long as Two and Thud were meeting at midnight, I decided I would call an emergency meeting of the remaining Chops to see if, together, we could call an end to all this and maybe rally around Two Down in his time of need.

At the worst, we could all get bail-bond drunk.

At midnight, we were sitting in the decrepit confines of Don's Mixed Drinks, where they actually still make Singapore slings, where every table is a red booth with a gray-speckled Formica table and where nobody ever delivers your drinks and says, "Enjoy!"

We were sitting there with a very drawn and weak Chunkin' Charlie, plus Cementhead and Two and Crowbar, together as always, and a few Fred Flintstone jelly jars of the ol' Robitussin, when Dannie walked in, looking plenty hacked off to be brought back in our company, the company she used to love. This whole thing had been one giant charisma bypass operation.

Dannie seemed to be a different person. She kept harrumphing and wiping off the grimy tables like she herself hadn't once danced the Maori haka victory dance on them after too many slings. She was wearing a Donna Karan kind of suit with a fancy hat and matching purse and shoes.

"Excuse me, Dan," Thud said helpfully. "Have you noticed somebody accidentally switched your clothes with Joan Collins's?"

"Oh, I'm sorry," she said. "This from a man whose entire wardrobe comes from boxes of Duz."

A nasty beginning to the evening.

"How come you never come around Ponky anymore?" Cementhead asked.

"Well, Browning doesn't like me hangin' around there anymore."

"Well, of course," I said, agitated. "Blu Chao blanches the arugula too long lately."

"So, let us in, Dan," said Thud. "What's his Stimpmeter rating?"

"Sorry, boys," she said, looking away. "You guys ain't gettin' no details from me. You'll just have to go home and play Fist Your Mister again."

"I don't know," said Patty O'Connell and her plus-5 tits. "You look to me like you haven't been laid by anybody recently."

"Not everybody thinks of 'recently' as the last half hour," said Dannie.

"I heard that, too," Two Down said. "You guys waiting for papal approval or what?"

Dannie slapped her hand on the table.

"You slobs don't have Clue A about me and Browning," she said, frying. "He's the first man I've ever met with real *honor and class*. Something you guys have never been within a par 5 of."

"I was right," said Patty, collecting glasses. "She ain't gettin' any."

There were many oooohs.

I tried to calm things down by saying, "Look, if she's not attracted to the guy sexually, that's her business."

I said this with a little hope inside that it was true, though I doubted it.

"Screw you, Ray," she said. "I'd blow him on the hood of my car with my dad inside honkin' the horn."

Very loud oooohs.

She gave me a manslaughter kind of look that made me turn away.

"Look, forget that," I said. "What we need to do is help Two right now."

"Screw you, Stick," he said, holding his hand gingerly over his stitches. "I didn't ask for your help."

Hey, kids, it's Screw You, Ray, Night.

"Oh, that's right," I said. "I always drive by the emergency room on my way home to check the cafeteria specials."

"All I need is for Thud to lend me a small item," Two said.

"Gt bnt," said Thud, munching his burrito.

"One lousy pine coffin from Thomasini, that's all I'm asking," begged Two. "And . . . maybe a little consulting work."

Two Down laid it all out about the kidnapping and Thud told him he could go screw himself, on account of him not wanting to end up with his old cell back at Bridgewater State.

"I stick my neck out for nobody," said Crowbar.

"*Tootsie?*" said Cementhead.

"*Casablanca,*" said Crowbar.

"Damn!"

"I understand, Thud," said Two Down. "You want to be honest at all costs, especially since you've been so up-front your whole life except for breaking most of the city statutes and codes by the time you could chew solids."

"I'm rehabilitated," he said. "But if you don't get off my fucking back, I can find some guys who aren't and give your head more holes than the Newton Putt-Putt, you get me?"

Silence.

Then I said, "Brilliant idea, Two."

"Pound gerbils," said Two Down, slamming his jar down.

He left with Crowbar, who kind of liked kidnapping generally.

"OK," Crowbar said on the way out. "Stupidest ransom notes."

"Shut the fuck up, Crowbar," said Two Down.

"I'm just sayin'!"

So now everybody had the red ass for everybody else and pretty soon it was just me and the Robitussin and Charlie.

Poor Chunkin' Charlie. He looked late for the sky. I'd never seen him thinner or more frail. I fumbled around awkwardly for a way to do something for him.

"Care to chase some balata tomorrow?" I said. "I know a wonderful little Ross course I can get us on, if you don't mind unplayable lies on the tee box."

He laughed. "Nah," he said. "I got a date with this babe named

Di Alysis starting tomorrow. They say my kidney is staging a work stoppage. Hell, I'm supposed to be at St. Luke's right now. I'm AWOL."

"Bring it along," I said. "I'll give it two a side."

He laughed again. There was just something so open about Charlie's face, even the way it looked now, that I could always tell him anything, so I decided what the hell, I'd tell him about Madeline. I hadn't told anybody else.

The whole time I described her he had a little grin on his face, but every time I asked him why, he said "Whaddya mean?" like it was nothing. I told him how I hadn't felt this way since Deisha, and in fact, I actually felt better, except for one tiny problem, which is that she recently threw me out and I haven't heard from her since.

"Sounds like a sensible girl," he said.

"Damn, Charlie, I'm being serious. I might actually be somewhat, nearly, you know, sort of, almost serious about this girl."

"And they say guys have a commitment problem."

"What would you do?"

"Tell her."

"She won't speak to me. She won't answer my letters. She's pissed off that I'm playing over at the Mayflower, playing with my father and other guys she knows I can't stand. She called me a scratch hypocrite."

"Are you?"

"Well, yeah, but it's just that I'm on the verge of getting my traveling game back. I just need to get a couple of those guys to pop for me for a year and I *know* I can make the Tour, you know? Courtesy Car Heaven? Posin' on your shots while Gary McCord says, 'Boys, that thing's longer'n the March of Dimes.' "

"At 30?"

"At 30."

"Hey, if that's what you want." He did not seem all that thrilled at my prospects. Or, for that matter, his. He looked tired and let down.

There was an awkward pause.

"I just want you to know," he finally said, "that it just hasn't been the same since that damn bet. Everything's changed. Ponky just isn't Ponky anymore."

I just stared at my Robitussin.

"But I will say this." Now his voice was choking a little. "Ponky was the most fun I ever had in my life. And I thank you for that at least. More fun than hotel sex."

He got up very slowly and threw $50 on the table for $12 worth of drinks.

I said I thought it could be like that again.

"I don't know," he said. "I doubt it. Besides, it's gettin' a little late for me and the Uglies."

Then he looked me right in the eye and said it. "I just hope it was worth it."

And he walked out.

Which left me and the Robitussin and an extra-large hole in my gut. I thought how Ponky was possibly going down the tubes here and how it was possibly my fault. Which was funny, since Ponky had actually saved me.

Two years after Deisha, I ran into Two downtown. I hadn't talked to him much in those three years. He told me he'd found a course where there was always action and lots of guys who didn't think their practice swings were televised and the greens committee hadn't yet outlawed laughing. He said as a matter of fact he was going right now to play and why didn't I come, just for old times?

"Where?" I said.

"Ponkaquogue," he said.

"Ponky?" I said. "I thought they turned that into a dump."

"They did," said Two Down. "Par 72."

It was like offering a lit cigarette to a man who hasn't smoked in two years. It was right there in front of me. Ponky. A place that was so decrepit it wouldn't remind me of any of the courses I'd played on and failed on. A place with no memories of my uncle or the career my father took from me. A place where I could play no-pressure, no-disappointment, no-tension golf and not possibly run into Deisha or that body or that face and not care if I shot 68 or 88 because who is going to care once you say you shot it at Ponky? Best of all, a place where my father would never go.

I went. And I went the next day. And I played 36 the next day. And I played every day there for two weeks.

I came to like Ponky so much that I moved to an apartment two miles down the road. Nobody cared where I wrote my little reviews. I'd just modem them in anyway. Who cared anyway? I was twenty-six, had no women in my life. No real family. I decided my family might as well be a bunch of fried-egg-eating guys named Thud and Cementhead and Two Down.

And I once again began a love affair with a 7-iron leaving on that perfect trajectory, juiced up with Tour cheese, just waiting to rip down some cloth; or the shot that was so pure you never even heard it leave the club, the kind of shot you don't even watch in the air, you only watch the pin, knowing that soon it will come floating down so close to the stick that you can holler, "Leaner!"

Now my surrogate family was getting a serious divorce.

Patty O'Connell tapped me on the shoulder and I jumped a little and she pointed at the clock that read 2 A.M. and said, "End of the road, Stick."

"Might be," I said.

....

With no pine box or Sunset *How to Kidnap* book at his disposable, Two Down had Crowbar drive him over to the Roosevelt Park projects for a little makeup audience with Thud.

It was the first time Two Down had ever stepped into the projects and he was actually surprised that every window was not boarded up and every door stoop not littered with crack pipes. There were kids playing out front and two families were barbecuing in the courtyard. Thud's little apartment was actually very neat.

Thaddeus "Thud" Jones was actually a lot like Two Down. He had a wife, two kids, a house and a Buick. He mowed his lawn on Sundays, and, like Two Down, was remarkably ingenious. Thud Jones was the only one among us who could actually outscheme Two Down.

It was Thud, after all, who sat down in the Pit of Despair one day and announced, "Five zops says I can drink all the Coke I want out of Froghair's Coke machine and not spend a dime."

And he won about five different ways, because this Coke machine was the kind where they load the bottles on their side and you drop your 75 cents in and open the long narrow door and pull the bottles out through the metal slats.

Thud simply took a bottle opener out of his black pouch, stuck his cup just underneath one of the bottles and flipped off the cap of a Coke bottle with the opener. The Coke poured directly into his cup underneath.

He was much hailed as the bulbous Edison that day.

Anyway, on this particular visit, Thud told Two Down he was sorry, but he had a policy against contract work and therefore could not see his way clear to kill Concorde, or even merely kidnap him.

"In fact," Thud explained proudly, "I use no violence in my work. I also refuse to deal in drugs or porno or anything tacky. I'm a style guy. You know, like Robert Wagner. *It Takes a Thief?* There aren't many of us left."

"Well," said Two Down, "you've got to help me or start showing me your line of Grecian urns, because this Concorde guy is going to get his money or call in my breathing license. Maybe both."

"What's in it for me?" Thud inquired.

"Uh, well," said Two Down. "See, I'm a little short for jing right now, but I could owe you."

"Wrong," said Thud.

"Thud," begged Two Down. "I'm desperate! Please."

"You'll owe me?" said Thud.

"Big! Big, big, big, big-big-big!"

"Wrong," he said, a huge blinding smile coming to his face. "You will give me three a side for the next year, whenever I want and for whatever amount I want."

"I gotta have a total loss max," said Two Down.

"Two Large," said Thud. "But no time limit, then."

"Bank, I guess," said Two Down.

"Wanna Coke?" said Thud.

Weeks later, when we heard how it was Thud nailed Concorde, we all agreed it was some of his finest work. Thud needed to tail Concorde for only four days before he had something.

"Almost every day he goes to the Copuley," Thud told Two Down.

"Copley?" said Two Down.

"Right. And bangs this tall, blond luscious. He gets there about three, goes up for a minute or two, maybe to get the room the way he wants or something, maybe leave a note or a whip or something. Then he comes back down and leaves a key at the front desk. She shows up there about four and goes up to the room and waits for him. Then he comes in about four-thirty and they probably get busy in there for an hour or so. And they both leave about five-thirty. He drives his turquoise Jag home to his wife and four kids in Brookline. I don't know where she goes."

"Any frameables of the happy couple?" said Two Down.

"Tomorrow," said Thud.

The next day, Thud was waiting in the lobby behind an opened *Herald* when Concorde showed up exactly at three. He had planned to follow Concorde up in the elevator to see what room he was in, but, instead, Concorde got the keys from the desk clerk, put one of the keys in an envelope, wrote a name on it, handed it back to the clerk and left.

Great. The one time he needed it, Concorde had completely skipped the going-to-the-room part.

Now Thud was stymied. He had planned to follow Concorde discreetly up in the elevator and get a look at the room number. But now that was mulch. He had not seen what name he had written on the envelope and he had not seen the room number on the key before it went in. He could not very well pretend the envelope was for him if he didn't even know the name or room number.

He went downstairs and picked up a pay phone.

"Yes, I would like three dozen flowers of whatever kind you got sent to the room of Mr. Stone Concorde, the Copuley Hotel, immediately," he said.

"Copley?"

"Right."

He put them on a stolen Visa he'd picked up on the T that morning and asked that no card be sent with them. He also tried to get them to bring him some food, but they apologized that they had none. He hung up.

When the delivery boy came walking into the hotel in ten minutes with this huge order of Birds of Paradise, the bellboy took them straight up to Concorde's room, with Thud right behind.

Simple. Room 832.

Now Thud went down to the parking garage, and took out of the trunk of his three-hole Buick a half dozen beautifully gift-wrapped boxes—white paper with purple ribbons and a pink-and-black-wrapped hat box and a huge red box with a green bow, all of them different sizes.

He carefully stacked the wrapped boxes on the ground by size, largest on the bottom, picked them up in one giant stack and began heading into the hotel, the huge column of boxes rising three feet over his head and obscuring his view. And though all but one box was empty and the whole mess of them weighed almost nothing, Thud did his best to make them look like they each contained anvils, staggering, weaving and groaning as he went.

You'd be surprised how nice people are to somebody with a bunch of brightly wrapped, heavy presents. A woman hit the parking garage elevator button for him, waited for him to enter the elevator before she got in. Once in the lobby, Thud staggered over to the room elevators and, naturally, people were only too happy to help him. They asked him what floor and he said "Eight" and they held the door for him getting in and getting out, too.

Now he staggered down the hall for a while just in case somebody might be watching him and when he realized he was alone, he made his way to Room 832 and began slowly pacing back and forth with the packages. This is a skill not a lot of people have. You must continually walk as though you just arrived, all the while acting as though the packages are about to give you scoliosis. Your style guys can do it.

After about ten minutes of pacing, a maid finally came out of a linen closet. She walked slowly down the hall until she saw Thud and his burdensome packages, obviously about to collapse under them. She ran to him.

"Miss. Could you . . ." Thud said, motioning with his head to the door, a man helpless to reach what most certainly was the room key in his pocket.

"Oh, *sí!*" she said urgently. She pulled out the master key that hung on a chain in her pocket and opened the door.

"Thank you *sooooo* much," said Thud, staggering into the room with the boxes. "I appreciate it."

Smiling broadly, the maid only nodded *sí, sí, sí,* and let the door close between herself and Thud.

He was in.

After waiting five minutes or so, Thud opened the door, turned the dead bolt so it wouldn't lock, checked the hall, took a bag of sophisticated Nikon camera equipment out of one of the boxes, took the rest into the stairwell and left them on the fourth floor, so that the maid wouldn't happen to see them. Then he went back inside, took his position in the closet, opened his lens to get all the light in the room he could, attached a 200-millimeter zoom and hunkered down for a lazy afternoon of watching skinny people fuck.

At about four-fifteen, he heard the door open. He had the closet door open only a crack. From the smell, he knew it was the woman. If she would try to open the closet door to put anything inside, he would be screwed, but Thud figured they would not need closet space for what they were about to do unless it was kinky, and he was right.

She was a blonde with legs that started weeks ago and what looked like full-grown fun bags, though he couldn't tell. She didn't have much of a curve to her butt. In fact, she had a very flat butt, indeed.

She went into the bathroom and came out in something sexy, though he only saw her from the back. It looked like gold lamé heels, extra-thick lipstick, and a paisley teddy that couldn't have held more than 98 cents of material but had to go for $200 at Pleasures on Newbury.

Thud munched silently on his favorite Little Debbies—perfectly quiet—while she checked herself in the mirror a few times, approved of what she saw, unmade the bed and fluffed the pillows. Then she went to the mini-bar and poured herself an industrial-size highball.

At exactly four-thirty, there was a knock. She answered it slowly. Concorde himself came in and immediately collapsed to his knees in front of her to do some major canyon yodeling, only to have the blonde give him what for with a wire brush she'd been hiding in her hand behind her back. He yelped

"No, Xanadu!" he said. "Pleeease!"

What the fuck, is what Thud thought to himself.

The blonde was remorseless. She only stared hard at him. Silently obeying, he took his pants and silk boxers off and lay over her lap in the chair. She let him have it about twenty-five times with the brush until Concorde actually cried, "No, Mommy, no! I'll be good!"

By this time, they were both so hot, they did a triple salchow onto the bed and looked like they were about to throw down with the kind of ferocity he had seen in nobody else this side of Jefferson and Finsterwald in *Cell Block C.*

Only that's when he noticed it.

The blonde had herself a serious Idaho Russet going. About a ten-incher, angry with a purple head. The blonde was not a luscious at all but a man. A foul taste gathered in Thud's mouth, his erection shrank. Still, he snapped away with his silencer.

He could only stomach about ten shots, but it was enough to prove that what you had here was two boys packing a lot but not going anywhere. The blonde's wig, teddy, heels and Wonder Bra were scattered all around the room. He kept the wire brush in his hand, though. Concorde seemed to enjoy it.

Thud did not go in for this sort of thing. He finished his shots and then closed his eyes and put his fingers over his ears. The last thing he heard was a delighted "No, not the fluorescent bulb!"

The Mayflower's fun couple eventually collapsed in a heap on top of each other, then made their way to the bathroom, both of them, not talking much, but the running sink allowed Thud to calmly open the closet door and walk as quietly out as a man named Thud can walk, taking the stairs in order to pick up his boxes.

He picked up the boxes and rode the elevator to the lobby, the boxes piled high. There, a policeman held the door to the garage elevator for him and admired the presents.

"Somebody's got the goods," said the cop.

"I'll say," said Thud.

18

AS LONG AS everybody's life was turning into a *Geraldo* show, I thought it was appropriate for my insides to do a Cuisinart. I wanted to talk to Madeline, to see her, to smell her, to play mattress tag with her, but she wouldn't answer my calls, telegrams, letters, postcards. So the only way I could see her was to continue playing golf at the Mayflower, which only made her want to talk to me less. That was the thing that brought us together in the first place—our shared hope that one day all the Numerals would contract the deadly plaid virus. The only way I could see her was to do the thing she respected the least.

On the other hand, my father and I were actually getting to know each other, which might have changed things in her eyes—"If you'd wanted to patch things up with your dad, I would understand," she'd yelled—but she wouldn't let me tell her. I even slipped a note on her seat while she was giving drinks to another foursome; the message said, "Gadzooks! My father remembers my name!" She read it, drove over to one of the trash baskets near the tees, set it on fire with a pack of matches and dropped it in.

Hey, at least she read it.

"Getting to know each other" was maybe overstating it. We played twice more at the Mayflower, mostly talking golf. Actually, we didn't talk so much about golf as golf clubs. One golf club. My driver.

I didn't know if he was just looking for a topic of conversation or whether he was infatuated with it or what, but he kept bringing it up. Finally, I let him hit it once. He caught it on nothing but the red insert.

"Did your grandfather hit it?" he asked, fondling it.

"I don't think so," I said, taking it back. "I don't think he even played golf, did he? He just bought it at the charity auction and then he gave it to Uncle Joe."

You could see him thinking, *Why the hell didn't the old bastard give it to me? At least I was a player.*

"Hmmm," he said. "Did Joseph use it?"

"Nah," I said. "In fact, I don't think he even kept it in his bag. He always hit his 3-wood."

"That's typical," said my father. "Why did he sell it to you?"

"He didn't," I said. "He *gave* it to me."

"He *gave* you Jack Nicklaus's 1962 U.S. Open driver? Why in the world would he do a fool thing like that?" He seemed stunned.

"I don't know. I guess he just wanted me to have it."

Very curious, his jones for that driver, but I didn't let it bug me. I was actually considering trying to become friends with him again. After all, we'd hung around together more in these last two weeks than we'd done in the last fifteen years. We'd finally found common ground—chasin' balata—and you'd be amazed what two guys can base a relationship on. The playoffs. Fly tying. Nine-irons. We aren't like women. We don't need to actually *know* each other. I've had lifetime friendships with guys and never known what their wives' names were. I mean, take Thud (the Almost Human). I don't know what he wants out of life, how he feels about his weight, his views on capital punishment or, for that matter, olestra. I just know that when he gets a candy bar, he licks the entire thing, from one end to the other, so nobody will ask for bites. Yet we're friends.

What did I know about Two Down? In six years, I'd never been inside his house, or out to dinner with him and Jane, or actually had a long dinner conversation with him. When Two Down sits down to dinner, he brings dinner dice. I didn't know what his brother in Chicago did for a living, or his dad, or how he stood on abortion. And yet I knew that every day he played he marked his ball with a penny minted in the '70s in hopes that he would shoot in same.

Take me and Charlie. We played golf against each other in the summer, bowled in the winter and pokered at night. We've probably exchanged the same $20 bill back and forth a hundred times and yet I didn't even know what he did for a living. And so what? Charlie and I shared more laughs and beers and funny stories and good times than half the married couples in America.

And so if my relationship with my father was based on cold-jumping 1-irons with a little high fade on them, so what? At least it was something.

And so, when he actually invited me inside the club for the first time to have a drink, I went. I waited thirteen years to play golf with him. I had waited thirty years to have a drink with him. I was ready.

Once I was in, I felt like a bottle of Ripple at a Provence wine tasting. The Mayflower was full of mahogany. The hallways were stuffed with 12-by-18s of exalted past presidents late for the taxidermist. Everything smelled like Clubman hair spray and marinating meatballs. There were only waiters inside—no waitresses—even in the parts of the club where women could go. They were all old, stooped-over black men who looked at their shoes when you spoke to them, the way they learn to do in the South.

In the men's grill, there were guys playing gin and cribbage, none of them smiling, all of them rolling and tossing and moving and then hunching over their little scribble pads to scribble, without saying much of anything. It was so quiet in there it made me ache for Ponky, where Thud might grumble, "Thrw the fkng crd alrdy," and Charlie might say back to him, "Whaddya know? A talkin' 4-H project," and everybody would laugh and Crowbar would be looking at the sausage and Velveeta sandwich Blu Chao had just handed him and say, "As God as my witness, I'm going to live through this, and when it's over, I'll never be hungry again."

"*Gunga Din?*" Cementhead would ask.

"*Gone with the Wind,*" Crowbar would say.

"Damn."

Then Dannie would burp real loud and we'd all break up. Grown-up stuff like that.

....

My father ordered Canadian Club, which gave me that old thirteen-year-old-kid panic in my stomach, and to combat it, I ordered a bit of the Robitussin myself, which I think gives you the full circle of life right there.

"Raymond, I've really enjoyed our golf together," he said, lighting up his one Newport of the day.

I believe it was the first kind thing he'd said to me in sixteen years.

"Me, too," I said.

"You're playing pretty well," he said.

I shrugged. "You're playing pretty well, too."

"Yes," he said. "I think I am, too. In fact, I've decided to make a run at the Senior Tour."

"Really?" I said. What I thought was: "Are you out of your frigging mind? Those guys would tear out your spleen and plunk it in your Efferdent."

Instead, I said, "Good for you. I've been doing a little thinking about trying the Tours again, too."

"Good. Well, that brings me to a little proposition I have for you," he said.

I got that little adrenaline rush, that little bird that escapes from your gallbladder and tries to fly out your throat when something big is about to happen. I was sure he was going to out with some large jing to get me another shot at those fucking courtesy cars. Yesssssss.

He sipped his CC and then said, "I'd like to buy that driver off you."

Six-second brain delay.

"Excuse me?"

"It's the perfect club for my swing. I've been looking for one half that good for years. I can't stand those big metal drivers. So tacky. Now, I've checked into the market for it," he went on, "and it's not as valuable as you may think it is, although, certainly, it is worth a pretty penny. The highest I've been quoted for it is $16,500, but I'm willing to give you $17,000 for it right now because I know it has sentimental value to you."

Is that what this had all been about? This is what all these rounds had been leading up to? A driver deal? No large jing? No Tour? No attempt at understanding each other? Just a golf club?

I know I had molten lava in my eyes. I took a sip and stared at the carpet and tried to calm myself and think. I knew the driver was valuable, but I'd never looked into it, I guess because I knew I'd never sell it. For one thing, I hit it so pure, and for another, it was my uncle's—and my grandfather's. But to hear I'd been hitting a $17,000 driver every day at a place like Ponky made my hands sweat.

"No," I said, trying to calm my voice. "I'd never sell it."

"Raymond, listen to me," he said. "Don't be a fool. Uncle Joe wouldn't have given you that driver if he'd known what it was worth. This is a man who ran a two-pump gas station, son. You don't think he could've used $17,000? He probably gave it to you because he thought it was just some old wooden club that he wasn't going to use anyway once he bought a metal one."

"Sure," I said. "You gotta be the world's leading expert on Uncle Joe, seeing as how you didn't even see him the last five years of his life. You didn't even come to the goddamn funeral."

"Do I regret that, Raymond?" he said, his voice rising a little. "Of course I do. But did I feel the urgent business I had warranted missing it? Yes."

"That must have been some urgent business to last five years,"

I said, my voice getting a little high. "What were you doing, foreclosing on Central America? You never even called him when he was in the hospital, for God's sake."

"Can we get back to the issue?"

"Let's. The issue is how there was only one life that was the model of living and that was yours. Doesn't matter what it was, nobody did it right enough for you. Nobody did it your way. Like the way you'd make me mow the lawn two and three times because you didn't think the lines matched up."

"I was only trying to teach you . . ."

"And then when Travis's lines didn't match up . . ."

"Don't you dare, Raymond . . ."

"Didn't quite match up right, when you thought he'd become an eyesore in the neighborhood, to your friends, like some fucking lawn . . ."

"That's not true . . ."

"You had to do it your way. You couldn't let us work it out. You couldn't let him go when he was ready! Thank God you came riding in to save the day! Well, how's the fucking day going now that you saved it, huh, Father? I guess he had more 'want to' than you that day, huh, Father? Do you see what it takes to win with you?"

"I was the father!" he bellowed. "I was the one who was responsible! Have you ever taken responsibility? Have you ever been the provider? Do you know anything about it? Look at you! If it weren't for self-pity, you wouldn't do anything well. You've got no wife, no family. You don't belong at Charles River. I checked. What have you ever had to provide for?"

"Oh, my mistake. I didn't realize providing takes three-fifths of Canadian Club a night?"

"And I see you don't drink now in protest."

"You taught me that at least."

"Can we just get back to business?"

"Oh, absolutely! Let's get back to business! The business here is that you invited me out here to play golf all these times just so you could smooth me out of a golf club. You didn't give a shit about *me.* You didn't give a shit about getting to know me again after, what is it, six years? No, no, no. Hell, make that thirty years. Tell you what, have your five millionth CC, lifetime, and call me when they find a real person inside you."

I was in full meltdown. I was up out of my chair and walking halfway out when he said, "You're right, Raymond. What I've done here is lousy . . ."

I slowed down.

". . . compared to you using *me* to win a bet."

Silence.

"I'm not stupid, Raymond."

Longer silence.

"I'll give you $18,000," he said. "That's my final offer."

I walked over and slugged down the end of my drink. "That's good," I said. "Because this is *my* final offer. If you ever so much as look up my phone number to call me again, I'll come down to your office or Republican National Headquarters or whatever you call it and floss your teeth with my 7-iron."

I started to walk out.

"Raymond, there's no need to get emotional," he yelled after me.

I went back to my apartment. I was humiliated and torqued off and hurt all at the same time, but mostly torqued off was winning big, so the first thing I did when I got inside was pick up a bottle of Glen Fiddich. Only it started to smell like Canadian Club, so I heaved it against the wall. The way the liquor smashed against the wall sounded so pleasing I decided to go triple OJ. I took every mug out of my cupboard and smashed them in the sink. What the mugs had to do with my fucked-up childhood is unclear. One of them took a very nice cut out of my right eye.

Then I went into my bedroom and started punching the bejesus out of whatever I could, the walls and the roof and the drapes, which got me back by digging one of their damn curtain hooks into my left ring finger.

Then I started beating on my water bed with both fists. Luckily, I broke before it did. The tears just started pouring out of me. I cried like Miss America. All that rage came first and then all that hurt. It was the strangest thing, but then I started talking like an eight-year-old kid, crying and saying, "It's not fair" over and over. I don't know how long I went on like that—five minutes or forty—but when it was done, I felt like whatever kid was inside of me finally got to beat up his father, which is a very nice feeling if you've been waiting thirty years for it.

Not that there was any reason to get emotional.

....

Two Down's problems weren't affecting him that much, other than the fact that he wasn't sleeping, couldn't work and kept laughing loudly into the toilet after every meal.

He stopped going to the Mayflower. His only hope was Thud. So the instant Thud called Two Down to tell him he had the pictures ready, Two called me and I might have accidentally mentioned it to a few guys and next thing you know it was a Chops convention at Don's Mixed Drinks, hungry for the floor show. It was the most eagerly awaited event since Crowbar premiered his edited reel of the Movies' Inadvertently Revealed Famous Nipples.

Thud walked in with a manila envelope and handed it to Two Down. Two Down played it out for drama, inching the print out slowly, painstakingly, with all of us huddling around him. At last, the two figures in the picture could be made out. And that is when he and I and a few others yelled in unison:

"Browning!"

For there he was, engaged in quite a number of non-Vatican-approved positions, up to and including what Dannie used to call the Baked Chicken, in which she would put her ankles behind her ears for convenience.

We were all mildly stunned. The love of Dannie's life, Mr. Tan-and-Teeth, the man she was going to marry, was delivering some serious room service to that snake Concorde.

We all agreed that the first guy that told Dannie about these pictures got their long irons bent and their bag slashed. Thud took the negatives.

Now that he had Two Down's approval, Thud called the Copley Plaza and checked a reservation for Stone Concorde. When they said, "Yessir, Mr. Concorde. We have you down for a half day for this afternoon," Thud simply put a set of prints in an envelope and left them at the front desk under Concorde's name. Along with the pictures, Thud attached a note, which he wrote with his left hand to avoid any detective work, that read:

Dear Mr. Concorde,
Kindly forget about Mr. Bingsley Colchester's little IOU, otherwise your wife and friends will get to enjoy these Kodak moments, too.

Signed,
Management

And this whole plan would've worked, too, if, within two days, Two Down hadn't felt good enough to go back to the Mayflower and play a little golf, unbothered by nettlesome little annoyances like death threats and losing houses. Equipped with a new lease on golf, he made a tee time for the following morning, hoping to continue uninterrupted on his mission to fleece most of Mayflower's industrial bankers of their fortunes, with maybe a soybean trader or two thrown in for variety.

And so it happened that at 8:42 one morning the started yelled out, "The Bingsley Colchester foursome." And Two Down happily and proudly walked up to the first tee with his group, much to the annoyance of Stone Concorde, who was hitting balls on the practice range. Stone Concorde did not do a whole lot of losing in this life and it was not sitting well with him.

"What did that man just say?"

The question was asked by a fortyish-looking woman hitting 5-irons next to Concorde, a certain Mim Smythe who had been around the club for years.

"What?" said Concorde, distracted.

"Did that man just say the Bingsley Colchester foursome is up next?"

"Yeah," said Concorde sullenly.

Mim Smythe looked surprised and puzzled.

"That's amazing!" she said.

Concorde was starting to get annoyed. Damn women. He stopped hitting drivers. "Why?"

"Because that was *my* name!" she said. "Of course, that was, gosh, I hate to say, seventeen years ago. But I always thought it was, you know, a unique name." She even went on to say that she couldn't remember ever hearing anyone else have that name in all her years at the Mayflower.

Concorde got very intrigued.

"I thought your name was Mim Smythe," he said.

"It's actually Bingsley Smythe," she explained. "Colchester was my maiden name. Well, I always hated the Bingsley—people called me Binky—so I started going by my middle name."

Concorde looked like he had just discovered electricity.

"Bingsley M. Colchester!" Concorde yelled.

"Exactly, Stone!" she said, a little flattered at his sudden interest. "That was my name!"

"You weren't a member here before you were married, were you?"

"Oh, I've always been a member, before and after. In fact, I was the first woman member of the Mayflower. My father was a member and so, as a legacy, I couldn't be denied membership. But when I married Chase, he was already a member, so we just got rid of my membership and I became part of his."

"Maybe not," Concorde said.

"Excuse me?" she said.

But by then, Concorde was off on a sprint to the clubhouse. All we can figure is he went to the general manager's office and checked on Bingsley Colchester. Somebody up there must've told him the truth. There was only one Bingsley Colchester, a female. Turns out that for the last twenty years the club has kept a few female members on the roster—at no charge—in case some feminist state legislator busybody starts coming around asking questions like how many women members the club has.

Grinning, Concorde set up at a table overlooking the 18th hole and waited for whoever this was pretending to be Mrs. Miriam Smythe.

When I finally got up off of that water bed, I believe I felt like a full-grown adult for the first time in my life. There were two people I wanted to call right away. The first was Madeline. I got a very depressing answering machine and it wasn't hers. It was New England Bell's.

"The number you have dialed, 555–4687, has been . . . disconnected."

So I sat there, thinking a while, sort of numb. I thought about what finally standing up to my father had felt like, and I don't know why, but I decided to call Charlie. Maybe because Charlie reminded me so much of my uncle or maybe because I liked him so much or maybe because for the first time I had room in my complicated little brain to worry about somebody else for once. I was connected to his room at St. Luke's.

"Yes?" said a voice, a youngish female's, kind of familiar, maybe not.

"Yes, speak to Charlie, please?"

There was a silence.

"I'm terribly sorry," said the voice. "He passed away two hours ago."

19

WHAT WE FIGURED Stone Concorde did was pay somebody to shadow Two Down as he walked home from the Mayflower that afternoon, fresh with 400 zops in his pocket from his first real kill at his new Ashworth hunting grounds.

We figured that's what happened, because at about nine that night the doorbell rang at his little pale yellow house on Waldeck Avenue with the golf-ball mailbox, the golf-ball doorknobs, and the golf-ball-shaped floor mat.

Jane, his long-suffering wife, looked through the flagstick-shaped door window, turned the putter-head door handle and found a man with a magnificently tanned face, perfectly combed hair, broad shoulders and a Steinway smile. Next to him was a very large Slavic-looking man in an Armani suit.

"Is your husband home?" he said.

"Sure," she said, and went and got him.

When he arrived, Two Down started to step back, thinking Concorde might crack his kneecaps for him, but the large Slavic in the nice suit already had hold of his left arm and gently flicked him outside onto the porch. Concorde closed the door behind them.

"Hello, Bingsley," said Concorde.

"Hello, Stone," said Two Down, white-faced. "You lost?"

"No," said Concorde. "No, actually, I think I just won."

Pause.

"Ohhhh," said Two Down. "You're probably wondering what I'm doing here. Well, this is business. You know, some of these middle-class people want to sell some of their old heirloom gems and, uh, you and I aren't above slumming it to turn a dollar now and then, are we, Stoney?"

"In your slippers?" asked Concorde.

Two Down looked down at his head-cover-shaped slippers with the little flagsticks coming off each big toe.

"*Very* hospitable folks out here in Dorchest . . ."

The Slavic man brought a very mean knee into Two Down's midsection. While Two was bent over, gasping for breath, Concorde whispered the following sweet somethings into his ear:

"Listen to me, Leonard Petrovitz. If I don't get my money in forty-eight hours, I'm going to make three calls. The first is to a buddy of mine. A Mr. Walker Singleton. You know him? President of New England Bell? Your boss? I think he'd love to hear what you've been up to, working as a cook at the club on company time. The second is to my lawyer. I want to ask him to break the current standing record for ways a lawyer can pencil-fuck a tiny little schmoe like you the rest of his life. Forgery, fraud, wire fraud, maybe a little tax evasion. The third is to a friend of mine at First Boston Bank. He owes me a favor. I'm going to ask him to call your loan. Would that be an inconvenience for you at this time, Leonard Petrovitz?"

Two Down didn't feel much like answering, as he was busy spitting blood. In the last two weeks, Two Down had seen more blood than the movie council.

"Ten thousand. Cash. Forty-eight hours. Deliver it in a wrapped box to the guard at the front gate of the club."

Concorde started to walk off, then turned around. "And if I EVER see those photos again, that lovely wife of yours will have a very hard time identifying the body down at county morgue. OK?"

The Slav kicked Two Down forward so that he was able to do a face plant on the concrete step of his front stoop.

That's about when Jane came out and shrieked in horror at her bleeding, scarred and doubled-over husband.

"Damn," Two Down groaned. "Those Watchtower people get pushier every day."

When the luscious you love has either left town or hidden and your father has once again treated you like a piece of smelt and one of your best friends had the nerve to go and die without any consideration of your feelings, there is only one thing to do besides hide the razor blades and the rope.

Go to the library.

I found a book on golf antiques and looked up my MacGregor 693 and read this:

> This may be the finest modern driver in existence, though there were only 250 made. Depending on condition, a MacGregor with a rosewood finish and a red center can be worth up to $17,000.
>
> The most valuable, though, may never be found again. Jack Nicklaus used his MacGregor 693 to defeat Arnold Palmer at the 1962 U.S. Open at Oakmont, the victory that is generally considered the turning point in Nicklaus replacing Palmer as the King of Golf. Unfortunately, Nicklaus, only twenty-two at the time and euphoric, turned over that club to a small Pittsburgh charity immediately after the win. Its whereabouts are unknown. It is estimated that if the club were ever found, it would be worth twice the usual amount.

This was not really exciting news to me, other than it meant I could go back on tour.

All I'd have to do is sell that club and I *knew* I'd be back out there. I had gotten my game back. Qualifying for the Nike Tour would be easy as Go Fish. My first reaction was to go tell Dannie all about it, but Dannie had blown me off like lint. Still, I could take Madeline with me. She wouldn't be a bad caddie, would she?

Sure as hell would look better than Squeaky. The question was, *could* I sell it?

As I walked to the checkout desk, I remembered what my father had said. *It's not as valuable as you may think.* Weasel.

I told Miss Big Hair behind the desk a small lie.

"You wouldn't believe what I found in that," I said. "A fifty-dollar bill."

"Like, seriously?" she said, snapping her Bubble Yum.

"Yeah," I said. "I wonder if you could call up the name of the last renter of that book so that I could send it to him."

"Guuuuuyyyy, you're soooooo nice!" she said.

She started punching keys until she seemed to find something.

"It's a William Davenport Hart," she said. "You want me to write down the address?"

"No," I said. "I know him."

"That's sooooooo lucky!"

"Isn't it?" I said.

Madeline quit.

That's what they told me the next day at the Mayflower gate. Nobody knew what had become of her. Nobody answered her apartment door. Nobody knew a forwarding address.

There was a very large black hole in my stomach, which I filled up with grog in the Ponky clubhouse. Dannie was behind the pro shop counter. At least the person who used to be Dannie. Now what was back there was some kind of Junior League Social Committee Chairwoman from Hell. She had on white pearls, a high-collar turtleneck with a business jacket over it and Chanel you could smell even through Blu's fried bologna and Cheez Whiz sandwiches, three of which were stacked in front of Thud. Nobody else was in there except Crowbar, and he was reading *News of the World.*

I missed Chunkin' Charlie already.

I had some time to think. My life was coming down to this: Either (a) Forget Madeline, sell my driver and go after the Nike Tour or (b) . . .

"You know what I'd like to see?"

"Oh, Christ," I said. "Not now, Crowbar. Please not now!"

"I'm just sayin'," he said, "you wanna know what I'd like to see?"

"No!"

I clutched my haircut.

"Well, you know how every game some guy rents a plane that flies over the stadium, right? And behind the plane is this big, long banner and it usually says something like 'Cindy, Will You Marry Me? Love, Jeff.' You know, something like that?"

"No. I have no idea what you mean."

"Sure. 'Cindy, Will You Marry Me? Love, Jeff.' So what I'd like to see, just one time, is another plane come along about five minutes later that says, 'No chance, Limpdick—Cindy.' Wouldn't you love to see that?"

"I'd consider my life whole."

"Me, too."

Or . . . (b) find Madeline if it took the rest of my life, screw golf, screw golf clubs and screw my father.

In my heart, I wanted to try No. 2, but I came to my senses. This ain't *Wuthering Heights.* I chugged the rest of my beer and chose No. 1.

I was about to get up and go call somebody at Club World or Vintage Golf Collectibles when Two Down walked in, shaking like Katharine Hepburn.

He had a big, ugly bandage on his forehead covering something you knew had to be uglier. His sweater was on inside out and his shoes were untied.

"Jesus, you look like something Thud coughed up."

He grabbed me hard by the shoulders. "Stick, you gotta help me!"

"Is every day with you *Rescue 911?*"

"No kiddin' around! This is serious!"

"Now what?"

He explained how Concorde and the Slavic dude had turned him into a sort of complicated blood clot and how his life was *this close* to being toaster crumbs and how he had an idea that would maybe solve the whole thing.

"Sck on an exhst pp?" Thud mumbled.

"Double or nothing," Two Down said proudly.

The Pit was stunned into quiet.

"Ohhhh, perfect!" I said. "Why didn't I think of that? It's so simple! This way, if you lose, you can be down $20,000 and not only won't you have your house, you won't even be able to afford one of those little urns Thud sells to put your ashes in after one of Concorde's hired hands turns you into soot."

"No, no, no!" he said. "It wouldn't be just me against Concorde. It'd be me and a partner against Concorde and his partner."

"Who?"

Pause.

I looked at those eyebrows. They were doing jumping jacks. I looked at Thud and Crowbar. They were enraptured.

They were all looking at me.

"No, no, no, no, no."

"I put up all the money!" Two said. "You're not up for any of it. Neither is Concorde's guy. It's all on my ass."

"Goddamn no," I emphasized. "Besides, you don't *have* any money. No."

"He doesn't even know I'm bringing you," he said. "Look, I've seen you play lately. You're fuckin' Van Goghin' it. I know you can whip anybody he brings. Anybody."

"Goddamn screaming bitch-ass no!" I enunciated, covering my ears.

"Too late," he said. "I already told Concorde you agreed. We've got to meet them over at the Bostonian Hotel in an hour to talk ground rules."

"Tell him you lied," I said.

"Stick, I made a big thing about Ponky, about how great the players were here, about how if the Numerals had to play Ponky, they'd never break 90 and how the best players in town are right here, not over there. How they're all spoiled by their perfect fucking greens and perfect fucking divots and no sprinklers going off on their backswing and nobody getting pleurisy at impact on them. He said I was full of shit. He said a Mayflower 20 could beat a Ponky 10 any day of the week and 36 on Sunday. He said a scratch at the Donkey would be a 12 there. It's a perfect setup! I really suckered this guy in, Stick!"

"Sucker him back out!" I said, holding the phone for him.

"Why do you care?" he said. "It's my ass on the line!"

"One, I don't wanna be responsible for your ass, or your wife's ass, or your house's ass," I said. "Two, look."

I showed him my black-and-blue left hand from my twelve-round decision over my apartment, then I showed him my eye socket by Ginsu.

"Shit," he said. His eyebrows dropped a story.

"Why the hell would Concorde agree to this bet anyway?" I asked. "Wouldn't he rather just beat you by himself?"

"Well, I told him a little lie. I told him I've got $20,000 equity in my house. I told him we'd play for that, but only if we did it my way. I think he knows it's the only way he's gonna get any whip-out."

"How much do you have in your house?"

"Maybe half that."

"Wonderful."

"Please? I'll never ask you for another favor as long as I live."

I thought about it. Blu Chao, Crowbar and Thud were all staring at me with hangdog looks, like I was the guy in charge of deciding whether or not to boil the puppy.

"No," I said.

They all groaned.

"Wanna know who *his* partner is?" Two Down asked.

"No," I said.

"Your dad."

I walked into the Bostonian in my holeyest jeans, my Smiths T-shirt and my decrepit UMass letter jacket.

No Red Sox hat, though, the one my uncle had given me. I couldn't find it.

I had no idea why I was doing this, except that I hated to see Two Down end up in some Slavic guy's trunk. Or maybe I wanted to do it to have one final shot at my father, play against him one time—no worrying about protecting the Captain's feelings—and make him hurt where it hurt him the most, in the little box on a scorecard where you have to write your score. *Honestly, I think I could beat you, Raymond.*

Screw "providing." Screw "business." The one thing that meant the most to him was being a better player than me. That was how he justified stiffing me for the money for my golf career. If he was a better player than me and *he* wasn't out there, how could *I* be?

Two Down was in that same phony Mayflower outfit he'd bought, a toxic explosion of planets Aureus and the Sears Johnny Miller collection. My father was in a tweed sports coat with a scarf, and Concorde was in some $1,200 Versace with a $120 silk tie.

I refused to look my father in the eye, staring only at Concorde.

He seemed surprised to see me, but he didn't say anything. We sat down without handshakes.

"Here's how it will work," I said. "We play the first 9 holes at Ponky, the back 9 at the Mayflower. My father and I will play scratch. Two and Concorde get 15 each. Total team score. Tomorrow morning at eight. I gotta be at a funeral at twelve-thirty. USGA rules. That's the deal or nothing."

"Excuse me?" asked my father, aghast. "You want to actually *play* Ponkaquogue? Ponky, the dog run next to the Mayflower? You want to play nine holes there?"

"Don't worry, Father," I said. "I know a guy who can get us on."

"Why play a shithole like Ponky," said Concorde, "when you can play the Mayflower? I mean, if you're worried about the guest fees, we'll cover those."

"Screw the guest fees," I said, the blood rushing to my cheeks. "Two Down was right. The best players I've seen are at Ponky. You guys couldn't find your ass with a map at Ponky."

I said I bet these two sweethearts with their starched underwear and their country-club swings and their orchids on their lunch plates wouldn't be able to draw it back at a real test of golf like Ponky. I mentioned that, top to bottom, our guys were better golfers, players who could invent shots from all kinds of trouble and lies, and that from what I'd seen Mayflower players need it to be sitting up like they just brought it on room service to make any kind of decent swing. I also told them that golf was invented in a muni like Ponky—St. Andrews—and not at some outdoor grass museum where the greenskeeper had all the burrowing animals on retainer.

"I like you two guys," Concorde said. "You're complete dreamers."

He looked at my father.

"Play the front 9 at Ponky and the front 9 at the Mayflower," Concorde said. "We're not allowed to start on number 10."

I looked at Two Down. Each 9 at the Donkey was equally horrific in its own charming way. And I thought the front 9 at the Mayflower was a little easier than the back, which we might need, since I wasn't sure Two Down could stay with Concorde straight up and my hand was not exactly going to be purin' it.

"Bank," Two Down said.

"There's only one little problem," said Concorde. "Where's the house deed?"

Two Down pulled it out of his shirt pocket, folded it up and flipped it to Concorde.

"What are you gonna do for the rest?"

"What rest?" Two Down said.

"The rest of the twenty in case you lose."

"Blow me," said Two Down skittishly.

At that point, my father took a sheet out of his briefcase and slid it across the table. "You have $10,300 equity in the house," he said.

Never try to bluff the bank CEO.

"My furniture and stuff has got to be worth five," Two Down said, trying to recover.

Concorde chuckled. "I've seen your furniture. When does *Sanford and Son* need it back?"

"Get bent, catalogue boy," said Two Down.

"What about a car?"

"I got a car," said Two.

"What is it?"

"A Ford sports sedan."

"What *is* it?"

Two Down gave up. "A sporty-looking Pinto."

They both laughed.

"It's got low mileage!" Two Down insisted.

They laughed harder.

I felt bad for Two.

"Zero, minus towing charges." Concorde laughed.

They decided all his worldly possessions were worth about $2,000.

"So that's twelve, total," Concorde said.

My father looked at Concorde. Concorde looked at his Rolex and his gold wrist bracelet and said, "Do you realize I'm *wearing* more than your entire net worth?"

Two Down just stared at the ashtray, embarrassed. Death by ball-mark repair tool would be too good for this sonofabitch.

"Let's forget the whole thing," said Concorde. "I'll keep the deed. I'll send somebody by with the papers in the morning. I expect you out by noon."

They both got up to leave, Concorde sliding the deed into his pocket.

Two Down had a fear in his eyes like I'd never seen. Just a nonblinking pure panic. He grabbed my thigh like a vise.

"Hold on," I said, prying Two's hand off me. "Just hold on. I'm good for the other $8,000."

Two Down's exhale almost blew the napkins off the table.

Concorde looked at my father, who nodded.

"Oh, Christ," Concorde finally said. "I'll do it. Probably the only way this loser is ever going to pay me."

"Then it's a wager," said my father.

"Bet," said Two Down.

"Bet," said Concorde.

I said nothing.

"What about you, Raymond?" said my father.

I took a deep breath. For the first time I looked straight at my father. I was in a do-or-die mood. The idea had been rummaging around in my head for a while, but now it was going to come out. Really, this testosterone was going to kill me someday.

"One more thing," I said to my father. "You and I play for the driver. Straight up."

"What . . . ?" he said.

"You heard me. We play for the driver. I know what it's really worth, Father—35 G's—and you sure as hell know it, too. We have the same librarian. If my team loses, you go home with the driver."

"And if my team loses?" my father asked.

"You sponsor me at the Mayflower."

He spit out his sip of CC.

"And cover my initiation fee."

"Why, you've lost your mind. I could never . . ."

"Bullshit, Father. I know how it works. I'm a legacy of a member. A cart girl I used to know told me all about it. A legacy is automatically in, as long as I have the membership fee. I can't be blackballed. What is it now, Father, about $37,500, right? The numbers crunch just right, don't you think?"

I knew that the $35,000 I might get for the driver wouldn't set me up on tour the way I needed to be set up. I needed to fly everywhere, not drive. You try to drive twenty-one straight hours from Stockton to Cheyenne and be ready to tee it up Tuesday morning in the qualifying against some phenom with brand-new graphite Calloways and his dad's Lear. I didn't want to have to eat Gainesburgers for a week in order to make it to Pensacola.

If I belonged to the Mayflower, I knew I could work those guys for some money. I mean, on the whole, they weren't all Roy Cohn, were they? I could get used to life there, couldn't I? I know I could, at least until I convinced somebody to sponsor me.

Two Down grinned. Concorde even allowed himself a smile. William Davenport Hart tried to stare a hole in my forehead.

I never blinked.

He pulled out his one Newport of the day without taking his eyes off mine.

He lit it, took one long drag and nodded.

20

AS I WRESTLED my pillow that night, I couldn't help thinking about what might happen if we lost.

My three best friends would be gone. Hell, two were gone already. Chunkin' Charlie, one. Dannie was pretty much a vapor already. I was toast on that no matter what happened. If she ever saw those pictures, she'd never speak to us again. And if she never saw those pictures, she'd probably never be around anymore anyway. My only hope was that she'd find out on her own, without photographic aid.

Two Down, three, would be gone for sure. He told me he'd probably go to Chicago and live with his brother, the mailman, until he could get a job there.

I don't know why he felt like he had to, except maybe he could not face life around Ponky if he went and lost the biggest match in the history of Ponky, not to mention my $8,000, which was going to be a bitch for me to scrape up and even harder to get from him in Chicago. Two Down was the Chops' Yaz, their knight in spikes, their patron saint of the double-back press. He was the little wiry guy who would take on King Kong with a Swiss Army knife and want half the action. He was a little man with huge dreams and hopes. He stood five-eight, five-nine tops, 155 pounds with all his change in his pockets, yet he shopped at Coppman's Big and Tall Shop in Newton. He'd find something he liked and tell the salesman, quite seriously, "Take the sleeves up a little on this and bring in the waist and it'll be perfect." The Chops loved him for it. If he left Ponky, they might all impale themselves on their spike wrenches.

Hard to believe I couldn't sleep. Ever since that day when my father rejected my request for money, I guess I'd dreamt of the day when I'd get him head to head and whip him like an egg cream.

Actually, when I thought about it, I knew it went further back than that. Deep down, in a dark, spinning ball somewhere inside me, begun on all those horrible tearful days on the course with him, I knew I had a hatred for him and yet a desire to make him proud of me, at last, to finally do something that kept him quiet; to finally do something that he just thought was, finally, silently, good enough and required no comment. Now, here was my chance.

Then again, I could very well pull the rare double tomorrow. I'd already lost the girl and now I could throw in the career, to say nothing of my own dignity. If I lost, I knew there was no chance I'd ever resurrect it again. If golf left me, too, along with the driver, Madeline, the Chops, I couldn't imagine what I'd feel like inside.

I really don't think my father wanted that driver to sell. I think he wanted the driver in the same weird way that I wanted to beat him—to show the old doc what he could achieve, to not only defeat his father but have part of his father with him. He might have felt it worse. One thing, though. He never got to tell his father how he felt. Even if I died penniless, homeless, driverless and Maddy-less, at least I had that now.

For Concorde, it wasn't just the money—though, unlike Two Down, he really *did* bet for the money and he didn't care if it came from his friends or his enemies or his mother. No, there was something more at stake for him. Word would be out. Concorde would be putting the Mayflower's reputation on the line here. If Bill Hart and Concorde Stone lost to muni hacks, to Dorchester dirt, they'd never live it down, not in the gin room, not at the Snowflake Balls, not at the member-member tournaments.

In that sense, we had nothing to lose. You can't fall out of a basement window. But if they lost, they'd need the Witness Protection Program.

Morning was a cloudy, chilly, morose affair. I went to the range at Ponky and I was surprised to see that already some country-club guys were hanging around. They were there in their fine wool slacks, $300 sweaters, Cole-Haan loafers and Ray-Bans. Even Captain Considine himself was there, ready to sniff and act official if necessary.

The Chops were out *en force,* too. Hoover was on the range hitting balls, his left leg encased in a blue plastic form that kept his knee bent. He had a strap that went around his body and his elbows to keep his elbow from flying on the backswing. He was also trying a Japanese gadget called the Power Tee, in which the ball sat in a little half cup of plastic on a small peg. That meant Hoover had now tried wood tees, rubber tees, pink lady tees, sponge tees, metal tees, Bakelite tees, cardboard tees, sand tees and now Power Tees. Every one of these gadgets he was wearing, he said, was designed to add 15 yards to his drive.

I remember Dannie once looked at him and said, "Hoov, I've been doin' some figgerin' and if all them things work, you'll be knockin' your tee ball dang near 450 yards. You'll have to be chippin' *back* to par 4s."

I walked up to him and said, "Hello, Hoover. Got a new driver?"

"Most certainly," he said. "The Colossal Cathy. Just came UPS. It's entirely grooveless. As you may or may not know, grooves are what impart backspin on the ball, which takes away distance. This is entirely grooveless."

"Sos yr swng," munched Thud.

All the other Chops were there, too, except Dannie and Crowbar. Blu Chao had actually changed the coffee filter and washed the pot in the ball-washing machine—twice—so it was indeed a gala atmosphere.

This moment was being savored by the Chops. They must have found it hard to believe that wealthy, important people were about to come to Ponky and not just as a place for their oil pans to drip during the Mayflower Carousel.

They were going to change their shoes in our gravel parking lot and set foot on our fallowed grounds. It was like the Visigoths coming to the Hun company picnic.

"Twenty thousand, huh?" whooped Meltdown. "Hoo-boy, I'd be nervous as a gerbil in a gay bar."

"You guys gonna play Reversals?" asked Cementhead.

"No," I said.

"Gotchas?" said Meltdown.

"No," I said.

"Murphys?" asked Thud.

"No," I said. "Not Murphys. Not Mandatory Mulligans. No Alohas. Not Pig and Wolf. Not anything except straight-ahead match play, both scores count, 18 holes, loser shaves head and leaves town."

Cementhead's eyes widened.

"Cement, I'm kidding."

"I knoooooow," he said, kicking at the ground.

The rules were pretty straightforward. We'd written them down on a napkin at the Bostonian the night before in case there were any arguments. It read:

Match play.
18 holes.
Front 9, Ponkaquogue Municipal.
Front 9, the Mayflower.
Strict USGA rules.
Total team score.

Since my father and I were about scratch and Concorde and Two Down were both about 15s and since both balls count, we decided to play the whole thing straight up. Two Down and I playing somebody straight up was such a delicious proposition a few of the Chops made some side wagers with a few of the Numerals. I saw Thud get $100 down with the Captain, though the Captain didn't have the Benji on him.

"It's OK," said the penitentiary-faced man with the knish crumbs on his face to the white Boston businessman. "I trust you for it."

Startled, the Captain just said, "Uh, why, well, thank you."

I had to slip Froghair an extra $20 to let us on without benefit of the pipe on account of he didn't seem to care that we were defending the honor, integrity and esteem of his little run-down vacant lot of a golf course.

Two Down showed up and had all his trophies out of the trunk and on the ground, looking for, gee, his golf bag, when Thud told him to hold the psych job this morning as his worthy opponents weren't there yet.

"Oh," he said, disappointed.

Two hit some balls but couldn't concentrate. He kept asking where Crowbar was every three minutes or so. It seemed to unsettle him.

"Two, would you forget about Crowbar?" I said. "We need Crowbar here like we need goiters. We just need to play relaxed. Play our game. I'm gonna julienne my father's ass and you're gonna stomp that cocksucker Concorde flatter than left-out beer. Christ, we should be 5 up by the time we make the turn, OK?"

"Yeah, yeah, OK," he said, but he kept looking around just the same.

At five minutes to go, Stone and my father pulled up in Stone's Jag and climbed out—in uniform. They were both wearing *the exact same outfits*—hot-pink pants and hot-lime sweater that had a logo on the chest and both sleeves. They each had two on their Titlist visors, one on the front and a little one on the side.

"Say no to Day-Glo," I whispered.

"Two dollars," Two Down said. "Logo violation."

"You boys workin' the late shift at the roller rink after?" Meltdown asked.

They paid no mind. Just behind them came their two caddies—Haircut and First-and-Third—arriving in an old Trans Am. The Numerals must've hit balls at the Mayflower and then drove over, not wanting the unnatural and unholy green stain on their clubs that comes from the lovely green Astroturf mats at Donkey Golf.

The Chops were already in awe.

"Jesus," said Cement. "Their *caddies* drive nicer cars than us."

Seeing them there felt so strange. How many afternoons had we fantasized about what it would be like to finally have a couple of chump Numerals walk through that front gate with American money in their pockets? And now, at last, here they were, right in front of our faces.

All that bull we'd talked was going to get tested now. Was all our bravado just a cocktail we drank to feel better about not being rich enough, successful enough, significant enough to make it through their wrought-iron gates? Now the lucky rich bastards from behind the gates had come to us.

I wore my usual fall ensemble—jeans, the Swarthmore sweatshirt with the firecracker hole. Sure missed my hat, though.

"So get on with your fucked-up little party," Froghair yelled from the pro shop. "I got a tee time right behind ya and I hate waitin' on idiots."

The Numerals looked at him.

"Charming staff," said Concorde.

"We insist on it," I said.

We all proceeded to the 1st tee, a dogleg left around the net. They won the tee toss. The match was about to begin.

I looked around for Crowbar to say something, but he was MIA, so I decided it was up to me.

"All my life I've wanted to lead a bunch of men in a desperate battle."

"Mr. Smith Goes to Washington?" Cementhead said.

"Patton."

"Damn!"

The Numerals stepped up and Concorde took a practice swing.

"Lord," Thud said loud enough to be heard. "Don't take that swing outta town cuz you cain't get parts for it."

The Chops laughed. The Numerals glared.

One of the stuffed-Polo-shirts got a good whiff of dump gas and cringed. "Good Lord! What IS that smell?"

"Do you like it?" Two Down asked. "It's Blu's special today."

Still and all, Concorde and my father both hit good shots, little right-to-left numbers that kicked into the wrong-sloping hill and rolled down in good position.

"Good swing, Stoner," said one of the Numerals.

"Yeah, Stoner," said Meltdown.

Two Down gave me a Milk of Magnesia look, put a whipsaw spinout nuclear accelerator swing on a driver and hit a screamer that was so low and hard it could've sailed under a Chevy Impala and touched neither earth nor oil pan. Still, it ended up all right.

"Did anybody see Two Down swing?" Thud asked.

"No, go ahead, Two, show 'em what you're made of," somebody else said.

Two Down didn't even smile. He looked like he was just trying to get the flashbulbs to stop going off in his eyes every time he inhaled.

I kissed the head of my uncle's driver for luck and put a Harley-Davidson grip on my driver, which was the only choice I had considering the bandage on my hand. Still, I jury-rigged it pretty well and drew a pretty little ball down there just past my father.

Professor had shown up and offered to be my caddie and he practically needed pliers to pry the MacGregor out of my hands, my grip was so tight.

"We're cool, Carl," he said.

Everybody hit their approach shots. My father and I were on the green to the right about 20 feet away, Two Down had unspeakable-hooked one into the driving range net left of the green and probably totally O'Brien, and Concorde had hit it to the left side of the green about 25 feet from the stick.

I kept an eye on him. He was walking ahead of us and fast and so I sidled over to my father as we walked and said, "Just between you and me, watch the creative ball-marking class your partner occasionally teaches."

"Don't be petty, Raymond," my father said. "It doesn't become you."

"Just watch," I said.

Sure enough, Concorde was up to his old magnetic self. He marked his ball with his left hand, leaning on his putter, which was about three feet in front of him and closer to the hole. Then he pulled the old switcheroo again. In the blink of an eye, a new mark was three feet in front of him and he had palmed the other mark. My father's eyes suddenly showed a whole lot of white.

"Classy friends you have," I said to him.

Two Down was caught like a grouper in the net, took an unplayable, tried to hit one, missed, took another unplayable and then chipped on for what looked like a sure 8. Then Concorde put his ball down, picked up the mark and started to study the line.

"Stone, no need to worry about the line," I said. "You just lost the hole."

Stone looked up and said, "Excuse me?"

"Sorry, Stoner," I said. "A caddie I know told me about you. The USGA rule book specifically says that putting your ball from three feet closer in is a violation. Picky bastards."

Concorde stood up straight and said, "How dare you insult . . ." and started toward me.

"Anybody else see it?" I said.

I looked at my father.

He looked at me, then at Stone. Then he began walking toward the next tee box.

"This is outrageous!" he yelled, standing there, red-faced and burning up. "This is outrageous!"

What can you say when your ass has just been caught colder than a Popsicle?

He hurried to catch up with my father.

"Will, do you know your son here worked as a caddie at the club until he was fired?"

My father looked at me.

"Is that true?"

I looked at Professor.

"Yeah," I said sheepishly. "But I hated all the black-tie functions."

Professor and First-and-Third grinned.

"You bastard," Concorde said to me. Then he looked at my father and his face went even whiter. "No offense, of course, Will."

Even the caddies busted out laughing then. Things were going nicely. We were 1 up and they hadn't even had to putt a Froghair volcano jar yet.

Two Down came up to me as we walked and said, "Nice job, pards."

I mentioned that maybe he ought to try and swing harder and faster at this next one in hopes of setting his shoelaces on fire.

On to the 2nd hole, the gruesome par 3 over Nuke Pond. My father looked like he'd just sucked on a lemon as he studied the hole. First of all, that's a mat tee there and I don't know if these two guys had *ever* hit off a mat tee. But we had. We were mat-tee aficionados. Depending on what decade Froghair had bought them, some mat tees were spongy, allowing you to hit a high shot, and some were old and hard and dry like this one, which meant you were not going to get the club down and through the ball, so the best you could hope for was to take one club less and knife one.

Unfortunately, Two Down put an unphotographable swing on his 4-iron and snap-hook-smothered one directly into the pond. Me, I toed one up there to about 25 feet from the pin. The two Numerals, however, had no clue about mats and blew what looked like 3-irons over the green.

"Nice facility," said my father.

"Yes," said Hoover. "Management spends literally *hundreds* of dollars a year here in maintenance alone."

Two Down tossed one down in the circle of shame—drop circle—and hit an 8-iron on and our two worthy opponents chipped on, too. But lo and behold, I drained my 25-footer for birdie and Two Down lagged up to an inch for his 5, which meant that one of the Numerals needed to make his 10-footer to tie us, both of them to beat us.

My father's putt jumped off a rock at the start, hit a dirt patch and skidded left halfway there and wound up about 4 feet short and 4 feet right. The Chops howled deliciously.

"Welcome to Ponky, boys," Thud said with a leer.

"Can't believe that putt didn't go in," I added.

Concorde hit a very good putt that looked like it was right in the heart, but as it approached the hole, sure and true, it hit the lip of a Froghair jar and pushed out right.

"L b dmnd," munched Thud through some Li'l Debbies.

"Something must've been wrong with that cup," said Hoover.

"No fucking joke, Einstein," said Concorde, staring bitterly at his golf ball.

"Yeah," said Meltdown. "Usually Froghair pulls those cups out a little worse."

Two up.

Just then, Two Down's face brightened. Up ahead, trundling alone in his golf cart, his ponderous gut cleaved by the steering wheel, came Crowbar.

21

YOU THINK OF all the wonderful ways somebody who had never played the Donkey might be thrown off his game—the brown greens, the cement tees, the tarmac fairways—but you never think of things like Crowbar.

The Numerals had no idea of the horror. What mind-warping topic would Crowbar want to bring up today that would drive them out of their gourds? Would he once again put forth his theory that guys who are cheating on their wives should always do it with somebody a foot taller? "Nobody believes you could hose somebody taller than you. They gotta think she's your secretary." Or maybe he'd muse about how nice it would be to have a little piano follow you around, so that anytime anybody got boring, they could start playing that little light piano music in the background like on Johnny Carson and you could simply say, "Well, this has been fascinating, but the music is playing. You've gotta go now." For once, I was actually looking forward to the King of the Non Sequiturs.

"Hello, Crow," said Two Down with a huge smile. "Sleep in?"

"Fuck you, Leonard," said Crowbar.

All the Chops in attendance were struck silent. In all their hundreds of rounds together, Crowbar and Two Down had never shared a sticky word between them. And now *Fuck you, Leonard?*

"What?" he said.

"You know the fuck what," said Crowbar. "Your last three checks bounced. I'm done working for your ass."

Two Down glanced around nervously. "What are you talking . . ."

"Yeah, it's out now, Leonard. Worked for you six years and you treat me like this. Well, it's over. I'm not doing your dirty work, today. I'm just out here to see you get your dick tied in a knot."

I looked at Hoover and he looked at me and it hit us at about the same time.

Crowbar had been Two Down's plant this whole time. He was a Two Down operative. All those games when Crowbar *just happened* to bring up some inane subject while we were about to hit the most important shot of the match. Turns out those were no accidents.

How couldn't we have seen it before? He *never* did it over Two Down's shot. Always one of Two Down's opponents. And what about our midnight round at the Mayflower? Wasn't it Crowbar who wrecked it for us, making all that noise, waking up Stretch, the guard? No wonder the fat slob wanted to come with us so badly that night.

Thud approached Two from one side. Hoover from another. Me from a third.

"Are you tellin' me you been payin' his fat ass all these years to fuck with our minds?" said Thud. "That's so, so *unethical.*"

"*That's* why he never played," I said. "I always thought that was sick."

"You evil man," said Hoover. "You soulless, evil man."

"Now hold on a second," said Two Down. "There's nothing in the rules against it. Besides, I always bought the beer, didn't I? And, I mean, it didn't always work. Remember when I lost that $300? It didn't help then, did it? I mean, sometimes he'd say such stupid shit that it would totally screw up my mind, too."

This did not seem to soothe anybody.

"We'll get you," said Thud. "Someday, we'll get you for this."

Concorde seemed to be especially enjoying this and the way it had changed ol' mo.

"Gentlemen," he said, "this is all very fascinating, but can we continue with our little game?"

What I should have done was, I should have just walked in and left Two Down out there to fight for his house with just him and his amphetamine phone-booth swing, but I had a little something riding on the outcome known as my life. I was stuck with the sloth.

I stepped in front of Two Down and said, quietly, "Let's just make some smooth swings and forget all this. You can win The Bet and make it up to us later."

It was no use. Two Down was toast. He stepped up to the third tee box and *whiffed,* then he cold-shanked his second shot O'Brien and hit his third fat. It went about 20 yards forward and 50 up and plugged in the middle of the fairway. He would be hitting 5. He wound up flailing at it six more times before I picked my ball up off the green and said, "Concede."

One up.

I noticed my father giving Concorde a big grin and a thumbs-up, which, coupled with the notion of Crowbar being a Two Down plant this whole time, got my blood pressure up and prompted me to try to knock the dimples off my ball. Instead, I wound up smother-hooking it.

"Keep hooking, sweetheart," Concorde whispered, which I thought was very sporting.

My father, meanwhile, put a creamy-smooth swing on his driver and was down there about 250, sitting up pretty and high as a sundae cherry. I had to chip out from behind the dirt mounds and made a bogey 5. With my father making 4 and Concorde making 5 and Two Down making 5, my bogey cost us the hole.

The match was even.

As we walked to the 5th tee, my father put his hand on my shoulder like we were longtime Rotarians and said, "Raymond, didn't I ever tell you that the woods are full of long hitters?"

I very much wanted to turn and land a wheelhouse right on his smug face.

"Let's see," I said, shaking out from under his hand. "I remember you telling me never to touch the liquor cabinet and to get me and my friends out of the house because you were trying to take a nap and I remember you making me park my car up the block because you said it was an eyesore, but no, I don't remember anything about the woods being full of long hitters."

"Everything has to be my fault, doesn't it, Raymond?"

"No, I think Mom broke her nose on the ironing board."

This was probably a stupid conversation to get into, as it got me shook up even worse, but it was too late. Like one of Blu Chao's specials, it was all coming up now.

When he stood up on the tee of the par 5 5th, with its splendid view of Beagle River in the distance, and the huge net protecting the 3rd green, and the 4th tee sitting right where you would like to place your second shot, the Numerals couldn't help but notice that there was no place to land their golf balls.

"Where do you think you hit here?" they asked their caddies, but even Professor and Haircut had never played a dump as sad as Ponky and thus had no idea.

"Perhaps I could help."

It was Crowbar.

"If it's permitted within the rules," he added.

Well, no, it wasn't permitted within the rules, as my father well knew. Only the playing partners or the caddies can give information or advice and Crow was an outside agency.

"Sir, what is your name?" my father said.

"Weasel," one of the Chops mumbled.

"Demetrius Howlings," said Crowbar.

Demetrius Howlings? It was the first time I could remember hearing his real name.

"William Davenport," he said, shaking his hand. "Would you care to be my new caddie, Mr. Howlings?"

"I'd be delighted," said Crowbar. "If I don't have to get out of the cart. I don't get out of the cart."

"Perfectly fine with me," my father said. He motioned Haircut to unhand the bag. Then he handed him a tenner and said, "That'll be all."

Then Hoover said pretty loudly, "I don't think I've ever seen a size Quadruple XL turncoat before, have you, Thud?"

"Npe," said Thud.

"The last time I saw anything that big it came with a two-car garage attached."

Haircut looked pretty pissed about the $10 buyout and walked over to Two Down. "Need a caddie, sir, at absolutely no cost?"

Two Down said well, yes.

"Fine." And as Haircut took the bag, he spun it so that it caught my father nicely in the kneecap.

"Now," my father said to Crowbar, rubbing the knee. "Where do you hit here?"

"Oh, you don't play the 5th fairway here, Will," said Crowbar, throwing his arm around my father's neck. "You hang a little 3-wood out into the 4th fairway, then, say, a 4-iron to the right of No. 3 green, and then just a 9-iron over the net there and onto 5 green."

"Who built this dump? Rube Goldberg?" said Concorde.

"I believe it's a Ross design," Hoover offered.

The Chops enjoyed that one very much.

I had counted on us winning this hole on account of no human who had never played it before could know where to hit it, but now Crowbar had screwed us. That was depressing, but then Concorde did something he'd regret. He had the tee box and he was getting ready to hit when he couldn't help but hear Thud snarfing down one of Blu Chao's Spam egg rolls, accompanied by the occasional slurping of his Monster Gulp Mountain Dew.

Concorde turned and found the source of the noise.

"Hey, Slim," Concorde said. "Do you mind? I'm trying to hit here."

Thud stopped.

Concorde looked back at his ball and then turned to Thud again. "Besides, you look like you could stand to stop once a month."

All the Numerals laughed, but Thud's eyes narrowed. If there is one thing you did not do, it was make fun of Thud's weight. He immediately got in his cart and drove down the middle of the 5th fairway by himself, over the Beagle River bridge and out of sight.

"Must be a sale at Winchell's," one of the Numerals said. More laughter.

All four of us hit pretty decent shots into the 3rd fairway. And then all four of us hit fairly decent second shots short of the 3rd green, in perfect position for our thirds.

Except that when Concorde got there, he found a very disturbing sight—the rotund and bulbous Thud standing over his ball, peeing on it.

Now this was no ordinary pee, of course. This was a wondrous, colossal, fire hydrant Thud of a pee, a beauty even for Thud himself. This was a Niagara Falls pee that other bladders talk about at union meetings.

It took just a moment for the vision to sink in on all of us. Finally, Concorde screamed, "Hey, you fat fuck!"

This did not deter Thud, who, we all knew, could pee longer than a bad play. Concorde tried to get to him, but he couldn't, on account of Thud continually turning his body so that the ball and his prodigious stream of ammonia-smelling urine was between him and Concorde.

By now, the ball was sitting in a small yellow pond.

"Nice try," Concorde said to me and Two. "But you just made a very bad mistake. You lost the hole. Your side touched my ball."

"I don't think so," I said. "Nobody touched your ball. Did anybody see Thud touch his ball?"

It was true. Thud had not touched his ball, or moved it in any way.

Concorde looked at my father. "Will, this is horseshit. I can clean it, can't I?"

My father scratched his head. "No, I can't think of any way you can, Stone."

At last, Thud had finished his prodigious and aromatic elimination. He zipped up and climbed back in his cart, returning to his egg roll.

"Classy friends you have," my father said to me.

"They do weddings, too," I said.

Concorde had no choice. He dug his rain suit out of his bag and put it on, zipping the neck all the way up. He put on his sunglasses and dug a rain hat out of his bag and put that on, too. Then he took an extra club, thinking the pool of fluid would slow his ball down, I suppose, though I'm not sure this is something *Golf Digest* has ever featured in an instructional.

He stood over the shot, waggling back and forth, with a castor-oil face. He waggled, stopped, rewaggled, stopped, swallowed hard and finally took a horrible little vitamin-deficient swing at it.

Hit the top eighth of it is all he did. It went about 12 feet, spinning a grotesque yellow wheel of pee as it went.

"Damn," said Cementhead. "You hit the piss outta that one."

Concorde walked up with the same club and hit it again, only he still didn't want to get too close to it, so the ball knifed into the netting of No. 3 green. The three of us played onto the 5th green and Concorde took four more before he even had it on the putting surface, at which point he took his wedge and smashed it toward Beagle River, taking a huge divot out of the green.

"Nice manners," said Meltdown.

"Concede," said my father.

One up.

Still, these Numerals were tough. Concorde rolled in a revenge birdie on the 6th, but I dropped some balata right on top of his ass for a birdie. Two Down, though, couldn't cover my father's par and we lost the hole.

Even.

And when Two Down got a panic attack on the 7th and slashed at one off the tee and into an old grocery cart, and my father hit a great shot to about six inches, we suddenly found ourselves 1 down.

"Who *are* those guys?" said Crowbar happily.

"The Great Escape?" asked Cementhead.

"Butch Cassidy."

"Damn!"

What we were finding out was that while Two Down was usually a nerveless money player, he was pulling an Alberto de Salvo choke special. Concorde, meanwhile, was a *big money* player. I was probably two shots up on my father already, but with Crowbar caddying for them, a lot of our advantage was useless. He'd tell them which sides of the fairways were pure cement and which sides were pure marsh. He'd mention which bunker they'd never get out of, on account of no sand being in there, and how this mat was going to move as they swung and that one wasn't. Your basic Donkey Primer. I guess Crowbar wasn't just daydreaming all that time after all.

The Chops were getting restless.

"C'mon, man," Cementhead whispered to me as I walked to the 8th tee. "Let's get 'em."

"C'mon, Stick," said Thud. "You can't let Numerals kick our

ass. This is our *only* chance at these guys. We need to win this hole."

Let's. Our. We. I wondered if these guys would find *us* a new career/$8,000/driver if *we* lost.

I got to the 8th a little after everybody else and I was surprised to see the Numerals' faces sagging. I'd played this tee shot so many times I had stopped actually thinking about it, but for them, it must've been like some horror flick come alive: the Bet Sematary.

Crowbar tried to explain to them that yes, it was possible to get your tee shot high enough to clear the rusted-out, wheelless, stripped, Jell-O-green '57 Chevy in front of you, but not so high as to clip the half of the *Boston Globe* billboard that hung over the fence and blocked your view of the hole.

"Do you get a free game if you hit it through the little hole?" Concorde said sarcastically.

"What hole?" I said.

Concorde chose a 2-iron and stepped up to golf's equivalent of the halftime half-court free-car shot. "Are you managed care or HMO, Stone?" Two Down asked.

Concorde stopped and turned around.

"Classy," he said.

"Hey, Stone," Thud yelled. "You think we oughta move back some of this gallery, just in case?"

Concorde realized he had to just swing and forget the gallery or it was only going to get worse.

"White trash," he said.

The man might've made a very good Chop about $3 million and fourteen cement estuaries ago.

His 2-iron managed to do the impossible, which is that it hit both the door frame of the Chevy *and* the bottom support beam of the billboard, after which the ball escaped onto Geneva Avenue, perhaps in hopes of a less violent life.

His second try hit the Chevy and bounced directly out of bounds, and his third try missed everything—the billboard, the Chevy, 8 fairway, 8 rough, 11 fairway, 11 rough, and landed *two fairways* over, on 12 tee box.

"Oh, yeah," Two Down said. "That's how the locals play it, Stoner."

My father clipped the billboard and wound up in the vegetables left.

Two Down and I did what we always do, which is hit 5-irons right through the hole with a little fade, hit another 5-iron on or near and get the hell out with bogeys. Actually, I made an up-and-down par and Two Down made a double bogey and the Numerals made your basic "other."

Back to even.

And now we came to the 9th, a fairly harmless par 5, except for being careful not to hit the golfers scuttling across the hole trying to play the 11th, but Crowbar warned them of that.

It was our box. I looked at my watch discreetly. Two Down saw me and discreetly looked at his. We both stepped up very quickly and hit hurried drivers. Mine kind of schlonked off the toe and wound up in the right rough and Two Down hit a low dachshund-killer about 190 yards. We snatched up our tees and offered the tee box to our worthy opponents.

Concorde was still frazzled by his disastrous score on 8, so he was taking his time. I again looked at my watch discreetly. Two Down looked at his watch discreetly. Concorde took his aim and waggled. Watch. Watch. Discreet. Discreet. One more waggle. Take it back, get to the top and . . .

CH-CH-CH-CH-CH-CH-CHOOOOOOOOOOSHHHHHH!!!!!!

You've got to hand it to the Massachusetts Transit Authority. Those T's are *very* prompt.

And that wasn't even the best thing. The best thing was that as Two Down was putting out for a 7 and a win on the 9th, there came from behind this huge "Fore!!!!" A golf ball hit the Mayflower Captain, Mr. Considine Roberts, right on the back of his fat, hairless skull.

It knocked him to his knees. Somebody put a towel up to the back of his head to stop the bleeding and the old Captain was able to pick up the offending ball and look at it. Then he looked back to see a man coming fast on his golf cart, waving his arms.

It was Froghair.

"Hey, you jerk!" Froghair yelled. "Whaddya think you're doin' pickin' up my ball? That ball would've made the green. I've never made this green in my whole life!"

Roberts glared at him, holding the ache on his head with one hand and the ball with the other.

"Is this your ball, *sir?*" the Captain asked archly.

"If it's a Titlist with three purple dots on it, you're goddamn right it is!" announced Froghair. "And who the *hell* wants to know?"

The Numerals stared at Froghair like he'd just shown up cradling the Lindbergh baby.

One up. Nine to play.

22

TO HIS CREDIT and my undying shock, my father insisted Crowbar come with him to the Mayflower for the final 9.

He didn't have to. He had First-and-Third to give him yardages and reads at the Mayflower if he needed them, which he didn't. But he insisted Crowbar come in with him, perhaps as a show of appreciation for what he'd done, but, knowing him, probably more because he knew it would rattle us Chops even more.

Here was a stuffy Numeral allowing a black man to enter the gates of the Mayflower when the black man's own buddy hadn't done it.

"Don't look at me like that, Ivan," Two Down told the gate guard as we passed. "They never found the real Butcher of Lyon, y'know."

Once they were in, there was no stopping every other Chop—Hoover, Meltdown, Cementhead, Blu Chao, even the eighty-five-year-old Stringley brothers.

The Numerals numbered about the same as the Chops, except, of course, for Captain Considine Roberts and two of his assistants, who had Froghair gripped by both arms last we saw and were grilling him about his whereabouts on that September night when a Titlist with three purple dots was taken from suspects trespassing on Mayflower grounds.

Teach his butt to shop the Dumpster.

I don't know why, but as we came to play the final 9, I wasn't nervous anymore. I'd played the front 9 in even par, which is not bad on a course with exactly eleven decent lies on it. I think Two Down was settling down, too. Plus, we knew the Mayflower by now. I'd played it half a dozen times in real daylight, and Two Down had been playing it pretty much every day for weeks.

We were allowed five minutes to putt on the green and the Chops used that five minutes to salivate. In all their years living in and around Dorchester, none of them had ever been any closer to Paradise than the hole in the hedge.

"Look at the size of that green!" yelled Meltdown.

"That's the fairway, stupid," said Cementhead, who declared himself the tour guide, having actually played it before.

"Wooooowwww!"

"Ahh, this sucks," said Thud. "I could never play here."

"Why on earth not?" asked Hoover.

"Too quiet," he said. "If somebody doesn't burp on my downswing now, I flinch."

We were about to get ready to walk over to the 1st tee box when the Mayflower's tan and buffed head pro came out and ahemmed a couple of times to get my father's attention. They huddled for a moment. Then my father returned to the group and said, "Gentlemen, I'm afraid no one is allowed on the course in dungarees," which is another thing I hated about my father, the way he called jeans dungarees. "I'm afraid we'll have to make some arrangements."

It wasn't going to be a small deal. Not only was I in jeans but so were Thud and Meltdown, which is all he ever wore—usually with giant holes in the legs held together by safety pins. Today wasn't as bad, though. They only had a few holes and a "SID" up one leg and a "VICIOUS" down the other, his dress-up pair. After all, today was Chunkin' Charlie's funeral.

Now, I knew that was the rule when I got dressed that morning, but I figured if we were behind, I could cancel the bet on grounds that dress isn't covered in the USGA rule book.

"Follow me," said Dudley Puttright.

We did, right into the pro shop, where he took us to the ugliest collection of pants this side of a Kiwanis convention—bright red, Christmas green and peach pants waited for us. The printed ones were even worse—lime green with whales on them, light purple with golf tees on them, combustible plaids and horrendously huge herringbones.

Both of them wanted to leave, but I asked them to stay for the sake of history. Thud picked a lovely pair of sky-blue Sansabelts, which I thought went lovely with his Homer Simpson T-shirt, "Mother" tattoo and stolen velvet Fedora. I selected the nearest thing to black I could find. Something inside Meltdown, though, just couldn't manage it.

"Not me," said Meltdown. "I don't do miracle fibers." He left the shop as a man fleeing Pompeii.

"I'll get these for you and your friends, Raymond," my Father said in an unctuous way.

"No chance," I said. Screw handouts now. "You sign for them now, but they become part of the bet. Winner buys 'em."

He shrugged and was halfway through signing and we were very close to being back out on the course when Thud yelped, "Holy Jesus!" and nailed me with an elbow in the gut.

He was pointing across the shop. There, standing with Dannie, was the leading cause of hardlegs among Boston's closet homosexual population, Browning Sumner.

"Shut up," I whispered, seeing as how Dannie suddenly had the evil eye on us.

He was beside himself with glee. "That's Xanadu!"

"OK, OK," I said.

"The fag in the pictures from that night!" he said. "At the Copley, remember? The spanker?"

By now, it was too late; Thud's pointing and whispering and laughing had gotten Dannie's interest.

She walked over. "What? Thud 'member a hilarious Quickie-Mart job?"

"Yeah, he got away with millions in unmarked corn dogs," I said, trying to get her off the trail.

Now, when Dannie is pissed, she gets physical. She backed me against a very painful rack of club ties, put one hand on my neck, squeezing hard, and the other on my injured hand. It was fun to spank Chester with a woman that strong, but now . . .

"What the fuck is he laughing about? Browning?"

"Nothin'," I said. "I think Browning reminded him of somebody he once mugged."

She shoved me so hard I thought a prong of the tie rack was going to lacerate my kidney.

"Stick, you tell me what in tarnation's going on or I'll shut you out like Sandy Fucking Koufax."

She had a look in her eye like she wanted to know. Dannie Higgins is not the kind of woman any sort of man could keep his hands off long and she must've been worried by now. I didn't want her to think it was her anymore.

"You were probably, unnggh, going to find out, owwww, soon enough. Two Down was trying to, oooh, frame Concorde with, uhhh, some photos of some luscious Concorde was shaggin' at the Copley and Thud was the shooter. Only the luscious wasn't a luscious. It was a guy dressed up. It was, uh, well, it was Browning."

All the strength drained from her. I checked for welts.

"What?"

"Sorry."

"You lie. You're just jealous. You have been from the start. Just 'cause you couldn't make a single relationship work in your whole pathetic life, just 'cause you couldn't stand to stick your neck out for one little second, you don't wanna see anybody else catch a break."

"Fine. Don't believe me . . ." I said.

"I won't," she snapped. She turned and walked away.

"But that sure is a sweet little butterfly tattoo he's got on his ankle," Thud said.

She froze. She looked at Browning. He was wearing long pants. He looked at her.

Browning started backpedaling like a cornerback.

"Sweetheart," he said. "I've been wanting to tell you. I just got so sick of the whispering at the parties. And my parents were *so* happy that I'd found someone. I'm going to tell them. I just wanted to give them a little happiness before I did. Is that so bad?"

Dannie walked out of the shop, looking like she was going to cry or punch somebody.

"Dannie!" Browning called.

"Shut the fuck up, Xanadu," I mentioned.

Suddenly, Dannie broke into a sprint toward the putting green. It took me a minute to figure out what she was doing, but then it hit me.

"Two!" I hollered. "Run!!"

But Two Down had no chance. He looked up on the putting green just as Dannie caught him with a beautiful punch 7-iron to the knee, followed by a nice uppercut to the nose, which immediately started your basic Red River going. Then she followed that with a knee in the groin. "Get yourself another hobby," she said.

Then she got in the middle of everybody and yelled through her tears, "Can I have everybody's attention? I have an announcement to make! Them two right there"—pointing at Browning and Concorde—"are goddamn"—pause—"low-rent"—double pause—"they're just . . ."

Concorde and Browning looked like their T-bills were flashing in front of their eyes.

"They're not what you think. . . . They're . . . just . . ."

And she couldn't finish, running off to the parking lot in a slobbery, gorgeous mess.

There was much murmuring in the crowd.

Concorde pulled Browning over to him with a big smile and said, "They just can't handle it when my boy Browning puts the old niblick off-limits, am I right, Browning?"

"Damn right," said Browning, his voice quivering.

The faces on the members lightened in relief and guffaws and backslaps.

As I leaned over Two Down, I knew I'd just lost my partner and probably The Bet. Dannie had opened him up like a 7-Eleven. It looked like Two Down's kneecap, nose and maybe dick were broken. He was definitely out of the match.

"You all right, Two?" I asked.

"Sure," he groaned, spitting out a tooth and holding his knee. "This is NOT my favorite putting green, y'know what I mean?"

••••••••••••••••••••••

The head pro brought some towels and ice for Two Down and one of the Numerals offered to drive him to the hospital, but he wouldn't hear of it.

"Stone," I said. "I've got to have another partner. Look at him."

"No way," said Stone. "That wasn't the bet."

"Fine. We win. One up."

"Wrong. You forfeit."

"Bullshit! We didn't say anything about injuries."

"We said strict USGA rules," said Stone. "You can't just substitute somebody during a match. We win."

"Bullshit," I said. "The rule book doesn't say anything about injury."

"Yes, it does," said my father. "You forfeit the match."

OK, so I forgot who I was talking to.

I looked around at the crowd of thirty or so Mayflower members watching.

I spoke up pretty loud. "So, Father, you want to win like this? By forfeit? When you're 1 down? OK, you get the money and the house, but everybody here knows that a couple slobs from the wrong side of the hedge beat you, 1 up, and then you went double weenie."

My father took a little look around and so did Concorde. There was a little grumbling in the crowd.

"Buck up, Will," one of the rich guys in the back said.

"Let the match continue!" somebody else yelled.

I could see Concorde starting to squirm.

"Just let me have *somebody,*" I said. "Anybody."

Suddenly, I saw Dannie out of the corner of my eye. She'd come back. "Except the girl," I said softly.

Concorde's eyes brightened. He turned and saw Dannie.

"Waaaaait a minute," he said. "The girl! Hey, that's a great idea, isn't it, Will? I don't suppose it would hurt anything to have the nice young lady . . ."

Suddenly, he froze. Then he spun around.

"Hold on one fuckin' minute," he said. "This is just what you want, isn't it? This was all a setup, wasn't it? The girl is a plant! How stupid do you think we are over here? This whole fight, this whole thing, all the accusations, they were just a setup so that you'd pick the girl and she'd be some dyke on spikes from the LPGA tour who would step on our balls and smoke a cigar later."

"Yeah, right," I said. "You caught us. I'm actually Dick Clark and you're on *Foul-ups, Bleeps & Blunders.*"

"Bullshit," he said. "It's the oldest setup in the world. Well, sorry. We're not buying."

"All right, who, then?"

He looked around at the collection of mutts who had invaded his precious club.

Crowbar whispered to Cementhead in a nerdy voice, "A course, I'm an *excellent driver.*"

"*The African Queen?*" whispered Cementhead.

"*Rain Man.*"

"Damn!"

Concorde kept looking. And then he saw him. The man he wanted. He pointed right at him. My heart sank.

"That guy!" he said. "The guy I saw this morning. That's your partner from here on in."

Every Chop groaned.

Hoover.

••••••••••••••••••••••••

Hard as I protested, the Numerals wouldn't listen. Stone said I was lucky they let me continue with anybody at all.

I tried to look on the bright side. As bad as Hoover was, maybe he'd accidentally skull one off a duck and into the hole or maybe just watching his swing would infect the Numerals' game. Hoover was better than quitting right then and there, but only by a little.

Hoover didn't want to do it. He was petrified. But we convinced him to run out to his trunk to get his clubs and they allowed him five minutes to warm up. But before he made a single swing I said one thing to him: "Hoov, just pretend it's dark."

He looked at me like he was just about to go to the electric chair. I gave him a wink and squeezed his shoulder. He was so tight he was not even there. It was like staring into the eyes of a chicken.

My advice really helped. On the 1st hole, he swung like a man trying to machete his way out of a Borneo jungle. He made a 14. Now we were even with the Numerals.

On the 2nd hole, he put a loop in his backswing you could have driven a Peterbilt through and made an 11. Now we were 1 down.

He played the 3rd hole a little better, reaching the green in 3, but then he put the Roberto Durán Hands of Stone stroke on his putt and it sailed off the green and into the longish rough, from which he became the first person in history to lose a ball off a putting green. He actually had to redrop on the green. Ten. Now we were 2 down.

As we got to the 4th tee box, I asked him bitterly, "How's that Colossal Cathy treatin' you, pards?"

"The kick point is a little high," he actually said.

"Oh, well, no wonder," I said, seething. "For a minute there, I thought you were just trying to ruin my entire fucking life."

He felt bad. I felt bad. Down 2 holes with 6 holes to play.

A couple of Chops tried to rattle Concorde. One time he hit his drive and Thud said, "Hoo-boy, you really *spanked* that one, huh, Stoner?"

And Cementhead said, "Yessir, he *spanked* that one hard!"

"Nuttin' like a good *spanking,*" said Two Down.

"God, yes. Nothin' feels as hot as a real good *spanking!*" Thud said.

But Concorde only blushed a little and kept staring straight ahead.

Soon the Chops' steps were heavy and their shoulders six inches lower. Two Down looked like the "before" half of a hemorrhoid ad.

"Jesus, Hoover," Two snapped. "Get aggressive. They slaughter the lambs in this world. When's the last time you ordered a lion burger?"

I personally couldn't look at my driver without feeling like crying. How many more times would I hit it?

Some of the Numerals' chums were already shaking their hands and saying things like "Well, congratulations, guys. I've got to go. You don't need me anymore."

The 4th hole at the Mayflower is nasty. The fairway is so tight, a fat guy like Thud could snag his pants on the rough on either side. It's 440 yards long on top of that, so you have to hit the driver if you are to have any chance. My father got up and hit a pretty decent drive down the middle, but Concorde bailed out way right, into the broccoli.

"Twenty dollars to the first person who finds that ball," Concorde announced. *"Inbounds!"*

I blistered my driver 275 down the middle. God, I was going to miss that club. And Hoover, upon my advice, hit a 4-iron that was ugly but actually found the fairway. I figured three 4-irons from him and two putts and a bogey and maybe we'd have a chance to tie a hole.

Concorde couldn't find his ball. Not only were he and my father searching but most of the Numerals, too. Hoover hit his second 4-iron in the fairway and all the Chops met right there in the fairway, waiting to see what would happen.

Thud: "You know, if we can win one here, we'd be only 1 down."

Me: "Yeah, right. And maybe Hoover is the ghost of Bobby Jones."

Thud: "You think Concorde's gonna find his ball?"

Me: "Of course. Don't you?"

Thud: "Nope."

Me: "Why not?"

Thud (pulling Concorde's personalized Titlist 3 out of his pocket): "Because I got it right here."

I had a sick feeling in my stomach, but the rest of the Chops were having themselves a very big laugh about it, when suddenly, from 50 yards up, Concorde hollered, "Found it!"

Ouch.

23

WHATEVER BALL THE lizardlike Concorde had slipped down his pant leg, he slashed it out of there, remarkably, very near the green and made the world's greatest bogey, especially for someone that had an 8.

What were we going to say about it? *That can't be your ball, because I have your ball right in my pocket!*

I made a very good 4 and my father made a 5 and Hoover chunked four 4-irons in all, plus a wedge for good measure, and wound up with a snowman.

Three down with 5 to play.

Maybe I could get interested in cribbage.

....

Of the many choices that were vying for the Most Sickening Thing About Losing, there seemed to be three front-runners: (1) Coming to another huge moment in my life and getting my neck stepped on again. (2) Coming to another huge moment in my life and getting my neck stepped on again by the one man on the entire planet I didn't want to have anywhere near my neck. (3) Seeing Ponky as I knew it go down the tubes.

If a T would've come by at that moment, I would have gladly gotten under it.

Instead, only Two Down limped by, with what looked like a larcenous gleam in what little sliver of eye he had left.

"How we doin'?" he asked.

"We're just about over Lockerbie now," I said.

"Don't give up yet," he said.

Then he walked away, mysteriously. Meanwhile, Concorde was about to tee off at the 5th, a simple enough 147-yard par 3, probably the easiest hole on the course. He lined up the shot, stepped up to it, waggled and was just about to draw it back when . . .

BBBBRINNNNNNNGGGGG!

"Shit," he said, falling away from the ball without swinging. "Probably my office." He went to his cart and picked up his cellular phone.

"Hello? . . . Hello? . . ." He flipped it off and went back to the tee box. "Idiots."

Concorde set up again. This time, just as he was beginning his downswing . . .

BBBBRINNNNNNNGGGGG!

Concorde lurched at his ball, sending it screaming off to the right and into what looked like maximum-security prison.

"Goddamnit!" he roared. "Who the fuck is it?" He ran over, flipped open his cellular, snapped off a hello, but, again, nobody was there. "Fucking idiots!"

"Just turn it off, Stone," said my father. Concorde, livid, did better than that. He turned it off and slam-dunked it into the little basket on the back of the cart.

That's when Two Down walked out from behind the tree and slipped back into the crowd, unnoticed.

My father and I hit decent shots and even Hoover laid it up short and left of the green, no problem. Concorde realized he'd never find his ball and teed up another one.

Just as he was at the top, somebody in the crowd said, "Call for Mr. Concorde!" and he stabbed another one in the exact same place.

That caused some pushing and shoving among the Chops and the Numerals.

"This is a motherfuckin' golf course, motherfuckers!" said Thud, whipping a Chinese semiautomatic pistol out of his black leather waist pouch. "Let's show some fucking civility!"

The Chops were very impressed.

"You do not meet a lot of twelve-time losers who know their way around both a Chinese semiautomatic and the word 'civility,' " I said to my father.

Thud put the gun back where it came from, but it had hushed the crowd.

"That man has done more for slow play at our course," Two said to nobody in particular.

Suffice it to say, we won the hole. I told Hoover to simply putt onto the green from 20 yards away, and even though he missed a 3-footer, he made a 5 and Concorde conceded on account of he was well on his way to enjoying a 9.

Hope never dies.

Two down. Four to play.

"How'd you know his number?" I whispered to Two.

"I still have a job at the phone company, for Chrissakes," he whispered back.

"*You* were the one calling Mr. Concorde?" Cementhead said.

"Of course, you moron."

"Well, he's right over there. I'll get him for you. Mr. Concorde!"

Thud put a cross-body block on Cementhead before he could get two feet.

"I'll handle this," Dannie said, finally speaking up. "I speak fluent Cement." And she dragged him off to the side to explain it all to him.

The win gave Hoover confidence, and as he stepped up, he actually put a slow swing on one and wiggled that sweet little aerodynamic Titlist 8 right down the middle about 190 yards. I stepped up and caught one a little thin down the left, but the Numerals busted good drives, too. Still, I wound up making birdie from a lucky lie and my father made a par and Stone made a bogey and it all came down to Hoover's 8-footer for a bogey to win.

Now, Hoover sinking an 8-footer for bogey is not something you want to put your house on. Hoover sinking a 4-footer for anything is not something you want to bet your pocket lint on. The only 8-footer Hoover has ever sunk is maybe a fence post.

In his whole life, Hoover had never made a big putt. He tried putters with level bubbles built into them. He tried putters with guitar-string faces. He tried putters with rollers on the bottom. He tried putters with rubber-band faces. He tried putters with mirrors on them, so that he could look down and see not only the ball but the hole at the same time. He tried putters that looked like Romulan space cruisers, with two giant-winged appendages, putters with convex faces and putters with concave faces. He tried a putter that was only four inches high, which he used on his knees. He even tried putters that stood up by themselves to allow him to misread the line better. Absolutely nothing helped.

And so as he stood over this one that we absolutely, positively had to have, I felt nauseous. Hoover had looked at it from every side but under, had backed off it twice and was now sweating on a 58 degree day. The only thing he hadn't done was bring in a surveying crew. That's when I had a very good idea.

"Hoover, hold on a second," I said.

I walked over to Two Down and had a little heart-to-heart.

At first, he shook his head, no, no, no. Then I got him to shrug a maybe, maybe, maybe. And then finally, reluctantly, yes. He walked to his bag and, as though it were radioactive, he carefully, gingerly, remorsefully extracted . . . Arnie.

Hoover's eyes bulged as Two Down walked slowly toward him. He didn't speak, only silently held back tears the way a first-time mother takes her kid to the bus stop on the first day of kindergarten.

"No!" yelled Crowbar to the Numerals. "Don't let him. Do not let him use Arnie!"

"Who the fuck is Arnie?" asked Concorde.

"Two Down's putter," said Crowbar. "The thing is deadly. It's unnatural. It's part of the occult. It came from behind the green fucking door! Just, look, I'm telling you, don't."

"Don't worry, Demetrius," said my father. "It's quite illegal anyway. It's against the rules."

Oh, God, the 14-club rule.

I turned quickly to Hoover. "How many clubs do you have in your bag?"

He looked.

"Nine," he said.

"Nine?" three of us said.

"Yes, well, it's a new theory the Japanese have come up with," Hoover explained. "According to Feng Shui, which is the science of creating positive energy flow through geomancy, having odd-numbered clubs in the golf bag blocks the clubs' ability to draw in positive life force. It is the same reason you should never stand near a lake, as it reflects negative energies. Through many hours of research, I became convinced that the odd clubs were drawing in negative *qi*, so I now carry only a harmonious grouping—my driver, 4-wood, 8-wood, 4-iron, 6-iron, 8-iron, wedge, sand wedge and putter. Nine."

"Nine," I said to my father, who shrugged.

"Still," argued Concorde. "You can't add a club from somebody else."

"You can," I disagreed, "as long as that someone else isn't playing in the match. Rule 4 dash 4."

Don't you love golf rules?

The way had been cleared for The Historic Borrowing. Two Down laid Arnie sideways into Hoover's disbelieving mitts, the way a doctor lays a newborn in a mother's arms.

"Speak gently," Two Down said. "He's never been this far from home."

Hoover tenderly took Arnie by his battered leather grip and

tried a gentle, slow practice swing with it. Then two. Then three. Suddenly, his stroke was smooth and patient, the same speed backward as forward. One-two. Like a pendulum. He smiled. For the first time in his life, he was looking forward to a putt. In his bony little hands was Excalibur itself.

A transformation had suddenly come over him. With a swagger, he adjusted his little Hogan cap, adjusted his skinny little shoulders, stepped up to the ball and looked at the line one more time.

"All right, Arnie," he cooed confidently. "Twelve feet forward and six inches down."

Then he put the sweetest little one-two on it you ever saw without lifting his head and that little ball dove in the cup like a homesick mole.

"We're on a mission from God," I said.

"Roots?"

"The Blues Brothers."

"Damn!"

One down. Three to play.

....

When the Chops finally got done throwing Hoover from shoulder to shoulder and Two Down finally got done trying to stop them in order to protect Arnie and Dannie was done yelling, "Boy, you're just as tough as a pine knot!" the sun did a wonderful thing. It came out from behind the clouds. Maybe God *was* a Chop.

"You know what, Hoover?" Two Down said, putting his arm around him for the first time I can ever remember. "Sometimes rats go hungry."

"And good men dunk 12-footers," I said.

He smiled to parts of his face the corner of his lips had never been.

We stepped up to the 7th tee, feeling the warmth on our faces for the first time all morning. It was a long par 5 and I let Hoover go first and he put a nice little swing on his 4-iron and hit it about 200 right to left, perfect spot. I hit one a little rightish, but OK, and then my father stepped up.

He was standing over it an extra-long time because the pressure was getting thick now and right then is when Hoover said an incredible thing, just out of the clear blue.

"Mr. Hart?"

My father stepped back off the ball, perturbed.

"What is it?" he said.

"Well, I don't know if you know this," Hoover said. "But I am quite a student of the golf swing. And I don't know if this will help, but . . ."

"Please, don't give me any advice. It would be against the rules."

He stepped back up to the shot.

"On the contrary," Hoover said. "I was just going to mention in passing something that I discovered."

"I don't want to know it."

"All I was going to say is that whenever I am having difficulty with my swing, I find it helpful to keep an eye on my shadow as I'm swinging. It's right there directly in front of you. See? It can be very helpful, but most people never even notice it. Can you imagine that? Not noticing your own shadow when it's right there in front of you the whole time?"

A chuckle went through the Chops. A gasp went through the Numerals. My father remained perfectly still.

"Understand that if you *did* notice your shadow, it would help your swing," Hoover continued helpfully. "You could see whether your club face was a little open at the top or whether your elbow was flying or all kinds of myriad things."

"Kindly shut the fuck up," my father said. It was the first time I'd ever heard him swear sober.

He backed off the shot and tried a practice swing. It was not the beautiful, languid swing I had admired my whole life. No, this one was out of the Hoover instructional video *Golf My Horrid Way.* It was herkier, jerkier, like a nickelodeon.

Hoover got an enormously satisfied smile on his face, topped in size only by Two Down's. Personally, I felt an ulcer forming.

My father stepped up again, clutched, double-clutched and then put a spasmic swing on his ball, which, déjà vu, went about 6 feet up and 8 feet sideways, bounced off one of the designer Smith and Hawkins benches they have on every hole and wound up behind a huge oak.

He chipped back out into the fairway, but there was the sun again and his shadow again. His face was bright red and he paced like a hyena. He could not get his shadow out of his mind. He skulled that shot, chunked the next, toed the third and heeled the fourth, golfing for the cycle.

My bogey and Hoover's double beat them by two shots.

"Looks like you'll have to triple the therapy," said Thud.

Two Down beamed. "I feel like a proud father."

Dead even. Two holes to play.

IF THERE IS a moment when the whole thing began to resemble the last day of Saigon, it was as we walked to the Mayflower's 8th tee with those 2 holes to go.

It got three notches past loud and one short of tympanum damage, partly because the Chops had invented "The Chop," which was, in fact, a total rip-off of the Florida State/ Atlanta Brave Indian tomahawk chop thing, and they were all chanting and whooping as we went

Nahhhhhhh, Nahhhhh-Nahuh-na-na.

Nahhhhhhh, Nahhhhh-Nahuh-an-na.

Meanwhile, the Sperm Dollars were starting to get on their boys. This is what happens when you lose three holes in a row to a phone call, a shadow and a putter from Voodoo Country Club.

"Let's get it together now, Will ol' boy!"

"Bear down now, Stoner!"

To lose to two guys who looked as ridiculous as Hoover and I looked in our ridiculous pants; to lose to two Lous from the wrong side of the hedge after having a 3-hole lead with 5 to play; to lose *at home,* my God! For the rest of their Mayflower days, they could never be sure that each chuckle, every muffled guffaw at every gin table in the clubhouse wasn't meant for them.

But that's when two things happened. One, the sun went back behind the clouds, where it was going to stay, much to my father's relief. And two, Hoover decided he was going to be Long John Daly and pulverize his Colossal Cathy, even though I thought we agreed he'd hit nothing but a 4-iron off the tee from here on in.

Before I noticed what he was doing, he was going after his drive with both cheeks. Unfortunately, he barely hit the top layer of enamel. It went absolutely straight down and plugged, not two inches from his tee. The Numerals nearly split their catheters with laughter.

Why Hoover decided he needed to do this scientists will never discover because the 8th is a 540-yard par 5 with a lake right in front of the green, not to mention a big willow which guards the left side, which means most pros probably wouldn't go for it in two, much less a schmoe like Hoover.

All he had to do was hit two 190-yard shots and he'd have been in perfect position. If the match had been televised, they wouldn't have had time to take a commercial time-out.

"Uh-oh," some Numeral yelled. "Didn't reach the ladies' tees. Gotta play with your dick out."

"At least he has one," Dannie observed.

I walked over to Hoover and held my hand out. He knew what I wanted. Cathy. He gave it to me. I threw it to Thud. He grabbed it. I nodded. He snapped it over his knee.

"You and Cathy just broke up," I said.

Now the pressure was on me big time. I tried to swallow down the nerves and put a smooth swing on it and I actually creased one right down the gut, the first drive I'd really hit in the dead center of the club face all day.

The Chops went triple certifiable, whooping and Chopping and carrying on. And I think Dannie turned to somebody and said, "Back home you'd have to change horses to go that far."

Still, the Numerals had their opening. The best Hoover could make now was 6 and probably more like 8 and so all they had to do was make a couple pars and they'd win the hole and have us dormie, which is golfgeek for 1 up with 1 to play.

We all realized that we were past all the pranks now. In fact, the prank cupboard was bare. The Chops had thrown everything they could think of at the Numerals that wasn't a violation of USGA rules and maybe some that were. Now it was pure golf.

Concorde crunched one long and into the light rough left and my father, after finding his swing again after about twenty-five practices, striped one down the middle, if 50 yards short of me. Off we went.

Then my father called my name. "Raymond, I want to say one thing to you."

I looked him in the eye, expecting, as always, maybe something big, maybe an apology, or an understanding or something from the self-help section.

"Raymond," he said. "I'll give you $20,000 right now for the driver and we'll call off our little bet."

I shook my head.

"Don't be a fool about this, Raymond," he said. "If you lose, you'll have nothing. I've seen where you live. I've seen your little friends. Take the $20,000 and I'll help you work out a loan for the other $15,000 for membership. If you ever want to make something of yourself, you've got to start circulating among the right kind of people."

I was so heat-flushed I couldn't think of what to say. The world is made up of two kinds of people: those that have the witty, excruciatingly perfect comeback and those of us that search for the right word like a set of glasses in the dark and finally say nothing at all. Most of us need a delete key and a cup of coffee and a few hours to get it right.

I think I said something like "Father, that is so . . . you are such a . . . forget it. Just forget it." And I walked twice as fast away from him, pissed at both of us.

I took about ten deep breaths while Concorde and my father laid up nicely to about 120 yards short of the pin, with only little 9-irons between them and the green and pretty certain pars. If Stone Concorde was a 15, then I was German Chancellor Helmut Kohl. The guy ought to go into the Sandbag Hall of Fame.

Hoover was a little behind them, about 145 yards out. Unfortunately, he was lying 3, which would be wonderful for him any other day but today. He was a dead-bolt lock for 6, at least.

Which meant it was my shot.

"One eighty-seven to the front edge of the pond, Carl," said Professor.

"How much to the pin?" I said.

"Who cares?" he said. "Jesus hisself couldn't reach."

"How much to the pin?"

He harrumphed.

"Ain't no point in tellin' you 'cause you got no club that'll ride you that far."

"How much?"

"Godamighty! Lessee. One-eight-seven plus fifty plus, say, three. Two-forty, I guess. But it might as well be two thousand forty. It's all carry, plus you got to bend it around that tree. Alls you want is a little 175 shot, 7-iron layup."

"Driver."

"Lemme ax you a question. Are you on crack? You can't hit a driver off the fairway over a lake with a draw!"

"Driver."

He handed me the driver and took a deep breath. Caddie code took over.

"Perfect shot for you," he said. "This club was made for this shot. Right outta the factory. If there's one man that can do it, it's you. Just smooth that little driver up there."

As I stood behind the shot, I tried to remind myself of the reasons I *had* to hit the driver here. For one thing, their team score was going to be 10 or less and with Hoover making at least a 6, I had to make a birdie 4 to tie. A par would do us no good. Plus, the last hole, the 9th, is a dogleg right uphill and narrower than an Alabama PTA. I did not like our chances of Hoover playing that hole. I didn't even like the chances of Hoover finishing that hole.

The one night he played that hole, he made a double bogey and it was the best he'd ever played the game. Chances were excellent that would be our final resting place.

The only way we were going to win this hole was by me making eagle or birdie. And if I was going to swing one club with my future on the line, plus Two Down's, I wanted it to be with my uncle's driver.

I put my Harley-Davidson grip on it, only even stronger for a hook, and I remember hearing a few people gasp and mumble as I set up over the shot.

I just stood over it for I don't know how long. Days, maybe. The weirdest things came to my brain, absolutely none of them about the moment I was living. I kept thinking about Ponky, what fun it was, all the times with Dannie, all the times with Two, and the mess I was suddenly in.

My brain just stopped functioning in the normal way. It needed a control-alt-delete to reboot.

Then I heard a familiar woman's voice that snapped me out of it. "Raymond?"

I turned.

It was Blu Chao.

"Fuck them in the neck," she said.

My sentiments exactly.

I am not sure what I was thinking about as I swung, but I know something weird came over me. I remember my last image was hitting balls with my uncle watching from his chair under the shade of that big willow at Fox Hollow, sipping his cold Falstaff. Maybe it was the big willow in front of the green that transported me back to those days. Maybe it was my uncle's driver. I don't know. It was just a feeling that swept over me.

Those were some of the first really pure shots I hit in my life. They were the kind that take off sort of low and then, 100 yards out, start climbing into the pink and purple early-evening sky, just drifting so lazily out there and finally coming down right over a pin or a bush or whatever it was I'd picked as my target. I remember the rush I got the first time it happened. And I remember my uncle saying, "Ray, you're makin' the range boy's job easy. You're just stacking them up out there."

I loved the rhythm of his voice, the relaxedness of it, maybe because my father's was just the opposite, and I thought of it and I tried to re-create that exact feeling as I swung, but I don't remember anything at impact and I don't remember how it came off the club face. The next thing I remember is seeing the shot in the air, starting out too low, but then rising, rising on that same gorgeous path into that cold sky and now bending left, gently, sweetly.

"Oh, baby, baby, baby," I heard Professor coo, "just come a little bit more, sweetheart."

And I knew it would.

I knew I'd hit it on nothing but that brick-red centerpiece. I knew it from the feel, which was nothing, and the sound, which is a sound you never hear on the golf course anymore, the pure sound of a crisply struck persimmon driver. Thank you, J. W. Nicklaus.

The ball floated lazily over the pond and dropped down sweet and soft as a parachuter with bunions, 15 feet right of the pin. If it ran 20 feet, I'll eat your visor.

"Lordamighty Jesus Horatio Christ!" screamed Professor. "I don't believe it!"

"Lucky bastard," muttered Concorde.

The Chops started screaming and rolling on top of each other. Thud even heaved his Baby Ruth into the sky and roared—until the horror of what he'd done struck him and he went looking for it.

Hoover practically gang-tackled me and Two Down started, too, until he got up too fast out of the cart and his lack of blood caused him a head rush. Cementhead was in a gang hug with Dannie and

Professor and they all eventually just clumped into your basic Plato's Retreat on the ground.

And then old man Stringley went right up to Concorde and said, "T-t-t-t-ake a s-s-s-s-suck a that!" And Concorde had to use the towel off his bag to wipe his face.

When things settled down a little, Hoover plopped his 8-iron over the lake and Arnie lagged up for his two-putt 6, just as I figured, and the Numerals each made 5, which meant I needed the 15-footer for eagle.

The way I look at it, there have been three perfectly pure putts in the history of golf. Boston's own Francis Ouimet's 20-footer at the 71st hole to lock up the U.S. Open at Brookline in 1913. Nicklaus's 10-footer at the 17th to take the lead for good in the 1986 Masters. And the brushstroke I put on my little Titlist late that morning on the 8th green at the Mayflower in Dorchester, Massachusetts.

"Son," Dannie told me later. "That dadburned thing goes in the center of a doughnut hole."

Eagle.

One up. One to play.

....

Two Down was using the one arm that wasn't holding the towel to his bloody head to pat Hoover and me on the back as we walked to the last hole. He yelled in our ears, "Kill 'em, boys! Screw tyin' this last hole! Let's kill! When this is over, I wanna be able to sop him up with a sponge! Remember what he did to me? Remember?"

To which Crowbar said, "Oh, Jerry, don't let's ask for the moon. We have the stars."

"Jaws?"

"Now, Voyager."

"Damn!"

All we needed was a tie on this last hole and the match was ours.

I looked over at Concorde. For the first time since I'd known him, he no longer looked like Joe Cocky USC Water Polo boy. He looked scared. His eyes looked like they needed recharging and he was licking his dry lips over and over again and his face was the color of spaetzle.

My father was nervously squirting his breath spray about every five seconds. Some of their friends were laughing at them. Worse, some of them were giving up.

One of them, a well-dressed older guy with silver hair, looked at his friend, another well-dressed older guy in a camel topcoat, and said, "We better get going," he said. "Charlie's funeral starts in half an hour."

Something cold went through my veins.

They started to walk away. I stopped them.

"Excuse me?" I said quietly. "Did you . . . did you say you were going to a funeral?"

"So?" said the taller of the men.

"Do you mind if I ask whose?"

"Charlie Thompson's," said the man.

My hands were shaking.

"You guys knew Charlie?"

"Charlie Thompson? He was only a member here for what, Bob, twenty-five years?"

"Oh, at least," said the other. "Except he didn't come around much the last few years."

The words kept snagging on my tonsils.

"He, uh, he was a member a long time ago or recently?"

"Well, until Friday, the day he died," the taller one said, a little perturbed. "May I ask why you want to know so much, buddy?"

"Oh, uh, well, he was a friend of mine, that's all."

"Sure he was," said Bob. "C'mon. We'll be late."

I felt a little dizzy. Charlie? A member of the Mayflower? This whole time? This *whole* time?

Hoover got up with his 4-iron and hit a beautiful little 190-yard shot.

I couldn't concentrate. Chunkin' Charlie, a Chop, was a member of the Mayflower this whole time and he hung around *Ponky?*

Not possible. Who would do that? How stupid would you have to be to hang around Chops, playing the widely acclaimed *worst course in America* when you can play one of the widely acclaimed best?

"Stick, you're up," said Hoover.

"Hold on," I said.

I turned away from the group and pretended to work on something in my eye.

Why? Why would he do it? Here's a guy with cancer, knows he doesn't have long to live, and he drives by the Mayflower gates every day—where he's a goddamn *member*—and keeps going to Ponky? It didn't make sense.

But then things started fitting together. The nice car. The thick money clip. The mystery about where he lived and what he did and the fact that he never talked about it. *He didn't want us to know.* He had a chance to take $1,000 from each of us on The Bet and he was the first one to no-bank. Every time one of us would ask him to be part of some scheme to get on, he'd walk away. Every time I'd bring up The Bet, every time I'd bring up the Mayflower, he'd get quiet and walk away. Or leave.

I remembered the night in Cementhead's truck. *This place isn't so bad,* he'd said. *Think of all the laughs.*

He played Ponky for the laughs. For the friends. For the camaraderie. He *chose* Ponky over the Mayflower. Every day. The reality of it sort of hit me in the back of the knees.

"Stick, you gotta hit!"

I stepped up and hit a weak driver into the left rough. It wasn't great, but it wasn't anything horrible. I hardly remember swinging.

Maybe I'd inadvertently slow-played the Numerals with the Charlie thing, because when they got up to hit, they were totally out of their rhythm. They both put death grips on their clubs and hit two of the sorriest shots of the day. My father's was a low liner that went deep into the jungle and Concorde hit a high slice that was possibly not findable.

A couple of Chops laughed with delight and Thud said to the Numerals, "Sorry. We're not laughin' with you. We're laughin' at you."

The two shots were so bad that they both had to reload. Concorde's, in fact, was never found (with the Chops overseeing the search) and Father needed a McCullough to get out from the maple he was under. Then Hoover skulled a 4-iron up to about 40 yards in front of the green and actually *posed* over it, and I was still so dazed, I bladed a 7-iron into the back trap, nothing I couldn't get up and down out of.

Unless a USAir 727 landed on our heads, we were going to win The Bet. I could make a double bogey and Hoover a triple and we'd win. We'd be laughing. Nothin' but teeth.

As I walked to the green, at last a winner, it wasn't the way I thought it would feel. Hoover was riding on the shoulders of Cementhead and Thud. Professor and Blu were doing I'm-not-worthies in front of me all the way to the green, but a sort of heavy emptiness enveloped me.

I mean, I was satisfied to finally beat my father. Even if I made bogey here, I figured I'd beaten him not only in match play but medal—about 71 to 78. I'd be a member of the Mayflower—the club Charlie left to be at Ponky—and I suppose something good would happen out of that, but I thought of Charlie and I felt ashamed.

I wondered if the Chops would treat me the same once I was a member. I think that's why Charlie hid his membership from us. He knew. Once they know you can be over *there,* you can't really be part of *here.* Once you're one of *them,* you can't really be one of *us.* I was missing those guys already and yet they were all around me.

But even *that* wasn't really the biggest part of the emptiness. It was knowing that when I played out this last hole, I was going to be alone. It was not having someone to share it with. If only . . .

Madeline.

There, at the top of the hill, to the left of the green, not far from my ball, stood Madeline. She was in a black cowl-neck sweater and black skirt and white overcoat. The crisp morning air had turned her cheeks pink and her chocolate hair was blowing away from her face with the wind and she looked more beautiful than even my sore memory remembered.

I walked straight to her, staring at her the whole time. I didn't know what I'd say, only that I'd do anything to have her back.

"Madeline," I said.

"Ray," she said. She was not smiling.

"You don't know how to get out of one of these darn sand traps by any chance, do you?" I said.

She was not laughing.

She tossed me my Red Sox cap. "You left this at my house," she said.

"Thanks."

I put it on. I was stumbling.

"Maddy, this is our last hole. If we just tie this hole, we win the match. Can we talk for just . . ."

"Don't," she said, holding up a hand. "I'm running late anyway, Ray. I just wanted to give the hat to you."

"Maddy, please."

"I know what you're playing for here, Ray. I hope you win. I really do. But I finally got a job. I'm going to be with the University of Arizona department of paleontology. We're doing a Costa Rica dig. I'll probably be there the next two years. I just wanted to tell you that. I just wanted to let you know I don't hate you. I think you sold your soul, but I guess I was doing the same thing working here. I don't hate you."

She started to walk away.

"Oh," and she pulled a note out of her coat. "Read this after I'm gone. I'm not going to the funeral. Uncontrolled sobbing makes my face get splotchy. I've said my goodbyes."

I was confused. Madeline was going to Charlie's funeral? She'd never met Charlie.

"Maddy," I called.

She kept walking.

"You gotta listen to me, I . . . that's not . . ."

She was nearly gone now. I felt sick, a black hole, doubling every minute. I looked at my ball in the trap. I saw the Numerals standing around the green, my new buddies.

I saw Two Down, wearing those stupid pro-shop clothes he'd been in the last month, his face aged five years in the last five weeks, his eyes swollen, his personality changed, his life just barely together, thanks to a bet.

I thought of Dannie and what she'd put herself through.

I thought of Charlie and the last thing he said to me. *I just hope it's worth it.*

I saw my father, standing fifteen feet from me, picking the six or so blades of grass off the bottom of his superbly polished spikes and going to the breath spray and I thought of how much I was turning out like him. I was, wasn't I? I was about to be a member of a bluenose country club, like him. I drank too much, like him. I'd never made a relationship last, like him. Never been a father, like him. And I couldn't give up on a stupid self-obsessed dream to be a golf hero again, just like him.

Who was I kidding? It was no more preposterous for him to join the Senior Tour than for me to join the regular one. I barely shoot par from the white tees on a course that isn't even set up for a tournament and I'm playing my *ass* off. That might get you another year on the Nike Tour, but it won't get you much past Lubbock.

I had always blamed my failures on my father, the near misses, the disappointments, the blowups, the lost years, the blown career. Hey, I was part of America's Dysfunctional Family Era. I *had* to blame it on my dad. That was the law, wasn't it?

But if I could blame my failures on my dad, could he blame his on his? And when do they do a quick-deed on your failings? When do they become your own? Eighteen? Twenty-one? Thirty? Mine never had. Not my failed writing. Not my failed marriage. Not my failed golf. Had his?

My father hadn't taken my golf career from me. I lost it. And it was actually a relief to realize, finally, I just wasn't good enough.

That was the funny thing, I guess. Now, as I looked at him, he didn't seem so endlessly tall to me. In fact, he looked small. For the first time in my life, I realized I was taller than him—at least two inches. And if a man that small controlled me, how small was I?

"Maddy!" I yelled as loud as I could. "Can I get a ruling here?"

She turned.

I picked up a rake and stepped into the bunker, maybe five feet from my ball. I looked at the ball. I looked at Professor. I looked at my father.

I took the rake, turned it upside down and jammed the handle into the sand.

Silence.

My father looked right into my eyes, shocked. I looked right back into his eyes and smiled.

"Hey, Father," I said. "I already know *the right kind of people.*"

Madeline was walking back toward me, grinning hugely.

"Dang," I said, turning toward her. "Look what I just did."

"What?" said Two Down horrified.

My father just stared at the ground.

"What? What?" said Two Down.

"Would someone explain to me what's going on here?" Concorde yelled.

Everybody was yelling and mumbling and crowding around the bunker until my father put his hands up to silence the crowd.

"I'm afraid my son has just lost the hole," said my father. "Rule 13 dash 4. Testing the surface."

"Yesssss!" screeched Browning, a little too effeminately.

The Numerals didn't notice. They were roaring their approval. The Chops were groaning.

"Bullshit!" said Two Down, aghast.

I threw the sand wedge to Professor and climbed out.

Madeline was walking away. She took one last look around at me and smiled.

"Don't you love golf rules?" she said.

Two Down was tugging at me. "I don't know what the hell just happened," he said, "but we've got sudden death. Let's go. Ten tee box."

"Wrong," I said. "We didn't say anything about sudden death. We said 18 holes."

Concorde stopped in his tracks and ran over. "What?"

"You heard me. The match is a tie. No blood."

"Hello? Stick?" pleaded Two Down in a panic. "I'm still down ten Large here! Let's go!"

By now, Concorde had started walking to the clubhouse.

"Stick, stop fucking around," Two Down pleaded. "Snidely Whiplash has my house."

My father just shook his head. "Raymond, are you sure you want to do this?"

I nodded.

"Stick!!!" said Two Down. "What about my house?"

"Right," I said. "About that, Leonard, I'll make you a deal. I'm going to give you my driver. You can get $35,000 for it."

Two Down rolled his eyes. Concorde turned to listen in.

"Yes, you can. Now shut up. I want you to sell it, give $10,400 to Concorde, give me what's left over and pay me back $100 at the corner table at Ponky every month until the ten grand is paid off. I never want more than $100 in any one month. But you've got to pay it in person. At Ponky. The corner table."

Two Down was suspicious.

"What's in it for you?" he said.

"I get free choice of the biggest golf trophy in your trunk, engraved with my name. And one for Hoover, too."

"Only don't engrave it 'Hoover,' " I said. "Make it 'Alberto de Salvo, Champion.' "

"That's all I gotta do?" said Two.

"That's all."

"Bank!" said Two Down.

I looked over at Hoover. His chest had suddenly grown four sizes.

Then I glanced at my father.

"And," I said, "I know someone who may have a sentimental interest in buying that driver."

My father smiled just a little.

Two Down walked right over to him. So did Concorde, holding the house deed in his right hand.

All the Chops looked bewildered, but I'd have time to explain it to them. OK, maybe not to Cementhead, but everybody else.

I remembered the note. I yanked it out of my back pocket. Madeline was gone. It had a St. Luke's Hospital letterhead on it and it was written in a wild, sprawling hand. It read:

Maddy,
That boy Stick loves you.
Worse than that, he needs you.
Make a dying old guy happy.
Make up.
Yours,
Daddy

It hit me like a cinder block upside the head.

Charlie was her father.

No wonder she hated the Mayflower. Charlie's brother—her uncle—had been turned down. Charlie left and yet she was stuck there, working for them.

"You know what I'd love to do right now?" I said to nobody.

"Go to a funeral?" said Two.

"Exactly."

"In those pants?"

We walked out. Hoover offered to take Two Down to the hospital. Two Down had my driver in one hand and Arnie in the other.

As we were driving out, Meltdown was leaning on the outside of the wall, underneath Ivan's window. When he saw us, he jumped to his feet.

"How'd it end up?"

"It was a tie," Thud said.

"Yeah," said Cementhead. "But it just as easily could've gone the other way."

EPILOGUE

CEMENTHEAD: WHAT DO you think this shot is for me?

Hoover: "I'd say, for you, somewhere between a bladed 9 and a chunk 8."

Cementhead: "Hey, thanks."

Hoover: "Stick, I'm about to beat you like a circus monkey."

Me (sinisterly): "If you're gonna shoot, shoot. Don't talk."

Cementhead: *"The Wizard of Oz?"*

Me: *"The Good, the Bad, and the Ugly."*

Cementhead: "Damn."

Two Down: "Remember, I got no bets with anybody. Except Thud."

Dannie: "Jeez, Two, I remember when one lousy bet wouldn't even get you out of bed."

Two Down: "Hey, shouldn't the game in itself be enough?"

That was just one of the best things that happened afterward—the fact that we got the Donkey back. There was a whole vatload of things.

For one thing, the Mayflower was forced to accept its first black and that great man was none other than a Mr. Howlings, Demetrius. Crowbar His Bloated-ness.

Apparently, what happened is Crowbar was walking along that final day with our match and started yapping with this suit about various topics hither and yon, and one of the topics was why people who build driving ranges are so stupid.

And the Numeral went, "Why?"

"Well," said Crowbar. "Everybody loves going to the driving range, right? It's fun. There's no walking. Your beer doesn't spill. It's great. But there's no game to it. It's just a rock pile, beating rocks at the rock pile is all it is. Fungoes. All day long."

"So?" the guy says.

"Well," says Crow, "what they ought to do is make it into a game. See, if I owned one, I'd set up these giant colored pits out on the range. If you knock it in the little 100-yard hole, the computer gives you 5 points. If you knock it in the 150-yard hole, the computer gives you 10 points. All the way up to the big 300-yard hole way the hell out there that everybody is trying to reach and get 25 points."

"Preposterous," went the Numeral. "They wouldn't know which ball was yours."

"Sure they would," said Crowbar. "Each ball would have one of those computer bar code things on it so the computer would know exactly who hit what ball. Pod 17. Five points. Like that. And the scores would show up right in front of you next to where you're hitting. You could bet your buddy. You could compete against what you did last time. You could bet against people all across the nation. You could have tournaments. Guys would be going, "Man, I think I can break 400 today!" Tell me that wouldn't be more fun than just beatin' rocks out there."

"That's so . . . so . . . brilliant!" said the Numeral.

A week later, the two of them were in business together, fifty-fifty, with some property the guy owned in South Boston. The Numeral's money. Crowbar's idea.

The thing apparently took off all over Japan and started heading to the States and Crowbar wound up getting Spielberg rich over the deal and so he thought what the hell, and applied at the Mayflower. Only they rejected him, so he sued. The Mayflower argued that they were a private club and had the right to refuse anybody they wanted, which is what they always argued.

Except that Crowbar's lawyer said, "Not if business is discussed on the grounds."

And the Mayflower said, "We don't allow business to be discussed on the grounds. It's in our policy book."

To which Crowbar said, "Then how did I get so rich?"

The judge let him in. Not that he actually plays golf there now. He just drives a cart and the members out of their minds. Somebody said they see him all the time, riding side by side with Stretch, who cannot ever seem to get away from him owing to the fact that only Crowbar's cart is able to do 45 miles per hour at any and all times. Wonder how come?

They had room for Crowbar on the ledgers because Browning gave in to his true desires and moved to Martha's Vineyard, where he opened up a unisex hair salon. They say you can get especially good brushes there.

Hoover you wouldn't even have recognized. Not only did he finally get a tan but he'd bet anybody just about anything they could stomach and he could hit the hatrack with his little Hogan cap two out of three times.

Two Down became famous for saying, "No junk. No in-flights. No double-backs." Not only that, but on Tuesdays his long-suffering wife, Jane, met him after work and played 9 with him, plus threw down a few Jell-O shots with us afterward, which only goes to prove you should never give up on family.

As for Chunkin' Charlie, the funeral was very nice. Chops outnumbered Numerals two to one. After the funeral, Thud secretly switched the remains with some divot mix and that night we all gathered around the putting green with the headlights shining on it and ceremonially poured his ashes into a clean divot bucket. Then we drove out to the 11th because that was the last hole anybody could remember him birdying. He'd chipped in and said his usual, which was "If you like golf, you *gotta* like that shot."

I jury-rigged the cart up with a tee again and Dannie and me and Two drove around and around that green, letting the ashes blow out and circle it with a fine gray mist.

"We miss you, Charlie," I said quietly as the ashes ran out. "See you on the back side."

"But we still ain't givin' you more than four shots," added Dannie.

Then Two Down proposed that Sunday Cotillion Night be renamed Chunkin' Charlie Memorial Study Hall. The motion was seconded and passed on the first measure.

Oh, and not only did we get rid of Crowbar but we got Dannie back, which has to be the best trade since Lou Brock for Ernie Broglio.

She took the Browning thing pretty hard, but that night, after the ash ceremony, she came up to me with those sea-green eyes and said some words that pretty much changed my life.

She said, "Stick, nobody ever said they were wrong much in my house. Couldn't give anybody an inch 'cause there wasn't any room. But I was wrong about you. What you did in the bunker showed me a lot of character. I know all the loot you gave up to do it. And I reckoned that all this time I'd been looking for somebody with integrity and he was right in my bed this whole time."

And then she took my hand, right in front of everybody.

When I'd finally caught my breath, I said, "You wouldn't want to go on a date with me, would you?"

"A date? Like a date date?"

"Yeah. Like a pick-you-up-at-eight date."

"Not a be-waiting-in-your-rubber-teddy-at-midnight date?"

"Nope. An Andy-takes-Helen-to-a-movie-and-a-burger-at-the-diner date."

"Well," she said, apparently confused, "it sounds so kinky."

And we did just that. We whispered all through the movie, laughed until they kicked us out, walked along for hours, laughed some more and held hands right out in public.

And then I took her back to her apartment, where we . . . kissed.

Once.

"Now *that's* sexy," she said.

And I went home.

It was the most erotic night of my life.

What we did was start over. We turned the Etch-a-Sketch of our lives upside down and shook it hard. And one night, when we'd finally stopped being fuck buddies and wound up lovers, she said, "So, want to see inside my locket?"

"What locket?" I said, being clever.

And you'll never guess who was in there.

Me.

It turns out maybe I could've had Dannie all along, but I didn't know there really *is* a need to get emotional about things, especially if you love somebody.

By March, we were married, right in the Pit of Despair. Blu Chao catered it and Thud sang. Turns out he has a lovely tenor. By June we were pregnant.

And even that wasn't the most shocking thing that happened. The most shocking thing that happened was Professor coming over to the Pit of Despair the day after the funeral and handing me a check for $16,276.49.

"What's this?" I asked him.

"Yo proceeds," he said.

"From what?"

"From that six grand you give me. You said invest it for you, so I did. Thems yo proceeds."

"I told you to split anything you turned and give me half," I said. "You were supposed to give yourself half of this."

"I did."

A very warm feeling entered my heart for this man.

"You did?"

"Yeah. See, y'know that merger that was supposed to go down 'tween Talbert Cable and Southern Bell?"

"No."

"Oh, man, *Barron's* was all over that shit! But I says to myself,

'No way does that man Metzger's ego fit in the same room with that man Rothstein's. This deal is gonna bust up like the *Challenger.*' So I put the five into 'puts,' which is just another way of bettin' the deal was gonna go up in flames. I bought 'em at 15/16ths of a dollar, which is 94 cents and I'll be damned if the deal din't go and take gas, and the stock went straight in the tank and my li'l 94-cent options went to $7 and you and I made $28,000 and them there's your proceeds."

"Professor?" I asked.

"Yeah?"

"Have you ever been French-kissed by a man?"

Dannie and I ended up taking that money, plus the $24,000 we got from Two Down out of the driver, who had indeed sold it to my father, and put it down on a little house close to Ponky. It even had a little writing room—which Dannie insisted on—and I even use the room these days to actually write things that didn't wind up roasting marshmallows. We even bought a beautiful big couch that Dannie just loves not to sleep on.

I did lose one very good friend in the deal, though. My main man, Glen Fiddich. Oh, we keep in touch. It's just that I learned opening up the scotch was a good way of closing me down to everybody else. Dannie and Charlie are mostly what I drink in now. Charlie being our son.

OK, so I gave up my golf dream. I was good, but I wasn't any damn Curtis Strange or anything. I really didn't mind.

I still love the game, it's just that I realized I don't need to drive a courtesy car up to a bag boy at an Andy Williams Shearson/Lehman Buick Open Presented by MCI to love it. I learned to love the shot I'm hitting right now and I not brood about the one that came before it. I have no choice but to think that way about Travis now.

I found out I don't need to beat my father to love it and I don't need to break 70 every day to love it and once I figured that out, I stopped needing to tie my 9-iron to a rope behind my car to punish the bastard quite as often.

I love golf for all the times when it's just the twilight and you and the crunch of your spikes on the fall leaves. I love it for the walk you get down the middle of the fairway after you pipe one or the way you get to hold your putter in your hand for 200 yards after you starch a 3-iron dead on the middle center groove. I love it for all the times you get to watch your ball fall against pink-and-purple skies.

I found out golf is a lot like life. Sometimes you're dancing and sometimes you're in the gunch and it's all your own doing. Nobody threw you a yellow-hammer curve or a fastball at the knees, or put overspin on a killer serve or threw a great block or fed you a perfect pass. Not your worthy opponent. Not your therapist. Not your wife. Not your inner child. Not your father.

True, I miss the Last Real Golf Club in America. I miss looking down and seeing that gorgeous grain, polished up nice, setting up so perfect, just lofted enough so that you could see the rosewood. But, hell, now I'm hitting a Titanic Tina like everybody else and the stupid ball just flies off there long and straight even when your swing sucks, which just goes to show you that you shouldn't hold on to things past their time.

Besides, I get to see my driver now and then.

It was about a week after the big Mayflower match. We were all hitting a few putts waiting for the Stringley brothers to get going off the 1st tee box and I was thinking to myself that I actually didn't care how long they took anymore, because I wasn't in a hurry to get done anymore.

I was thinking that maybe it doesn't matter if the grass on the other side of the hedge is lush and green and the grass on yours is dead and brown as long as the people are alive and rooted in something.

And I was thinking that life to me was one happy MCI Friends and Family list when I saw that big old gold Cadillac with the personalized plate pull into the gravel lot.

And out of the Cadillac came a tall, thin man dressed in third-degree flammables and at least two logos over the limit. And we all knew it was my father and so we all stopped and stared.

And what he did was, he opened the trunk, put on his shoes, took out his monster tour bag and threw it over his shoulder, closed the trunk, walked over near the starter's window, dug in his bag for a ball, brought it up slowly, looked at us, dropped it in the pipe, looked right at me and gave a little smile.

We were all a little shocked, except me, who was frozen solid.

And then Two Down said, "You see, George, you really did have a wonderful life."

"*It's a Wonderful Life?*" asked Cementhead.

"Damn!"

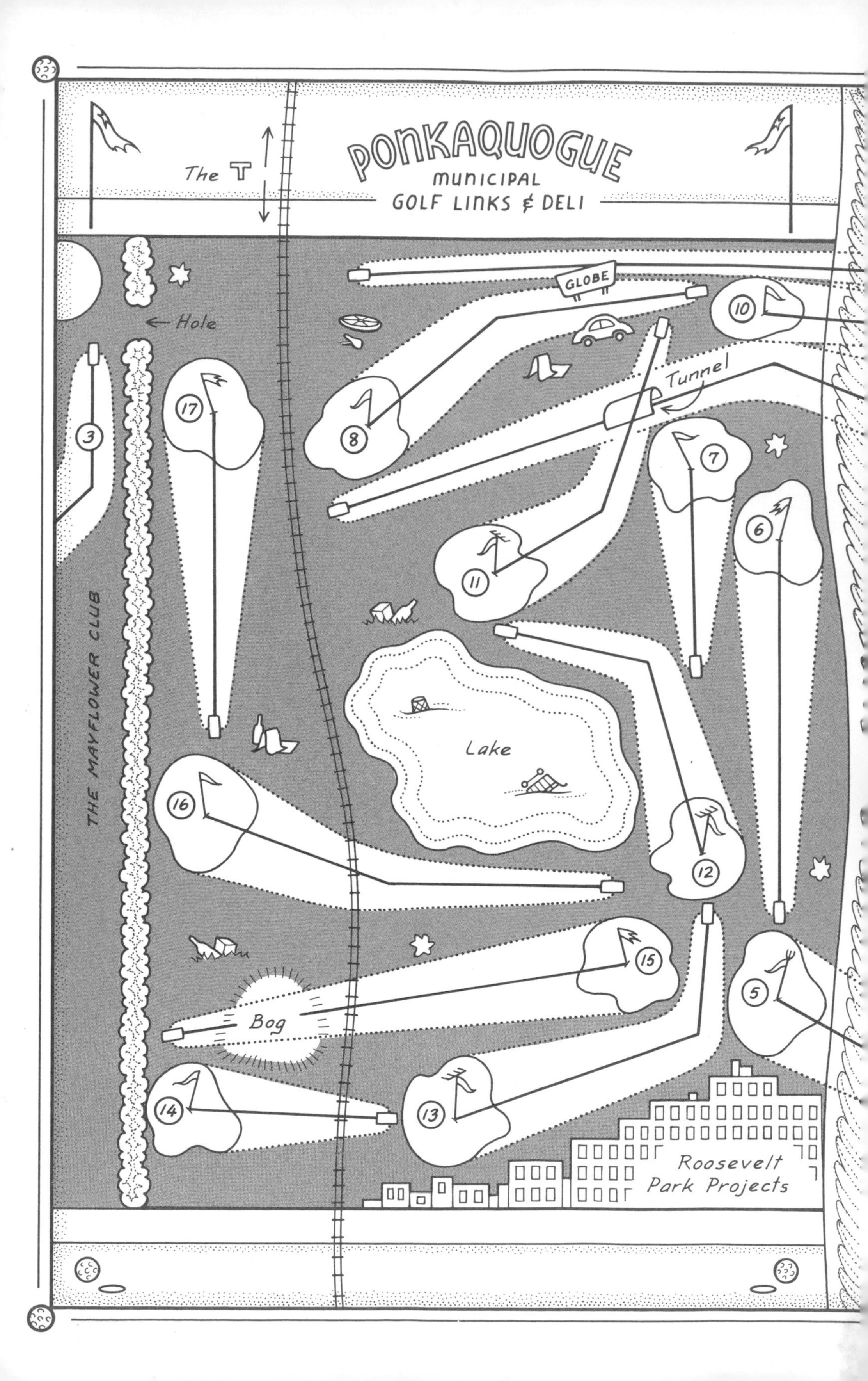
PONKAQUOGUE
MUNICIPAL
GOLF LINKS & DELI
The T
Hole
GLOBE
Tunnel
THE MAYFLOWER CLUB
Lake
Bog
Roosevelt
Park Projects
10
8
17
3
7
6
11
16
12
15
5
14
13